Ophelia's Fan

ALSO BY CHRISTINE BALINT

The Salt Letters

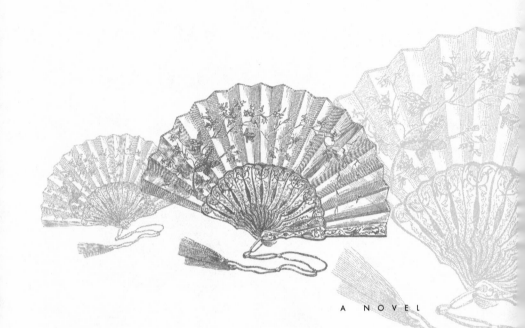

A NOVEL

W. W. Norton & Company

New York London

Ophelia's Fan

Christine Balint

For information about permission to reproduce selections from this book, write to
Permissions, W. W. Norton & Company, Inc., 500 Fifth Avenue, New York, NY 10110

Manufacturing by Quebecor World, Fairfield
Book design by Barbara M. Bachman
Production manager: Anna Oler

Library of Congress Cataloging-in-Publication Data
Balint, Christine.
Ophelia's fan : a novel / Christine Balint.—1st ed.
p. cm.
ISBN 0-393-05925-1
1. Berlioz, Harriet Smithson, 1800–1854—Fiction. 2. Berlioz, Hector,
1803–1869—Marriage—Fiction. 3. Composers' spouses—Fiction. 4. Irish—
France—Fiction. 5. Actresses—Fiction. 6. Ireland—Fiction. 7. France—
Fiction. I. Title.
PR9619.3.B314O64 2004
823'.914—dc22

2004007450

W. W. Norton & Company, Inc., 500 Fifth Avenue, New York, N.Y. 10110
www.wwnorton.com

W. W. Norton & Company Ltd., Castle House, 75/76 Wells Street, London W1T 3QT

1 2 3 4 5 6 7 8 9 0

For Rupert

At once he took his Muse and dipt her
Right in the middle of the Scripture.

—W. HAZLITT, *LIBER AMORIS:*

OR, THE NEW PYGMALION

The aspiration of the mind is after the highest excellence,
its longings are after immortality: its performance
is generally as nothing; its triumph but for a moment!

—OXBERRY'S PREFATORY REMARKS TO *JANE SHORE:*

A TRAGEDY BY NICHOLAS ROWE

Part One

BENEVOLENCE

Mme Harriet Berlioz
Rue de Londres
Paris, 7 May 1838

My dear Louis,

I write to you in English for in French you have never known your mother. I long for the lands of English where words flow like song and do not catch their sharp edges in my throat.

I collect my writings and papers because I am compelled to make you understand the lands and journeys that made me. A great many things happened to me before I was your mother and your father's wife.

Do not let them tell you I am melancholic, for it is the perpetual forward movement of time which breeds melancholy. We are the sum of all we have been, all we have read, all we have played, and all we have dreamed. My mind is not lost, it is merely wandering the passages of my life.

Today your father brought you to my room and you touched the fan now so gray and threadbare on my bureau, before asking softly about Ophélie. Your father wept when he heard you. For the story of Ophelia you must wait.

I will bind this manuscript and ask Joséphine to give it to you when you are grown. By the time you read this, you will have long forgotten such childish moments.

Your loving mother,
Harriet

The Birth: Ennis, County Clare, Ireland, 1800

*T*HE WINTER BEFORE Henrietta Smithson's confinement was the worst in living memory. Ice glazed the streets and doorsteps. The poor locked themselves into cottages with stale bread crumbs, and their body heat nurtured a fever that would spread like fire through the town.

In Simms Lane, the Smithsons were away from the fever. Many of their patrons, including Father Barrett and Lady Castle Coote, sent the salted meat and preserved vegetables they could spare in gratitude for last season's performances. As the ice melted, Smithson embarked on a new season of theater.

On the night his daughter Harriet was born, Smithson left for the theater in the late afternoon. As he kissed his wife, he saw that her face was paler than usual and her cheeks felt like the warm dough of his childhood. It seemed to him that all her skin was becoming more malleable in preparation for the birth.

"*Romeo and Juliet* tonight," he shouted as he left the house. "Rest, my fair Juliet."

Although Smithson had built the theater himself, he felt an initial resistance on entering it. The building was small; the stone walls were close together and it was as though they would swallow him up in the musty dimness. Whenever his theater was full, he would look over the crammed house. His heart would beat madly, and he would pray that on this night the candles would not set the house on fire. Smithson still hoped that he would one day have the funds to build a grander theater like the one in Limerick. He imagined himself as manager of such a theater. He believed this was one role he could perform very well.

On the night Harriet was born, her mother screamed lines from Shakespeare to dull the pain. The midwife was puzzled by words of love and death.

Ennis: 1800

*F*ATHER BARRETT RETURNED from the lodge feeling warm and merry. He had spent a very satisfactory evening with the brethren, enjoying the Freemasons' singing and the ceremony which he did not have to lead. News of the child's birth had come from Smithson himself, who had left his wife in the care of a friend.

Father Barrett tried to imagine the child Smithson had described. Clear blue eyes and thick dark hair. Her name was Harriet and she was going to be a great actress, Smithson had said. And he had shaken his head tearfully. The reverend had patted the arm of his friend and shuddered imperceptibly. She had an expressive face, the new father said, even in her newly born redness, her unfocused eyes, uncontrollable movements, and limpness. Barrett felt a connection with this child he had not yet seen, a Protestant child who would not be christened by his hand. Later, he would long to christen her one hundred times over as though bearing his cross would prevent her bearing any other.

"Father, if we cannot . . . if it is better. . . . Will you look after her?"

At seventy-nine, Father Barrett knew few people older than himself and many younger. He had little left to learn but much to teach. His very mind quickened at the thought of a child hungering for learning in his library. He nodded.

Ennis: 1806

THE SMELL OF ENNIS permeated everything. It slipped between the cobblestones and saturated bed linen. It stained clothing so deeply that the few people who had ever left the town had written home that no amount of scrubbing restored their clothing to cleanliness. Even when old Ennis clothes were torn to shreds and used as dishrags, they still retained the alarming sourness of home.

The streets leading into the town were rank. Odors of mashed potatoes whirled among oily hair and the boiled onion smell of sweat. Dead, ill, and tired air blended into a deep pungency. Hot, thick lumps of horse manure became part of the air breathed by the town and remained unnoticed until a workman slipped on the cobblestones and cursed.

The lopsided walls of the workers' cottages lining the streets looked like cards. They were constructed with the haphazardness of a child's game. A small boy, waking confused to find himself alone in the bed he normally shared with five other children, once stood and began jumping on the mattress. The shaking of the walls was visible from outside. His mother shouted, and a quick shudder moved up from the foundations. A tiny earthquake. A warning not to overstep boundaries.

The people of Ennis were accustomed to living with death. Too much rain had blighted crops. Tiny black insects could be found on the soft skin of babies and could carry them off within the day. Lack of fuel could bring on rasping coughs. Stories of the 1745 famine pulsed through their veins and made them grateful for potatoes. The old Franciscan friary overlooking the fierce brown Shannon reminded them that the river had swallowed the life of little Annie Rich who had slipped off the stone wall lining its slippery banks. Winter puddles were large enough to drown children. Many families were said to be hoarding corpses beneath the floorboards for fear that the Church of Ireland would snatch them and bury them secretly in unconsecrated Protestant ground.

In Ennis, it was not unusual for the dead to speak. They had much to complain about. It was common over cups of tea in the morning to be told that Grandpa Tippett had whispered words up through the floorboards during the night. Children sometimes crept back to the kitchen after dark and held glasses to the floorboards. Little George received a belting on the day he told his father that Uncle Michael had asked for his hair comb back. Sometimes the dead incited mischief. If Ennis boys were beaten for stealing the pennies from their father's purse, they would scream that Aunt Ellen had made them do it. Their mother would pause, tell them not to speak ill of the dead, and then remember that once Aunt Ellen had, in fact, stolen pennies. Occasionally the dead did nothing more than take rasping breaths. Those who could find no peace were said to groan fit to bring the roof down. Dead children wailed like banshees. Those seeking revenge could throw cooking pots, leaving gashed walls slowly crumbling as a reminder of their pain.

FATHER BARRETT TRIED to keep the sourness of Ennis away with morning prayers and sweets. He preferred the strawberry sweets; they distracted from the brownness of his teeth, dyed his lips crimson, and made his gums look as though they bled. But if Bridie, the maid, was unable to find them, sugar cubes would do. Each morning and then every hour or when required. This sweetness was warm when you came in the oak door. It rubbed off Father Barrett's hands and infused everything he touched. It left a trail around the house so that Harriet always knew where to find him.

Harriet knew there were many words that could be used for him, but she could never remember the correct order. *Barrett, Dean, Doctor, Father, Reverend*. She knew that if she called him *James*, he would nod vaguely and peer somewhere behind her while Bridie gasped and her cheeks turned purple.

Sometimes Harriet liked to make Bridie angry on purpose. It meant that she would feel strong fingers gripping her arm while Bridie bent down to hiss at her. It made Harriet feel strong being touched like this. Then she knew that what she was doing mattered. It was like being wrapped. There was nothing Harriet loved more than the feeling of being wrapped in a towel after she was soaked and scrubbed in time for the Sabbath. She liked the tightness on her limbs, the moisture being blotted from her skin, and the warmth of being rubbed dry. At other times, Bridie's touch would make her jump and she would have to hold back from hitting her. There was only one person who had ever really held her. Harriet thought she remembered Mrs. Fudge. Mrs. Fudge had looked after Harriet in Father Barrett's home when Harriet was very small, before she had learned to read. Harriet had a faint memory of standing in the parlor, clinging to Mrs. Fudge's thick thighs while the woman's whole body had heaved with sobs.

"Don't make me leave my girl," she had said. And Father Barrett had stepped from his left foot to his right, scratching his left temple and frowning.

"Come, come, Mrs. Fudge," he had said. "Harriet does not need your help any more. I will teach her."

Now that Harriet was nearly six, she knew that if she did not make too much noise, they would leave her alone. Then she could give herself up to the spirits in the dusty air and old books in the nursery. Once Harriet had pulled one of Bridie's old gray aprons over her pinafore and made a feather duster from clothing scraps. As she dusted someone else's long-forgotten toy soldiers, Harriet's voice became full and sweet. Sounds she had never made before began to pour out of her.

> *You remember Ellen, our hamlet's pride,*
> *How meekly she blessed her humble lot,*
> *When the stranger, William, had made her his bride,*
> *And love was the light of their lovely cot*
> *Together they toil'd through winds and rains,*
> *Till William, at length, in sadness said,*
> *"We must seek our fortune on other plains;"*
> *Then sighing, she left her lowly shed . . .*

"Whatever are you doing, child?" Bridie had appeared after some time in the nursery. Harriet had not heard her climbing the stairs. She noticed that although Bridie's eyes were stern, her lips were curved into the hint of a smile. Harriet closed her mouth and turned back to the soldiers.

"And I did those shelves only yesterdy!"

THE SONG ABOUT ELLEN reminded Harriet of Mother Mary and Babyjesus. Harriet knew that she was lucky to live with Father Barrett, even if he was not like other people's fathers, because he had been there when Babyjesus was born. He had told her all about it. Each Christmas they celebrated the birthday of Baby-jesus, and everyone wanted Father Barrett to go to *their* house for lunch to tell them about the night that Babyjesus was born. Just before Christmas every year, Harriet was allowed to go with Father Barrett to find Babyjesus in the church. She would put on her very best Sunday dress, and Father Barrett, with unusual per-ceptiveness, would peer down at her and say, "Harriet, your pretty dress will soon be covered in dust."

She would puff out her chest, stand on her toes, and say, "I am visiting our king." Father Barrett would grin and let his fingers hang low so that she could hold onto them. His pocket would be heavy and bulging from the Christmas Key when they arrived in the church.

"Now then, Harriet," he would say, "do you remember where we left Babyjesus last year?"

She would nod proudly and say, "Yes, in the crypt down below." Father Barrett was lucky she was there, Harriet thought, because otherwise he would never remember where he had left Babyjesus and then all of Ennis would be without Christmas.

The crypt was dark, and they had to light a candle to see their way down the stone steps. Harriet would slide her hand down the banisters, trying not to trip as she ran ahead while Father Barrett stumbled behind her and his voice echoed, "Patience is a virtue, Harriet! Be careful you don't slip!" Harriet would slow down, knowing that still she would be the first person in Ennis to see Babyjesus.

Father Barrett found her crouched in the dark corner, gently unraveling the rags, which Harriet knew were really silk cloths, in which Babyjesus was wrapped. She laid Babyjesus on her lap, stared at his dusty and fading eyes. By candlelight she wiped his face with a velvet sleeve. She leaned over him and kissed his cheek.

Every Christmas Harriet was Mary. She cradled Babyjesus as she carried him home. She bathed him in the porcelain basin in her own bedroom, in water that was Neither Too Hot Nor Too Cold. Gently she shook the water out of his joints and wrapped him in clean cloths. She took him back to the chapel with Father Barrett and laid him in the manger for all Ennis to see. She collected him after the Christmas Day service and picked the straw from his face. She arrived at Christmas Lunch with Father Barrett, cradling Babyjesus and staring up into the faces of grown-ups with large, pious eyes. But this Mary was never satisfied with her Joseph. One year Tommy Kiley dropped Babyjesus on purpose in the ash of a dead fireplace. Another year, Johnny Owen swung Babyjesus around by the left arm. Babyjesus had never quite recovered, and his left arm was still a little longer and more flexible than his right.

FATHER BARRETT WAS GOOD at telling stories about the events surrounding the birth. So much so that Harriet longed for him to tell her own story.

"What happened?" she would ask at dinner when they were alone and she was allowed to ask him anything she wanted to know. "What happened on the night I was born?"

In the beginning, Father Barrett had only told Harriet about

The Irishman in Naples and *Romeo and Juliet*. One night she asked, "What else, Reverend Doctor? What else happened on the night I was born?"

Father Barrett murmured quietly to himself. His eyes were so misty that Harriet wondered if he could see at all.

"After *The Irishman in Naples* and *Romeo and Juliet* there was," he cleared his throat, "a distinct view of Mount Vesuvius on fire and," he paused, "a solemn dirge and funeral procession."

The words were sweet and warm as milk. She rolled them around in her mouth as she waited for Father Barrett to tell her the stories. He stared at the portrait of an earlier priest on the wall.

"Hmmm," he said slowly, thoughtfully. He looked down at his plate and gently sawed at his mutton. Harriet sat still, her back straight, her hands clasped in her lap, her meat growing cold.

"Hmmm," he repeated. That was all he said.

So Harriet had been forced to embellish the stories herself. She painted her face with black ink in front of her small hand mirror, a gift her mother had slipped to her at the end of one of the family visits. The mustache was nearly perfect, apart from a slight drip down to her chin. She pulled her hair behind her head with a ribbon and found a misshapen hat in the chest. If she shook her head too much, it covered her eyes. Harriet knew she could learn to walk without moving her head. She also knew that Naples was in Italy and there were nice churches there. She remembered a friend of Father Barrett's from his Paris days, an old Italian man who had once come to visit. Harriet remembered that he had talked a great deal and waved his hands about during the meal. It was only when Bridie came to clear the table after the men had gone that Harriet noticed he had barely touched his Irish stew.

Now Harriet stretched a skipping rope across the nursery so

that one half of the room could be her father's theater, the other her parents' small cottage, somewhere up in Simms Lane. She spread a blanket on the floor for her mother and found her doll to play the part of herself. Soon she would be lying on the blanket playing the part of her mother; for Harriet knew babies came to women while they slept. She peered over the rope to where the theater was going to be. She stared back at the doll and realized that she did not want to play this role.

Slowly, Harriet wound the skipping rope around her left hand. She returned the blanket to Bridie's linen press. She leaned the doll against the shelf. The doll became her audience, and Harriet began her performance.

Harriet moved around the nursery, waving her hands in the air because she was sure this was what Irishmen did in Naples and this was what her father was doing in the theater on the night she was born. Harriet had climbed down the stairs and was on her way out the back door when Bridie caught sight of her in braces and still wearing the hat, which had fallen down over her eyes. Bridie gasped and grabbed her arm.

"Just you come with me, young missy. You're never again to dress up in men's clothes as long as you're in this house. Father Barrett is not to find out you ever had a mustache," Bridie ordered, scrubbing Harriet's stinging face with surgical spirit down in the kitchen.

Her mustache faded a little every day. Father Barrett did not seem to notice the black lines or the raw redness of Harriet's face.

HARRIET NEVER MISSED the Thursday market. She would be woken before sunrise by the regular rhythm of horses' hoofs pulling carts of produce and the occasional rude sled being dragged bumpily along the cobblestones. Bleating sheep and groaning cattle beneath her window would always remind her of staying with her friend Molly on the farm. After breakfast she would tell Bridie she was going out into Chapel Lane to play. She knew Bridie would never allow her to be seen at the market on her own, but going with Bridie in the afternoon did not offer the same pleasures: Harriet was overlooked when she was with Bridie. On Thursdays there was a great deal of foot traffic in Chapel Lane, and she would meet many women from the congregation and their servants carrying baskets on their way to the market. The women would pat her head and ask after Father Barrett, so Harriet would walk with them a little. She would find herself in Market Square, filled with the vivid tints of vegetables and flowers, the sounds of bleating and clucking farm animals, and the rank smell of meat. Harriet rarely had a penny to spend, but this did not stop her from looking. Most of the sellers knew her by name. Mary O'Conner would ask after Father Barrett and hand her an apple or a pear. Farmer Donald would let her hand-feed the calves and lambs. Once he even let her borrow a small yellow chicken for the morning. Harriet cupped it gently in her left hand and carried it around the market, showing it the coarse fabrics to hide under, and the turf stall where there were always seeds sprinkled in the dirt.

On the days when Molly came to play later in the afternoon, Harriet would beg her to return to the market as the sellers were packing up their wares. There was always a good chance of some slightly wilting flowers or hardened sweets that a tired seller did not wish to carry home again. But Molly disliked the market intensely.

"When you come to my house you can see all the animals you

like," she said. But they both knew it was a long time since the reverend had taken Harriet to visit.

"Oh, Harriet, couldn't we please look at the town shops? At the dresses we will wear when we are grown up?"

IF PEOPLE WERE really in trouble, Father Barrett would invite them to dine. Harriet remembered sitting at the dining table while Father Barrett and Mrs. Irons forgot she was there and Mrs. Irons sobbed into her soup that her husband had committed *adultery*. Harriet had wanted, very badly, to ask what that meant. She knew it was in one of the Ten Commandments, but Father Barrett's eyes grew misty whenever she recited them and he merely nodded and said, "Yes, yes, keep going, can you remember the rest?"

From time to time, Harriet was allowed to go with Father Barrett to visit families. On these evenings Harriet would spend many hours staring at her feet or at the tablecloth. She was always seated with the children, and they wanted to know what it was like to live with Father Barrett.

"Do you have to pray all the time?" Tommy Kiley asked her.

"No."

"Does Father Barrett snore?" Tommy and his brother laughed so hard at this that their mother asked them to leave the table.

Harriet knew what it meant when Father Barrett lifted his hat, revealed his yellow teeth, and said he was going to do his duty by Mrs. Baird. Bridie would nod, clamp her jaw together, and blot the corners of her eyes with her cotton handkerchief. *Duty* was a strange word, Harriet thought.

The first time Father Barrett took Harriet with him, he began to tell her about Mrs. Baird's Irish stew as soon as they left the house.

"Thick," he muttered. "Hot, salty, full of onions." Harriet learned that when Father Barrett went to do his duty by Mrs. Baird, he was really going to eat a hearty helping of Irish stew. She wondered whether there might be a secret reason for Mrs. Baird wishing to feed Father Barrett. She wondered whether Mrs. Baird might be a witch trying to poison him.

"Watch where you step, Harriet." Father Barrett said, clutching his parcel of salted mutton. "This is no time for you to trip on stones."

Harriet imagined Father Barrett had been a soldier before he was a father because he was good at marching. The rhythm of their feet on the uneven stones helped her to think. She had learned that while Father Barrett quoted the New Testament she only needed to say "Yes" every few minutes and she could still play pretend inside her head.

IT WAS ONLY a few weeks since the last visit from Harriet's mother and father. Bridie spoke of them as though they were very important. But Harriet did not really know why. The Woman Who Was Her Mother was thin with a long face. She limped slightly, and her hair drifted in wisps around her face. Her teeth were thick like horses' teeth and twisted around each other. She was quiet and liked to peer at Harriet and grip her arms, so that Harriet wanted to run away and hide under her bed. But just as she knew that Father Barrett's duty was to eat Mrs. Baird's stew, Harriet knew that her own duty was to let the Woman Who Was Her Mother leave large bruises like fingerprints in the smooth skin of her arms. The woman's eyebrows were thick caterpillars that, whenever she spoke, crawled across her forehead. Harriet liked it when she spoke because at those times she needed her arms to wave around like ribbons in front of her, and this would force her to set Harriet's own arms free.

The Man Who Was Her Father spoke a language of laughter with Father Barrett. Harriet thought that even the Woman Who Was Her Mother did not understand the meanings exchanged between Father Barrett and the Man Who Was Her Father. The man entered Father Barrett's library, and Father Barrett would offer him one of his lime sherbet sweets. He would wink and greet Father Barrett with the words "If music be the food of love," and Father Barrett would show his flecked and crumbling teeth which meant he was trying to be polite, stretch out his right hand, palm upward, and say, "Play on."

Then the two men would collapse into long stretches of laughter, nodding their heads up and down and clutching their bellies. Harriet only ever saw Father Barrett lose his composure like this when the Man Who Was Her Father came to visit with his theater troupe.

For some years now, these visits had been decreasing in regularity. Three years ago, Harriet's father had begun hiring out his beloved theater building, claiming the population of Ennis could not support many theatrical performances in a year.

IT WAS A LONG WALK to the dairy farming district outside Ennis. Mrs. Baird, when they arrived, balanced one twin on her right hip while the other clutched her knee.

"Much obliged," she muttered, feeling the weight of Father Barrett's parcel and blushing. "There seem so many more of them since Francis passed on," she told Father Barrett. "But we are lucky the McKinleys have allowed us to stay on the farm."

Harriet slipped out the back door to find Molly.

Molly's clothes flowed in shreds around her body in a way that reminded Harriet of the Erin in folk songs or one of the Marys in the Bible.

"I've been waiting for you, Harriet," she said, taking her hand. Harriet knew from the brightness of the sunshine that there would be magic in this day. They ran up the hillock behind the house, ignoring the cries of small William who could not keep up.

"I'll play with you later, Billy," Molly called. He stopped running, stared after them, and began to sob.

Harriet squinted and the daisies studding the grass became a thick golden carpet.

"We can make crowns," Molly said, sitting in a patch of gold. They picked so many daisies that they left a circle of grass among the gold at the top of the hill. She showed Harriet how to split the end of a stem and thread another stem through. The tips of their thumbs and forefingers became green and sticky. In the sunshine on top of the hill, the two children crowned each other.

The butterfly's wings were large blue irises. Harriet pushed her nose into the grass as she had watched sheep do and blinked in time with the wings. She said, "I wonder what grass tastes like?" She closed her eyes and smelled sunshine. She heard Molly laugh and say grass tastes like horses' hoofs and dandelion seeds.

"It can't be very pleasant, Harriet. I wouldn't try it!"

"What else," Harriet wanted to know. "What else does grass taste like?"

"Frogs' gizzards and the golden dust of fairies' wings. It tastes like Mikey's tears when he needs a wash. And cow's breath. And Father's toenails."

"Oh." Harriet lay on her belly. Moisture from the grass crept through to her skin like invisible ants. Once she had flattened the tufts, the ground was hard. She smelled earth. It smelled like darkness, a deep heavy scent different from the lightness of sunshine.

"Harriet? Harriet, what are you doing?"

"Watching the ants." She should never have lied. But as soon as she uttered the words, Harriet saw lines of tiny ants; red, purple, and yellow, marching across the horizon of her eyelids.

"Molly, if grass is so dirty, then why is milk so white?"

"Come and see the chickens!" She heard Molly's small voice from the chicken shed farther down the hill.

"Holy Mary, mother of God," Harriet whispered, just in case the grass was poisonous, "pray for us sinners now and at the hour of our death. Amen." She got up on all fours and gripped tufts of grass between her teeth. Harriet closed her eyes and chewed. She could not taste horses' hoofs or dandelion seeds. Nor could she taste frogs' gizzards or the golden dust of fairies' wings. Harriet could taste nothing but green. It was the green of satin ribbons. The green of lime sherbet sweets.

With green buzzing in her belly, Harriet skipped down the hill to the chickens next to the vegetable patch. Molly was sitting in a dirty corner of the chicken coop, hunched over with her arms outstretched. One dusty gray chicken sat on each hand while another huddled in her lap.

"Let's teach the chickens to fly!"

Harriet creased her brow. "But how are we going to do that?"

Molly tried to stand, hitting her head on the roof of the

chicken coop and causing a flurry of chicken feathers. She crawled out of the cage and stood next to her friend.

She tugged at the ribbon holding Harriet's hair. "Shake your head."

They ran, laughing, to the top of the hill, holding hands. At the top, Molly caught her breath. "Ready?"

Harriet nodded. They stood apart and held their arms horizontally from their bodies. They ran slowly at first, flapping their arms up and down like wings. When Harriet's legs were stretching as far as they could, and the wind rushed past her ears, she leapt into the air just in time to land in a muddy puddle at the bottom of the hill. Her dress and the fringes of fabric around Molly's legs were patched brown. They laughed so hard that it was some time before they could stand. As they made their way slowly up the hill, Molly said, "Our boots are slowing us down." She sat and began tugging at the laces. "Come on, take your shoes off."

Harriet did not move. There was something improper about bare feet, Bridie had said. "Never let Father Barrett see you in your nakedness," she had told her once, as Harriet ran up the stairs in her nightdress after a bath.

"Look at those toes. Little grubs. See how ugly they are when they wriggle!"

Harriet had nodded and wondered how any part of her could be ugly when it had been made, Father Barrett assured her, in the image of our Father. But perhaps Bridie did not know this, Harriet thought. Or perhaps her toes were more ugly and grub-like than Bridie's own. Bridie liked to make sure that every part of Harriet was either hidden or fastened into place. The reason Harriet liked wriggling her toes so much was that most of the time she was unable to do so. And not everyone had their toes so tightly bound, Harriet knew that. When the Man Who Was Her Father came to visit, she noted with great satisfaction that his shoes were not only loose and floppy around his feet, but they even had holes. Harriet wondered whether perhaps this was why Bridie seemed to dislike him so much. While the Man Who Was Her Father laughed and shook hands with Father Barrett, Harriet could see his toes wriggling through the holes in his shoes. She noted with delight that even his stockings had holes in them. His feet were wide and flat as though he were not used to wearing shoes at all. When Harriet chanced to look up from the feet of the Man Who Was Her Father into the face of the Woman Who Was Her Mother, she noticed that the face looked uncomfortable and that its jaw was as tight as her own feet in their boots.

Molly tugged at Harriet's bootlaces. Harriet looked down at her friend sitting in the grass at her feet, one bent leg on either side of her right foot, tugging at the lace. She bent to help her.

"We'll have to pray hard tonight," Harriet informed Molly. "For letting God see our nakedness."

"Our nakedness!" Molly scoffed. "God sees our nakedness whenever he likes. He can see right through our clothes, you know. That's why we have to wash. Because he can see the dirt on our skin."

"Oh."

Harriet followed her friend into the chicken coop and squealed as her hair caught in the wire. Molly kicked up dust and straw which rose like steam and stuck to their skin.

"Here," Molly held out a chicken, clasping its wings. "You take Josephine." Harriet was not at all sure about the good intentions of Josephine who struggled in Molly's arms and wagged her head about as though waiting for soft flesh to sink her beak into.

Not to mention the clawed feet. They were exactly as Harriet imagined crocodile feet to look.

"Don't be scared, Harriet. It's just a chicken. It makes nice eggs and drumsticks. Josephine won't bite you, she only eats grains."

Harriet climbed out of the chicken coop with Josephine. She had collected a spiderweb in her hair as well as chicken dust under her fingernails, and she thought that, like Molly's, her face must also be dirty. Her belly still buzzed with green, and the smell of sunshine grew stronger. Harriet knew that she would be able to fly. She imagined Father Barrett's face as he and Mrs. Baird stood outside the back door shielding their faces from the sun with their arms, their mouths wide open in surprise. Harriet felt the lightness of her body and saw birds flying around her in the sky. She and Molly would fly together away from Ennis, away from Ireland and all the way to Paris.

She could not run as fast with Josephine in her arms. It was hard to balance while running down a hill clutching a chicken, and Harriet was worried she would fall and land on the bird. Mrs. Baird would be upset if Harriet killed one of her chickens. And Harriet knew that Father Barrett would think she had committed a dreadful sin. Perhaps even more than one. Was Harriet stealing Josephine? No, she decided, just borrowing. But if Harriet killed Josephine, even by accident, that was definitely murder.

Harriet could no longer see Molly as she began to run. The hills around Ennis blurred. Just as she thought she was going to fall, she threw squawking Josephine into the air and shouted, "Fly!" But Harriet could not stop running. Her legs stretched more and more as she moved faster and faster. She leapt into the air and waited for the wind to carry her up into the sky. But before she managed to fly, Harriet landed heavily, and with great disappointment, in Mrs.

Baird's cabbages. She sat still for a few moments and caught her breath. All of a sudden she heard a scream and Molly came soaring down from above to land next to her.

"I flew, I flew!" Molly said breathlessly. "Harriet, did you fly?"

"A little." She realized, sadly, that between them they had murdered Mrs. Baird's cabbages.

"And I taught my chicken to fly too! She'll be able to leave now if she wants to. But she doesn't. See, she's landed over there."

The ruffled chicken pecked indifferently at the grass.

"Harriet?" Molly peered accusingly at Harriet's face. "Where's Josephine?"

Harriet noticed in alarm that the cabbages were carpeted in feathers. She wondered whether the lump she could feel underneath her was a chicken.

"Harriet?"

"I don't know." She sniffed.

"What have you done with my chicken?"

Trembling, Harriet stood. She turned around slowly and looked at the flattened cabbage leaves she had been sitting on. She turned to Molly.

"Perhaps I taught Josephine to fly," she said.

"I don't think so." Molly climbed out of the vegetable patch. "I think you lost her. Come on. If we don't find her, there'll be trouble."

Harriet could no longer smell sunshine. The sky was darkening with gray clouds, and the trees around the house were buffeted violently by the wind. She turned in a slow, wobbly circle and peered as far as she could along the horizon. Molly was already making her way toward the house.

"Maybe you scared her," Molly said, bobbing under the window so her mother would not see her. She wondered if she wished hard enough whether Josephine would reappear. She wished she had helped Father Barrett do his duty, and eaten Mrs. Baird's Irish stew even if it was poisonous.

Molly pulled open a tattered wooden door. "She might be in there. You have to go and have a look."

Harriet smelled stale dust and damp air. She saw spiderwebs and blackness. She turned to Molly. "How could Josephine have opened the door?"

"It's always open. Someone must have come along and shut it after she went in."

"Couldn't we look around the garden before we look in there?"

Molly shook her head. Harriet took a deep breath of windy air and ducked her head under the small doorway.

"Josephine!" She called. Her voice was swallowed by the darkness. There was nothing frightening about darkness, Harriet told herself. It just made it difficult to see. She would have to tread carefully. But if someone were to light this space with a candle, she would see wooden stumps and spiderwebs. She could be backstage in her father's theater. There was no reason at all, Harriet thought, why ghosts or other such creatures should choose to hide here in the dark underneath Mrs. Baird's house. Harriet heard a knocking sound and jumped. Her back was beginning to ache from being hunched over. She sensed the ceiling caving in. She reached up to steady herself. The boards crumbled slightly under her fingers. They were vibrating. Something was banging unevenly on the ceiling. Harriet realized that one of the other children must be jumping on the floor.

Harriet ignored the small voice calling her and dug her feet into the dry earth. It was almost as she imagined sand to be. If she closed her eyes, she could be by the seaside. She did not want to play with Molly anymore. She feared what Molly would make her do next. You could never be sure what was in Molly's imagination. If Molly thought Josephine might have found her way into the stream, she would make Harriet search for Josephine in the water. Harriet decided she was far safer in the dark place under the house. She heard crackling leaves outside and a whistle of wind. She closed her eyes and imagined brightness. Something furry brushed her hand and she jumped. Harriet could smell rot.

Harriet was in a cool dark crypt. Father Barrett had begun telling her the real story of Romeo and Juliet. She smoothed out the dust to make a long, narrow strip that she could use as a bed. As Juliet, she sat on the strip and straightened her muddy dress so that no one could say she was not a lady, even in death. She lay back stiffly, spreading her hair around her shoulders and straightening the crown of daisies on her head. Her first real performance would be in the dark where no one could see her. Harriet closed her eyes and imagined cold, clean, white marble. Sleep came in the shape of thick rose petals falling from the sky like scented rain and showering her in pink and mauve.

She woke to the sound of wailing. A chorus of wails of different sizes and pitches through a small hole a few feet away. Thick leaves rustled somewhere in the wind.

"Harriet? Harriet, are you in there?" Before Harriet could remember what had happened, she answered Mrs. Baird.

"Come out, dear. There's nothing to be afraid of."

Harriet opened her eyes, which were crusted over with dirt, and sat. Her neck ached, and her thighs were stiff from being held so tightly together. She stood and felt the crumbling ceiling. Harriet blinked in the light.

"Good lord," Mrs. Baird said. "Harriet, you look a fright. Molly, run and tell Aunt Ruth to warm water over the fire. You both need to be scrubbed. I can hardly see your noses under all that dirt."

※❧

"I WON'T TELL MOTHER about Josephine," Molly whispered, lifting strings of Harriet's hair to find her ear. Harriet felt sleepy all of a sudden and did not mind, when she looked into the brown, grainy water, that she could not tell Molly's limbs from her own.

"You two have grown a second skin," Aunt Ruth said. "You first, Molly." Molly stood in the tub, her hair in tails around her shoulders while Aunt Ruth, a pink glow in her cheeks and smelling of lavender, leaned over and scrubbed her with a rag.

Harriet stared into the crackling fire. One of the logs glowed deep orange while gray ash collected under the flames. At home, Bridie was always quick to sweep away ash. She said it reminded her of death and that if too much of it built up, it would bring bad luck. Yet Father Barrett had told her that ash was purified and clean. There were even some civilizations, he had said, that used ash to thicken up open wounds on their bodies.

"What did you see under the house?" Molly asked when Aunt Ruth went to get towels.

"A tomb," Harriet replied. "It was all marble, and I was inside. And," Harriet peered at Molly's wide eyes, "a solemn dirge and funeral procession. And a distinct view of Mount Vesuvius on fire."

"Just as well we came to find you, then."

Harriet smiled.

Aunt Ruth rubbed her dry far more gently than Bridie ever did. She even let Harriet and Molly sit in front of the fire without any clothes on to warm themselves, without saying anything about God seeing their nakedness. Aunt Ruth pulled a nightdress that was too tight over Harriet's arms. Harriet could not move very well, but she did not mind. She wondered if Father Barrett would let her live here with Molly forever. Mrs. Baird said that Father Barrett had left as he had to prepare a sermon. Harriet asked if Father Barrett had done his duty by her, and Mrs. Baird looked puzzled.

Aunt Ruth placed a steaming bowl under Harriet's nose. Harriet watched Molly dig her spoon into the stew, close her eyes, and chew. Molly swallowed and opened her eyes.

" 'Tis good, Harriet," she said. "Try it." Harriet looked at Mrs. Baird and thought that perhaps she was not a witch after all. If she had been a witch, she could easily have left Harriet under the house. And if Molly was eating the stew, perhaps it was not poisonous. Harriet lifted the spoon in her right hand, dipped it into the bowl, closed her eyes, chewed, and swallowed.

Juliet

I KNOW I HAVE NOT yet the wisdom of years to guide me. Though these past days could have filled books and years. I can now say I have lived a life, though others would say my life has but begun. The rest of my days, should I survive them, will be not a continuation of this life but a new one with no past. With this opiate I shall drown the life I know and birth that which is unknown.

I wonder, had my mother not come to me with word that I must marry, whether love would have known to flutter within my breast. For it is true that I had never until that moment thought upon it. Oh, what sweet days I had known! My nurse did love me more than a mother, bent to my wishes, held me to her breast. And oftentimes in the day I would walk the streets of Verona with those young ladies I have always known.

But I confess when my mother told me that I was to marry Paris, I looked forward to such a change in my life. For it had been the same as long as I could remember. My nurse even now could not be stopped repeating those tales of when I took my first steps and spoke those first words. Sometimes I would stare at her and wonder whether she had not slept through my growing years. My mother had told me that her own father had found my father for a husband, and she had always seemed happy enough. For some hours I lay under the orange tree, a white and fragrant mist coating my dreams of marriage, in which I was allowed all manner of beautiful objects and all gowns of my desire. I held balls for all the ladies of Verona, I chose exquisite meals and furnishings. Within this dream, Paris was nowhere to be seen. While these imaginings occupied me for some hours, they never seemed more serious to me than my childhood dreams of sailing the seven seas. And it certainly did not occur to me that they would be any more binding.

With the milk from my nurse's breast I know that I drank the bitterness of hatred for the Montagues. My nurse was well taught, and my mother and father did not need to tell me whom to hate. For I slept to the sounds of her tales. There were swords and battles. There was stolen land and sheep. I believe even a tale of one murdered in his sleep. There was not room in Verona for us all. And the nurse played her part by averting her eyes whenever we chanced to come across a Montague or his servant in the marketplace.

As a small child I played with my nurse's daughter, Susan. My mother had not asked the child to be banished which was as well since the nurse would have left her employment rather than abandon her daughter. As babes we sucked at the same breast, and as we grew we ran together in the garden while the nurse sat under the oak tree watching. I remember thinking that Susan was my own angel come to look after me. For she climbed the branches first to check their strength and ate the green fruit, saving me the sweetest and plumpest we found. And so I tried not to dirty my dresses, which were always crisp and bright and well laundered. In this way they were only slightly worn and faded when they became Susan's, for she was smaller and thinner and paler than I. It was Susan who slipped into the pond early one winter's morning while I was still sleeping. Peter happened to be passing and hauled her out by the hair. He wrapped her in his own greatcoat and carried her to her mother. And that was the only day my nurse did not come to me. When I was told of Susan's quiet passing, I wondered what she had seen in that pond and whether something dark lurked there and she had wished to protect me from it. And if it is true that something of the soul is imbibed during an infant's sucking, then I had lost my sister. A sadness came over me and my nurse then, and she moved her cot into my bedchamber, swearing never to let me out of her sight.

When I was five years old I recall visiting the marketplace with her. She led me by the hand, chattering all the while. I do believe my nurse taught me how to listen well. When we arrived she began speaking with the fishmonger. She let go of my hand so she could point into the different boxes which held the glimmering fish. I stepped backward, for the smell overcame me like something rotten and I felt faint. And three steps away I saw another thinner, sterner nurse reaching for a cabbage while a small boy stood quietly at her feet. The boy was a little shorter than I, and there was not a hair out of place on his head. We stared at each other, and after some moments I lifted my hand and waved to him. He stood thoughtfully for some time and then looked back at his nurse, who was now feeling the weight of a melon. Then he gently lifted his hand and waved back. And suddenly my nurse was grabbing roughly at my hand while his nurse jerked his arm and led him away.

"A Montague," my nurse hissed. "And that was the youngest boy, Romeo."

Now Paris I had known all my days. Many mornings when I was taken to see my mother after her breakfast, she would tell me that my father was unavailable for he was entertaining Lord Paris in his drawing room. Occasionally I would glimpse the two of them in a cloud of black smoke through one of the windows from the garden. As I grew older I was sometimes required at dinner with Paris, my father, and my mother. During these meals I ate very little. I spoke quietly and carefully, answering everything Paris asked about my days and my books. But then he and my father would move to other subjects, and my mother would lower her eyes. She would attempt to converse with me a little, and eventually I would be dismissed.

After my mother told me I was to marry Paris, I wondered if he would continue to visit my father so often. I wondered whether he would still think of polite and meaningless questions to ask me. I wondered whether he and my father would continue to make that foul-smelling smoke that drenched and darkened the curtains. Sometimes I imagined we were already married, for were we not already living as my mother and father did? And in the moments when the thought of such a marriage made me feel ill, I consoled myself that he was old and would soon leave me a widow of considerable means and liberties.

On the night of the ball, Mother left the room and the nurse fussed over me, helping me dress in a new gown, combing my hair until it was soft, adorning me with jewels and flowers. She spoke of Paris all the while, saying what a handsome figure he was and how fine a gentleman and that there was none better. And so it was only with slight disappointment that I descended the stairs to the ballroom where my father was entertaining a large number of guests to supper. For although Paris himself was of little interest to me, the life of a married lady appealed to me more than continuing maidenhood.

And so began a merry evening. Servants were all about opening doors, serving cakes and sweetmeats. Musicians piped and swayed, silks flowing in vivid hues around them. Everywhere people clustered or danced, laughed, and ate. The house was awash with candlelight, and there were places to hide among the shadows.

In the earlier part of the evening it was our duty to stand in the hall and greet guests as they arrived. My nurse stood near me, ready to adjust my hair should any lock chance to stray, or to straighten my gown if any sudden movement caused it to slip. At times she beamed with tearful pride as though she were my own mother. At other times she chattered absently with whoever would listen, or to herself when she lacked an audience. I discovered my good cousin Tybalt, who joked with me and told me wild tales of galloping across the countryside on his horse. And I felt a pinch of sadness that those early days, when Tybalt's adventures were confined to the garden and I was free to join him there, were now gone and we were being forced more and more into the separate spheres of life preordained for a man and a woman.

It was growing late in the evening and black as pitch outside. The servants had closed the door, and my mother and father were beginning to move into the light of the ballroom when a knock sounded.

"More guests!" my father exclaimed in delight, and moved to open the door himself. It was with some surprise that I noticed a band of nine or ten masked men. These men were in fine condition, slim and strong and not a gray head among them. If they were my guests, I had not been told about them.

And my father welcomed them, called them to dance. Oh, how often I have recalled his warm invitation and wish'd he spoke thus and knew to whom he spoke! The musicians began a lively jig, and the servants began clearing the tables and folding them away. Something called me then to look at Tybalt for he was of a like age to those men and I thought he would know them. He had wide eyes and a thoughtful expression but did not echo my father's invitations. After I had followed the crowd into the ballroom, I turned and saw Tybalt and my father in animated argument. He alone could reason with my father, soften his countenance, and bring a smile to his lips. It was often as though he were my father's son while I the tiresome child of some other. If I could be granted but one wish it would be to know of what they spoke. For this could have been the making of me or the undoing.

It was understood that these masked young men would be the last guests to arrive, and so we moved into the ballroom where the servants had stoked the fire and all was aglow. After the greetings at such gatherings, my father and my mother would be occupied with entertaining their guests, allowing me the freedom to speak with whomever I chose. It must be said that there were rarely any young people invited on such evenings, for my parents thought only of their own pleasures and social obligations, with little attention to mine. And it was of interest to them that I should be able to converse easily with those older than myself.

So it came about that I had the chance to weave among the people, to feel the warmth and savor sweetmeats and punch upon my tongue. When I look back upon this night I like to pause here, for this was the last hour of my contentment. My life was a straight line, the past still visible and the future an unwavering road into the distance, uncluttered, uncomplicated, and whole. I would go to Lord Paris, not happily but without objection, and would thus follow the life my parents had wished and planned for me, remaining within the fold of the family and the people of Verona who were my parents' friends.

Then suddenly a masked man was before me. Beneath his mask I discerned a handsome countenance, and I was not afraid when he took my hand, for his hands were soft and gentle; a gentleman's fingers. And when he spoke those honeyed words, I drank them in and his kisses were the sweetest fruit I ever tasted. He did not know my name, and as my nurse called me away all tolerant thoughts of Lord Paris were forever banished from my mind.

It was as though I had awoken from a deep slumber. I was like a kitten suddenly learned to see or a babe opening her eyes for the first time. And before me were no longer beautiful objects or gowns. I no longer desired to hold balls for all the ladies of Verona, or exquisite meals and furnishings. I wished only to see that face unmasked and to taste those kisses once more.

I bade my nurse discover the man's name and whether or not he was married. On my nurse's return, it was no longer the possibility of marriage that would weaken me but something that seemed far worse. This man was the same fair blue-eyed boy from my childhood. The Romeo whose eyes I had stared into and who had waved to me as though passing a secret message before we were whisked away, each by our own nurse. The son of my born enemy. But I had known his kisses, and this promised me to him.

When finally I was alone and all believed me to be in bed asleep, I crept to my balcony. For it was a warm night, and at times when I have trouble sleeping it is my custom to whisper my thoughts to the moon. On this night the moon was full, casting a glow over the garden. The air was warm and sweet with summer blossoms. So I stood in my nightgown and told the secrets of my love to the heavens and was most astonished when the heavens replied. Then I saw that it was not the heavens but my love himself, returned, for he could not keep away. On this night I promised myself to Romeo in words.

That was but days ago, and I have lived since only in a dream.

I remember not my days or how I spent them. It was only my nurse who knew my troubles, and she tried to tell me that I should wed Paris. For she could see all that he was and that he would look after me as Father did. But when she saw that I spoke and breathed only for Romeo, she consented to assist me in my plans. For suddenly I understood the meaning of marriage and that this marriage was more important to me than my own life. In my heart I hoped that once the deed was done my mother and father would forgive me. For had they not told me themselves that it was time I married? While my mother and father planned my marriage to Paris downstairs, my nurse prepared me for my marriage to Romeo in my bedchamber. It was a quiet and fast ceremony, and Friar Laurence prayed it would finally unite the Montagues and the Capulets.

Oh, how I wished I had kept my lover with me that afternoon, or calmed my beloved cousin's fury and sat with him under the apple tree. For fate was not to keep them apart, and I cannot choose but feel that what struck that day was intended to punish me for the rest of my days. My nurse soaked me and scented me, smiling all the while as she prepared me for my wedding night. My thoughts were full of Romeo, of holding him in my sleep and not having to let him go. And at this time I did not know that thunder struck the streets of Verona, that brewing furies could no longer be contained and a fight broke out among the young men. I have seen the battle one thousand times in my mind. Romeo could not be killed on our wedding day, so buoyed was he by his love and his dreams. They strengthened him as air in lungs. And my sweet Tybalt's heart was poisoned by hatred for the Montagues as he reached to strike. Romeo slew him dead, and the prince ordered Romeo banished from Verona.

Now that I knew what sweetness could be contained in kisses, I could not give my lips to another man. And it was as if my father breathed the fury from the air for he swore he would never again speak with me if I did not marry Paris. What strange remedies my father dreamed when choosing this time of grief to hand me to his friend.

Last night I did dream that I stood with my Romeo in Friar Laurence's cell. My mother and father were there, and Lord and Lady Montague. They did not smile, nor did they object as I stood in the white gown my nurse had found for me. I shook under so many gazes and stumbled over my vows. I seemed unprepared for such ceremony and was wearing no shoes. But then the town crier shouted over me and I learned that my wedding was to be the execution of my beloved. I looked up to find his eyes but a second before he had bolted from that room pursued by my mother and father and the Montagues. And then suddenly it was just myself and Friar Laurence, standing together in his cell where he has heard so many of my confessions. He smiled and asked me to be seated. So we sat silently, and I wondered whether I had been married or no.

My Romeo came to me after dark for his farewell. We drank every drop of sweetness as though it would be our last. And I could not bear to think that the next night would be my wedding night with Lord Paris. I did not tell Romeo of these fears, and he said it was not safe for me to go with him. After he left in the dawn I went to Friar Laurence to see what could be done. I wailed and wrung my hands as though struck again by death. And then Friar Laurence contrived a plan. He gave me this vial which I now hold before me. He said that it would make me appear as though dead for long enough to have me laid in the tomb. Then I would awake and be taken to join Romeo in Mantua.

And so I hope that this vial is indeed something to slow and not stop my heart. But if this night be my last, then at least it can be said that I have known joy. And as I fall into deep sleep I will dream of my life in Mantua with my love. We will live together in a small cottage, and there we will bring up our children. And in a few years we will write my mother and father. They will be so pleased I am living that they will forgive me for what I have done. This is my prayer.

Part Two

LEARNING

Advice to the Actor

Practise entering and taking up a position in your own room frequently. Although a lady's dress conceals her legs, it is equally essential for her to attend to this rule, in order to preserve a natural and graceful attitude.

In making a rush on to the stage, commence the movement several feet from the point where you will come in sight, and take particular care that your steps are firm and decided, unless you have to represent indecision, fear, or any similar feeling. See that there is nothing to impede you, such as an awkwardly slung sword or badly arranged drapery. . . .

When leading on others, or pursued by an enemy, your face should be directed towards the entry, but your body should have its full front to the audience. Let the head be a little thrown back. Entrances of this kind are most effective when made from the Left, because the right hand, especially if grasping a sword or baton, can be used most effectively, and the whole figure can be displayed to the greatest advantage. . . .

When a person is carried off the stage in a faint, or dead, great care is necessary to keep up the natural representation. These exits should be carefully rehearsed, and not, as they usually are, left to chance at night. . . . If possible, the person selected to bear off the actor should be sufficiently strong to do so, without faltering, but if, as must frequently be the case, this actor should have to carry off a much heavier person than he can bear he should have one to help him, and by a little contrivance at rehearsal, he may appear to support the person who is in reality sustained by the other. Take care that the dress is clear of the wings. By proper rehearsal and arrangement, the folds of robes may be made to fall picturesquely, adding greatly to the effect of the exit.

Be particularly careful not to touch the head of the actor you are supporting or his wig may come off.

—NINETEENTH-CENTURY ACTING MANUAL, QUOTED IN
VICTORIAN THEATRE: THE THEATRE IN ITS TIME

My fate, whatever it may be, shall never separate me from my mother.

—ELIZABETH INCHBALD, *LOVER'S VOWS*, QUOTED IN
OXBERRY'S "MEMOIR OF MISS H. C. SMITHSON OF
THE THEATRE-ROYAL, DRURY LANE"

Ennis: 1808

*L*ORD CASTLE COOTE was one of the Protestant landowners of our parish. His wife occupied herself with charity works, which caused her to have a good deal to do with Father Barrett. After their meetings, the door would be flung open and Lady Castle Coote would enfold me in warm fabrics and the smell of roses. She would kiss my cheeks and stroke my hair. I do believe Lady Castle Coote had always longed for a daughter.

She never forgot that first performance of mine, dancing a pas de deux with Mrs. Helme just before the death of Father Barrett. My father had decided that Ennis should be the place of my performing debut, and somehow he convinced Father Barrett of this. I wonder whether Father Barrett, sensing the end was near, agreed to this opportunity for my performing under his own watchful eye. He immensely enjoyed the theater. His only wish was that I should be protected from the low company of fallen women and cavalier men, their breath sweet from drink. And so I imagine that he had a solemn interview with my father and Mrs. Helme. During this he would have instructed my father on the nature of my performance and that I was not to witness the rest of the theatricals that evening. Rehearsals with Mrs. Helme were to take place in the parlor and not in the theater itself. Mrs. Helme was to take utmost care while instructing me. During all these discussions, I am sure Lady Castle Coote was in the background somewhere, using her silent powers of persuasion to prevent the ruin of a child who had until then been so carefully guarded.

On the day of my first rehearsal, my father sat with me for some time. "Now, Harriet, you must be very respectful of the great Mrs. Helme. Pay careful attention to everything she says to you."

And when the lady herself arrived, I soon came to understand the nature of her condition and that my father had a number of reasons for referring to her as "the great Mrs. Helme." For she was swollen and enormous with a painfully upright carriage. Three weeks later she would give birth to twins.

It was from this breathless woman that I received my first instruction. She emphasized the importance of deportment, eyed me carefully, and then informed me of my most handsome side. "Always endeavor to have your left shoulder closest to the audience," she said sternly. "This will show you to greatest advantage on account of putting the dimple upon your right cheek into shadow."

At first she stood before me, beating her loosely closed fists to the rhythm of the music inside her. I wondered whether those two heartbeats, as I thought of them then, beat in time with each other. And then, when I thought she was going to join me in dancing, she sank her large body into one of Father Barrett's armchairs and called directions. Left foot, right foot, point, turn, counting in between, praising often. At the end of the morning she pronounced me very gifted. That was my only rehearsal under the direction of the great Mrs. Helme.

Two days before the concert, my father brought me a copy of the *Clare Journal and Ennis Advertiser* to show me the evening's program in print. He had often shown me his advertisements in the newspaper, but this was the first time my own name was featured. He gave me the copy to keep. I memorized those words as though they were Father Barrett's Latin grammar. I remember them still.

ENNIS, 1 FEBRUARY 1808

LAST NIGHT OF MRS. HELME'S ENGAGEMENT AT THE ENNIS THEATER

Mrs. Helme most respectfully begs leave to acquaint the Ladies and Gentlemen of Ennis and its vicinity, that her BENEFIT is fixed for WEDNESDAY, FEBRUARY 3rd, being positively the last night she will have the honor of appearing before them; on which evening will be presented Shakespeare's tragedy of

ROMEO AND JULIET

In the course of the evening Mrs. Helme will dance

the celebrated

BROAD SWORD HORNPIPE

A PAS DE DEUX

by Miss Smithson and Mrs. Helme

and a DOUBLE HORNPIPE

by Mr. Waring and Mrs. Helme

To this day I am disappointed to have missed viewing the great Mrs. Helme in the role of Juliet.

Father Barrett attended the evening's entertainment in its entirety. I believe most of Ennis was there that night, including the Castle Cootes and the Freemasons of lodge number 60, of which my father was a peripatetic member. The brothers appeared in full regalia, and their heavy cloaks drew my attention. I was taken along for the dancing by a disgruntled Bridie, deprived of her night of rest. After I had been indulged in the rare privilege of a bath, Bridie dressed me in my new green gown that had been sewn by my mother for the occasion. She arranged my curls neatly about my face and helped tighten the laces on my boots, which would be exchanged for satin dancing shoes before the performance. It was a short walk to Cooke's Lane in my dark cloak; occasional lamps pushed balls of light into the frosty air. Bridie crossed herself as we entered the lane and muttered under her breath. Like many other Ennis residents, she tried to avoid the street where the jail had so long stood.

Bridie knocked quietly at the stage door, which was opened by a large man with long, tangled hair. He nodded to her before taking my hand and leading me inside. It was dark, and the boards were dusty. Mrs. Helme herself, wearing a crimson gown that made her glow, led me to a small room where she instructed me to change my shoes. The walls seemed paper thin, and I fancied the audience could see us moving about as they shouted, laughed, and applauded. And then suddenly I was on the stage.

I stood still, frozen in dim stagelight. And then there was soft laughter coming from the audience before plaudits. As the applause grew louder, my sight returned and I could see Mrs. Helme smiling at me from the other side of the stage. Then the musicians began playing from somewhere in front of me and I began to move, trying to remember the steps I had been shown a few days earlier. For someone so large, Mrs. Helme moved deftly and with nimble feet. However, the dance itself was untidy and under-rehearsed. While I believe Mrs. Helme tried to follow my steps so that we danced together, after the first few seconds I danced alone. I had forgotten her presence. I sensed the audience's delight with me, and the applause was as exciting as thunder. I felt as though I had moved the world.

Waterford, County Waterford: 1809–1814

MADAME TOURNIER'S WAS a school for Catholic girls, most of whose fathers had been educated in England or in France. They were the daughters of doctors and barristers, sent to Waterford to be taught what it was thought they needed to know. We were taught a little French, and we read passages from the Bible. Once I let slip that I had read Shakespeare and Madame Tournier glared. Young ladies did not need to know Shakespeare.

At Madame Tournier's we learned to sew samplers. Some of the other girls became very interested in this pastime and would sit in bed late at night, trying to finish embroidering perfect crimson flowers by candlelight. I am sure many of them already had weak eyes by the time I left at fourteen. I would hide my head under the covers to block the light. In my dreams I returned to Chapel Lane.

We learned singing; my voice was not as strong as the voices of other girls. There was one girl, her name was Anastasia, who could sing very well and wanted everyone to know it. "I will be the next Mistress Siddons," she announced one day, flicking her hair behind her head. The other girls stared at her in shock. I stared at my feet. I could not imagine why anyone would wish to live the life of a player.

Madame Tournier took little notice of me, and I did not speak much when called upon in class. She never failed to look surprised when I topped the class again in French, Latin, or British history.

For when I closed my eyes I could see pages of books or slates of text before me, and I never had trouble recalling information. After school there were lessons to complete, usually French grammar or a few sums. Then there would be supper. When our stomachs were full and our bodies weary, we were sent to bed. Oftentimes I whispered Lamb's *Tales from Shakespeare* to the other girls in my room after the candles were snuffed. I knew some of the lines from Father Barrett and my father, so I would color the stories with these, imagining myself to be someone else, embellishing, deepening the sounds. It was my capacity to entertain which finally drew the other girls to me. Sometimes their laughter would bring Madame Tournier running from her quarters.

When the other girls asked me questions, I developed ways of answering. Yes, I had a brother and a sister, my father was a manager. I soaked up those school days like sunshine before a storm. Some weekends I traveled with them to see their families. Mothers would shake their heads at hearing how far away my family was, and that there were only rare opportunities for us to meet. Apart from these explanations, I rarely thought of my other life. I was always one of a crowd of children. And as we grew older, the other girls began speaking of young men and marriage.

DURING MY SCHOOL YEARS I spent many summers with the Castle Cootes. Their Irish country estate was the most grand I had seen. In Ennis, uncultivated land was overgrown and tangled. In Waterford, the lawn at their estate was trimmed and the gardens brimming with fresh flowers. I came to know the three Castle Coote boys as though they were my brothers. Charles was around sixteen at this time, and he had the most time to spend with me. George was in his final year of boarding school, and Edmund attended Oxford University. It was only in summer that the three boys would be reunited for this longer period, and I was pleased to be included in their games. In the evenings we learned plays, and whenever there were guests from England we performed for them. It was during this time that I experienced the thrill of performing for the second time. I found that after one or two readings I could remember the lines. I was still completely untrained and already acquiring bad habits, but I found it easy to slip in and out of character, which I was frequently required to do, being the only girl. One summer we performed a version of *The Merchant of Venice*.

We spent most of our time preparing the courtroom scene in which I, as Portia, disguised as a man of the law, defended my husband's friend Antonio against Shylock, the Jew claiming Antonio owed him a pound of flesh. The afternoon of our performance, Charles found me alone in the library. He stood facing me and held a garment in his hands. "Your costume, my lady," he said, bowing. He lifted the cloak over my shoulders and arranged it about my neck.

"Thank you, sir," I said quickly, trying to hide my blushing.

I still remember the earnest Edmund, robed in a suit of his father's, his face contorted and falling to his knees. He flinched and it was clear he had fallen harder than he had intended.

I am a Jew. Hath not a Jew eyes? Hath not a Jew hands,
organs, dimensions, senses, affections, passions?

And as he spoke, Charles and George stood to the side, stifling their laughter at Edmund's melodramatic posture, his cracking voice. From her seat in the front row of the Castle Coote theater, Lady Castle Coote raised an eyebrow, while her husband looked down as though attempting to comprehend the words.

I moved as close to my audience as I could. I looked Lady Castle Coote in the eye, with more boldness than I would usually have dared. Wearing the Castle Coote cloak, slowly and clearly I began:

> *The quality of mercy is not strained;*
> *It droppeth as the gentle rain from heaven*
> *Upon the place beneath: it is twice blest:*
> *It blesseth him that gives and him that takes;*
> *'tis mightiest in the mightiest. . . .*

Lord Castle Coote watched silently, barely breathing while his wife held her fingers to her right cheek and sat motionless. At the end of the scene they paused for a few seconds, waiting for me to become myself again, before applauding and shouting "Bravo! Bravo!" in accents that could be mistaken for English. And while the boys bowed awkwardly, I curtsied as I sensed I should, eyes lowered.

Occasionally my parents visited. Although Lady Castle Coote was very polite to them, I saw the way she looked at their post chaise, the boxes overflowing with properties, and the costumes untidily cluttering up the lawn. And she most certainly would have refused my father's request to have the mule housed in the Castle Coote stables, had she found a polite way to do so. Once, after they had gone, I heard her telling her husband that she had wanted to grasp my younger brother and sister and plunge them into a tub to give them a good soaking.

Lady Castle Coote had satin gowns sewn for me by her seamstress. The boys never had to ask for a new saddle or a book. Members of the family gave me many books of poetry and British history, and I was also permitted to use the library freely. But after summer I would have to leave my books behind, for fear Madame Tournier would disapprove. I also left my gowns, for there would be no use for them at school. And so after spending such a rich and happy season, I always returned to school in a small carriage with nothing but my battered trunk and a few pinafores.

In what was to become my final year at Madame Tournier's, a play was planned. Madame Tournier had written it herself. It told the story of nuns opening a school for the poor in Derry. I believe it contained very little in the way of plot. Rehearsals began after lunch one day. Madame Tournier listed the characters and who was to play each one.

"Harriet Smithson," Madame Tournier said after my many years of near silence in her presence, "is to play Mother Superior. I presume she has inherited a great acting talent from her parents."

My body grew hot as coals and I quivered. The girls gasped and stared at me. Then they turned around one by one, seeing by my reaction that what she had said was true.

At supper the other girls turned away from me, and I was left to learn my lines alone and tearful. I played Mother Superior to the best of my ability, and the parents who came to see the play applauded in their ignorance. But from the day the roles had been cast, even my closest friends turned away.

THAT SUMMER, Charles and I spent much time together. We would sit in the orchard, peach juice dripping down our chins, and speak of a shared future in which we toured the world, visiting the great castles and gardens, riding horses through valleys, bathing in the sea.

At breakfast one morning during my fourteenth summer a maid brought me a letter from my mother. Correspondence from my parents was more unusual than their surprise visits, and a shadow hovered over me that morning. Charles had gone to town with his father; I went to sit in the orchard under an apple tree. It was there that I read of the difficulties that had befallen my family. My father was ill with a weakened heart; the doctor thought he had not long to live. He had retired from the stage immediately, and my mother had returned to acting. But her income was too little for a family of four. I was ripe for a career on the stage, she wrote. She and my father had been discussing this prospect and decided that I stood every chance of success.

The time had come for me to begin to repay the gifts I had been given. I felt ill prepared for such a profession.

"Do not be too hasty, Harriet," Lady Castle Coote said. "Give my husband some time to enquire after a post of governess among our friends. Otherwise, we shall speak with Mr. Jones from the Theatre Royal and see what can be done for you."

Desdemona

*I*T WAS MY FATHER WHO tuned my ears to the sounds of stories. Oh, I had nurses and maids to sing me to sleep, but none had the power of Father, whose soft words would send me to dreams of other worlds. And though I grew and learned to read, though my head was filled with books, I never lost my need for the purity of fresh-told stories. It is true I had a happy childhood and wanted for nothing, but I did grow tired of my own company. My nursery never held for me the excitement of battles through desert storms and valleys.

My father had many friends visit the palace. And he chose his friends for nobility and intelligence, not for color, breed, or education. For this I admired him. In the evenings it seemed my presence was not enough and he would desire the company of men. At these times I was not permitted to be fully present but instead would flit about like a moth, relieving the maid of the tea tray and whisky bottle until the men had had their fill and I could listen to their speech. My father would grow merry as the evening darkened, and sometimes I would be called on to tend his headache the following morning. On such mornings he often asked how I liked Organo, Felano, or Felicio, for each of them desired my hand. I begged my father not to give me to them, for I was happy in the palace and did not wish to leave. I could not tell him I did not feel these men were of superior mind. My father patted my head and nodded. He told me I did not have to go.

And for some months after, I remained mainly within the palace walls, my books for company. Oh, how I loved tales of adventure! And then it happened that my father began to invite Othello to talk with him in the evenings. Father admired this Moor and was intrigued by his life. Othello was polite and attentive toward me when I poured his drink, although my father would press him impatiently for more of his story, not looking away from that man's face even as I took away his teacup and handed him his whiskey glass. And I became glad that I had relieved the maid of these evening duties, for Othello's story was the most pitiful I had ever heard.

He began with tales of a boyhood wandering the countryside, hunting with the men and returning in the evenings with his catch for the women to cook over the fire. Such boys are already made men, he said, and his work made him strong. And so he caught the attention of those with shackles and chains, those evil men who captured him and sold him into slavery for a good sum. As a slave he met men whipped to shreds, with blankness in their eyes. But Othello was young and strong, and he tended the fields well. In time he received the admiration of those he worked for, and they freed him to become a soldier. As such he has fought many battles for us without a white man's fear of death. He has traversed deserts and quarries, he has seen heaven from a hilltop.

I spent time alone with Othello. Sometimes my father was occupied with business matters and I kept Othello company while he waited. Other times my father was unwell and Othello remained talking with me until well into the night, long after Father slept. How could I choose but love such a man? He carried me to other worlds with his stories and then brought me back to the kindness and the best of this world. And so I told him that had he a friend who loved me, he could woo me thus. Othello asked if I would be his wife.

It must be said that he wished immediately to go to my father. It was I who stopped him, for fear my father would rip the joy from my breast. For although he loved Othello, I do not believe he had ever considered a black for a son, let alone one with little fortune or education. It was my plan that we would be wed in secret and then would go to my father and tell him. I was sure he would come to seeing my view. He knew the goodness of the man who had won my heart. But I betrayed my father, and I fear the heavens will not forgive me.

I had never imagined it would be so easy to be wed in secret. I was in my marriage bed before my father knew I had gone. But I was awoken from my slumber by hammering and shouting at the door.

Those who captured him could not see the beauty of his form, his strength, the smoothness of his skin. I would that my father had believed the truth of my love for Othello. My husband told me afterward that they accused him of wooing me with witchcraft, and I laughed at the thought. What spells, what herbs, what magic could he have given me? It was nothing other than the stories that drew me to him. I testified thus before my father, and after some time he did believe me. His voice cracked and he furrowed his brow. I saw the lines of years across his cheek when he told of the pain of losing his daughter. At that moment I loved him, for it was losing me that pained him, and not losing me to a Moor. This sadness is a shadow over me like an ill omen.

The moment was soon over, for suddenly people were shouting that we were at war with the Ottomans over Cyprus and my father was collecting himself and calling to Othello that he must go. There was some talk of my staying, but I would rather have died than lose the chance of my first adventure and of accompanying my husband, and finally they all agreed.

I was quite ill during the voyage and pleased to have Emilia, Iago's wife, to care for me. My husband traveled behind with soldiers. On the island we were housed immediately in comfortable lodgings, and as I lay upon my bed a fierce storm came over. Emilia whimpered and I bade her under the covers with me. The walls shook with thunder, and lightning blazed like fire. It was as though the heavens wished to punish me. I prayed that if Othello were drowned I would be struck by lightning in my sleep.

This morning there is pale sunlight and a playful sea breeze. I sit in the sunshine, waiting for some news. Boat timber has been washed up on the shores, and I fear this gentle weather has something to hide.

Dublin: 1814

I COULD SCARCELY BELIEVE my good fortune in being invited to perform at the Theatre Royal. If I had to enter the acting profession, this was an auspicious beginning. Lady Castle Coote held one last dinner in my honor; all her sons attended. Present, too, was Mr. Jones, who had offered me my new position of employment. He seemed particularly friendly with the Castle Cootes after a few glasses of wine. There were speeches and toasts. Lord Castle Coote wished me well as "a member of our warm family circle," and I fancied Charles looked a little wistful.

After Mr. Jones had left in the wee hours of the morning, all other members of the family retired until I was left alone with Charles. He stared at the thick carpets and then at my boots, until finally his eyes met mine. And then he said, "Miss Smithson, I will think of you often," before reaching into his pocket and pulling out a box which he placed in my open palm. The gift was a small silver thimble, bordered by curled engraving. It had been his great-grandmother's, he said, and would protect my lady's hands. He hoped that whenever I looked at it I would remember him.

I WAS PLEASED to be spared returning to Madame Tournier's school for young ladies. Lady Castle Coote helped me pack a trunk that had once been hers. When she thought I wasn't looking, I noticed her slipping small muslin parcels of dried lavender and rose petals between my underclothes, a surprise sweetness that would mean so much to me once I had left the pastures of Waterford for the cobbled streets of Dublin.

"There is much to see in Dublin. You must visit Christ Church Cathedral," Lady Castle Coote told me. "And you will enjoy being with your family again." I will never forget her standing in my bedchamber with an armful of gowns, her cheeks slightly flushed from the exertion.

"Harriet, won't you take some of these?" she asked.

"Perhaps one or two. I think I have outgrown many of them. I expect I will spend most of my time working in Dublin. I shan't have many opportunities to wear such fine clothes."

I stood before her in my day dress, and one by one she held the shimmering fabrics against my body, leaning back and squinting. Several of them were now too short, and it was clear they would not fit over my shoulders and hips.

"They are yours, Harriet. Perhaps your sister would wear them?"

And when my bedchamber was bare of trinkets, most of my books boxed ready for a charity school, and the wardrobe empty, I stood alone before the full-length glass staring at my bony figure in its new curves and the silk underclothes Lady Castle Coote had bought me. I stepped into a pink satin gown I had worn to a recent dinner and pulled it up around myself. I could still move inside this one. I folded it into the trunk and lifted a pale blue cotton day dress from the previous summer, holding it against myself. It still held the shape of my thirteen-year-old figure, but I would not be able to wear this one again. And as I stared into the glass, I noticed tears trickling down my cheeks and I held that dress as though it were my life.

Lady Castle Coote accompanied me to town in one of her carriages. Her driver lifted my trunk into the mail coach, and Lady Castle Coote peered anxiously at the driver of the mail coach, in his torn coat, who was chewing some foul-smelling plant.

"Harriet—are you sure we cannot send you with our own driver? I am worried to allow you on your own—"

"It is all arranged. And there will be other passengers. I'm sure I will be safe." And as I spoke these words, I wondered if it was too late to change my mind, to travel back home with her and live out the rest of my days as a lady in Waterford. She turned back to me and sniffed.

"I must let you go then. Good-bye, sweet child. A safe journey and love to your family." Briefly, she enveloped me in her soft cloak and the scent of white roses.

The journey took many hours, and we stopped overnight in Wicklow. I was grateful for the presence of an older lady on her way to visit her grandchildren in Dublin, though at times her chatter became too much and I feigned sleep to encourage her silence. We shared a room at the inn, and if it was not for old Mrs. Kennedy, it is possible I would have slipped away in the night, away from the carriage that would take me to my family, or instead I might have cried myself to sleep. But Mrs. Kennedy told stories of all her children and grandchildren, and this passed the time and distracted me from my worries. As the carriage jolted up and down, I imagined a vibrant city with many cobbled streets to explore, beautiful shops, and churches. But I could not help feeling I was leaving my real home for a place where I would always be a visitor.

My dress, once pressed, was creased and stained when I arrived. Although I had combed my hair in preparation for arrival, I knew it was dull and dusty and out of shape from my dozing in an upright position. My mother met me coming off the mail coach in Dublin. I did not notice her at first, a woman cloaked in worn dark cloth, among other similarly attired Dubliners. She touched my shoulder and kissed my cheek quickly, looking down as though not sure she was allowed to take such liberties.

"Harriet, you have grown so beautiful. Is this all you have?" She looked about me at the cobblestones, watching as the driver finished unloading trunks. I carried a small case containing a little embroidery, a copy book, my Lamb's Shakespeare, my Bible, and one of the gray pinafores I had worn at school.

"I also have a trunk," I said. My knees buckled and I steadied myself, dazed.

My mother took my case. "Joseph, help your sister."

It was then that I noticed a small thin boy, eleven or twelve with dark curls, standing a discreet distance away. He smiled shyly. I moved to where my trunk had been left by the side of the road.

"This is mine," I said and watched him quickly try to gather it in arms, struggling with its weight, finally trying to drag it behind him as he began his way back along the road.

"Joseph!" I smiled. "Let me help you."

He turned.

"We'll carry it together." And so we began our slow walk to my parents' lodgings, holding the trunk between us like a bridge between islands.

"Harriet, I am roasting some mutton and potatoes for our supper. You must be worn out from your journey. You will have to share a room with your sister, but there is a bed all of your own." My mother smiled proudly and then sniffed. "I cannot recall when we last ate a meal all together. The five of us. Your father—your father has been poorly. But this last week he has talked only of your return. He will be proud to see you so grown, so lovely and with such learning as he never had."

My father was standing in the narrow hallway blocking the entrance when we arrived at the shabby Dublin lodgings. The building held the savory aroma of roasting meat and wood smoke.

"My girl!" he said, holding me in his arms until I felt the beginnings of tears. "Let me see you," he said breathlessly, holding my shoulders away from him. "A fine Juliet! Won't she make a fine Juliet, Hetta."

"A fine Juliet, yes. Now let us in, William, I need to see to our supper downstairs."

"Come." He led me by the hand to a sitting room with some faded brown armchairs.

"Harriet!" My sister was sitting in an armchair, her legs invisible, a woolen rug draped over her.

"Hello, Anne." I leaned over and kissed her cheek, pushing her hair away from her eyes so I could see her face. She was pale and thin with bright dark eyes. She looked much younger than her ten years. "May I see your sewing?"

She held the cloth out to me, shyly. "I am making it for you. Mother buys me cotton from the market."

I peered at the fine stitches. The canvas was bordered by a weaving green vine with small blue flowers. My full name was embroidered in a fine red copperplate, and she had begun to sew a mask beneath. I turned it over in my hands. It was difficult to tell the front from the back.

"It is very good, Anne. What an excellent eye and a steady hand!"

She grinned as I handed it back to her, sinking into a chair.

That evening we ate crammed around a table that should have seated only four and wobbled under the weight of the chipped unmatching crockery. I noticed they had saved the most comfortable chair for me while Joseph perched on a stool and my mother propped herself up with blankets so she could sit tall enough to cut her meat. Each plate contained a morsel of hardened meat and some well-roasted potato pieces. My father had found some sour wine which we drank from preserving jars. Before we commenced our meal, he held his own jar up in the air.

"I would like to thank God for the safe arrival of our Harriet," he said.

"The safe arrival of our Harriet," my mother and siblings chorused, Joseph and Anne raising their child-like voices and their almost-clear drinks heavenward.

As I began to saw at my mutton, I noticed Anne giggling. Joseph, a moment ago so pious, was now rolling his eyes around and around in his head.

"Children," my mother smiled. "Eat your supper now. It will get cold."

At the end of the meal, the room began to spin around me and I felt faint. My mother stood and grabbed my arm.

"Come now, Harriet, you are exhausted. I have made up your bed with extra blankets in case you get cold." She pulled me up and led me from the table.

"Good night, then," I said to the room at large. My brother and sister watched silently from the table.

With a tenderness I did not remember from childhood, my mother helped me undress and wrapped the blankets around me. She sat on the bed and I closed my eyes, feeling as though I was falling from a great height.

"Harriet, you must never think that we did not love you. But look at you, now. So strong and clever and beautiful. We could never have given you the life and the education that Father Barrett gave you, bless him. Sleep now. We will speak more in the morning." I felt her lips on my forehead and sensed the dim candlelight moving with her shadow out the door.

DURING THOSE EARLY WEEKS in Dublin I came to know my father. He told me that as a young man he had had no interest in the theater. He was a stonemason, as was his father before him. He said there was warmth in stone, in the very center, and that buildings made of stone would outlast everything else. It was a childhood friend of his who invited him to go along to the theater the night he met my mother.

My mother was sixteen and performing the part of Belvedira in *Venice Preserved*. She remembers nothing of the night she met my father except the shy man who tried to shake her hand after pushing his way through the rowdy audience to meet her. My mother says his hands were calloused yet tender as she held them in her own.

After I was born, my parents toured Ireland for a year, taking me with them. But with both of them working, they frequently had to leave me with strangers. The decision to leave me with Father Barrett was made one night after they collected me, screaming, from a neighbor, my face splattered with sour milk and my clothes soiled.

I know there would never have been any question of my parents giving up Joseph, the second child. My father was overjoyed to behold his only son. Joseph became a part of the theater world from the day he could walk. I know that this means he spent hours on his own, crawling among moth-eaten costumes and abandoned props. That occasionally a leading actress would give him sweets and stroke his blond curls. And the rest of the time he would have to find his own morsels of food, snatching bread from actors' belongings, curling up among the carpetbags when he was tired. But for all this neglect, the theater was in his blood more so than it was in mine.

After the birth of Joseph, my father said my mother was afflicted with a deep melancholy. She did not eat for months, and then she would only eat barley. She grew swollen and was prone to bouts of crying. She was eight months pregnant before they guessed. Father said he started feeding my mother vegetables and mutton. He could scarcely afford to feed himself, but he knew that she needed to eat well for the strength of their child.

Anne was born breathless and blue, tangled in the umbilical cord. She was curled in the shape of a cashew nut, and no one could straighten her arms or her back. She did not cry for days. My mother never stopped fearing she would die.

❦

I DID NOT SLEEP for weeks leading up to my debut performance, and had I been any older this would have shown itself in heavy shadows under my eyes. And while part of me could not sleep for excitement, the other part could not sleep for shame. As an actress I would be admired by some; I also knew I would be reviled by others. And once on the stage there would be no removing the experience from my past. As I thought about Lady Castle Coote, Father Barrett, and the girls at my school, I felt the beginnings of a deep shame that pride would force me to become a working woman.

In Dublin I spent hours reading my scripts in bed. In the mornings and on performance evenings my mother would leave for rehearsal in a great flurry of drapery and calling out instructions to heat soup and boil potatoes as she closed the door. We could not afford to eat meat, and to this day I do not understand how she made meals on the small salary she must have earned. We ate a good many potatoes during that time, but my mother always found a few herbs, an onion, or some butter, and so our meals were flavorsome and nourishing enough.

After my mother left, I would wake my sister and help her dress. I would prepare some gruel for breakfast and sit her at the table with Joseph and my father.

"Who are you this morning, Harriet?" my father would grin.

"Albina, Father."

"Lovely," and small flecks of gruel would spatter the tablecloth. Anne would screw up her nose, and Father would pretend not to notice.

"And shall you marry the man or not, then?"

"I shall."

"Very good."

"Mind you treat him well. Feed him up and remember to darn his stockings."

"He shall darn his own stockings, Father."

"No!" he feigned shock.

"What sort of man is he, then?"

"One that likes cotton and thread, Father." At this, Joseph and Anne would begin to giggle.

"Well, I'll be."

There was great anticipation surrounding my debut perform-ance, and my father requested to hear my lines once a day. Lying there with his eyes closed, he would offer advice on inflection and intonation. He suggested gestures and clicked his tongue at the bad habits I seemed to be acquiring.

"Stop *swaying*, child, for heaven's sake! You are not a pendu-lum," he said. He put much time into preparing careful instruc-tions for me. He said the Crow Street Theatre had only just been reopened after rioting spectators damaged the building.

"Aah, the people of Dublin have too much time on their hands. They rioted on account of a dog withdrawing from the stage over a pay dispute."

Dublin was an excellent theater, he told me, and a fortuitous beginning. I wonder now whether I could have stayed in Dublin and made my mark there, sparing myself all that was to follow. I knew the Theatre Royal to have been a step in the careers of many actors and had heard that a number of the better known London players performed there in summer. I hoped to see the great actors Kean and Macready there. My father said that Edmund Kean was known for his love of pomp and circumstance, and that certain theater managers had been required to hold parades in his honor before Kean could be persuaded to appear. And Macready had a dislike of reciting lines, even those written by Shakespeare, and would frequently add his own or change what had been written. But each actor had such a gift that he could forget himself upon the stage and become the very essence of the character he represented.

My father told me that Mr. Jones was a gentleman and he was pleased I was in such safe hands. At first I was astounded at hear-ing how much I was to be paid. I had never had my own money before, and my mind filled with the colored fabrics, shoes, and jewels I could buy. Then I remembered that my parents had not accompanied me merely for my own protection. They wanted their share.

Although I knew my lines from the first, the other actors were not always kind to me in rehearsal. I could barely open my mouth before Mr. Jones would beg me to make more sound. He was a small and gentle man, but this made his requests all the more powerful.

"If you please, Miss Smithson, could you speak a little louder?" These frequent interjections only served to increase the self-doubt I nurtured, and to make my voice, if anything, quieter. During the rehearsal of my scenes, the chatter around me frequently rose to such volume that Mr. Jones's instructions were inaudible. He waved his arms at the other actors in vain. I would pause and close my eyes, biting my lips together, willing myself to remain composed. Then I would commence my lines again, with slightly more conviction, and Mr. Jones would allow me to continue for the sake of the rehearsal schedule. In performance, Mr. Jones was known for his peculiar way of rolling his eyes.

Years later I came across some of the Irish players in London, and they seemed surprised I was capable of uttering my own speech. They heard me recite lines often enough, but during rehearsals I watched and listened in silence. It would not be until the performances that I managed to lose myself in the character I portrayed.

Although I could never have told my father, the theater in Dublin was grander than I had ever imagined, my only experience of theater being the one in Ennis. I had heard that my father's theater was now a school, though I did not like to ask him. In

Dublin the stage was spacious and there were a number of entrances to the building. The balcony railings were gold, and altogether the brilliant colors were like Christmas. In the coffee room it was possible to procure mulled wine and other refreshments.

The Theatre Royal was also known as the Crow Street Theatre, and to us it was simply the Old Crow. My mother and I would leave Father and Joseph with Anne and walk to the Old Crow in the evenings. We had to walk fast for we were usually running late. As my own thoughts became preoccupied with the role I would soon play, I was reminded of an occasion when my parents had visited Ennis. On the night of a performance, I had tried in vain to gain my father's attention. He had seemed absent and had later said he had been picturing the forthcoming scenes in his mind.

Mr. Jones had a hold on his actors. The English system of fines would be nothing by comparison. At the end of each rehearsal he lectured us all on our conduct before and during the performance. If anyone was found to have had so much as a drop of wine, he would not merely be fined but would be banned from performance for at least an evening. Not one of us could risk losing a whole evening's wages, and so it happened that the actors at the Old Crow were a respectable society for a young girl.

ON MY OPENING NIGHT in *The Will*, I sat by myself in the greenroom, hoping my skirts were straight but reluctant to examine myself too closely in the glass in front of the other actors. And then I noticed someone standing before me. I stood.

"Miss Smithson?" A young woman smiled. I had seen her before but could not place her. "I am Eliza O'Neill." She shook my hand in a way I had only seen men do. "I have been watching you in rehearsal. I think Albina is a perfect role for you."

"I still have much to learn. But thank you." I smiled. My father had told me about Eliza O'Neill. I knew that she was the favorite of the London audiences, but she had also begun her career in Dublin.

"Are you performing this evening?" I asked.

"Only later in the second drama. Come, sit down." We sat together on a bench. "Do you have a charm for your first night?" she asked. I shook my head. "Then you must borrow mine," she said, reaching inside her skirts so that I had to look away.

"Here." She dropped a ball of soft fur into my palm. "My brother caught it years ago. I always have it with me when I perform." I examined the white hairs and realized I held a rabbit's tail.

As I stood in the wings that night, I entered a state of numbness where I was deaf and barely breathed, my mind completely empty. And then suddenly someone gave me a great push and I was on the boards, lit from below, and through the fog I could discern an audience. People laughed and conversed, but they were focused in my direction as I began to speak. And as I spoke, I became Albina; my life until that moment dissolved.

All through *The Will* that night, Eliza sat with me in the greenroom. She asked me about my scenes in advance. "Now, what is Albina thinking in the next scene? How can you show this through gesture?"

When I came off stage, she greeted me with glasses of water and her own soft applause. At the end of the performance she helped me seek out my mother who was standing in the foyer speaking with some of my colleagues. My mother paused in her conversation when she saw me approach.

"Mother, have you met Eliza O'Neill? She is recently arrived from London."

"I don't believe I have." She held out her hand. "But I have long admired your work, Miss O'Neill."

"Thank you. Your daughter Harriet has great talent, Mrs. Smithson. I believe she will soon be seen in the greatest roles. It is rare for a new performer to receive three separate plaudits after a debut performance."

Eliza O'Neill was a commanding presence and performed throughout my first season. Her eyes were an unusual shade of dark blue, her hair blond and curled. She had a prominent forehead and a large nose. She was tall and large-boned and rarely laughed. Although not considered by many to be beautiful, Eliza was much admired. From the day I met her, I would strive to be everything Eliza O'Neill was.

Our season together in Dublin seemed short. Her family guarded her closely; her father and brother were never far away. She attended church every Sunday, and occasionally I accompanied her. The relaxed friendship between the O'Neill men and the players protected her from untoward attention.

At the end of the season, the O'Neill family invited me to stay with them before the summer touring season. I savored those days as though knowing such times would not be possible again. Eliza seemed to have no end of stories inside her. She had so much to tell me about her family; she could keep me entertained for hours without repeating a word. One by one I learned about them all. It was usually late by the time everyone retired for the evening. And in Eliza's bedchamber she whispered stories to me in the darkness.

"My mother was a lady," she whispered to me one night. "As

a girl she learned piano and painting and French. Her parents disowned her when she married my father. We had to make our own family; there were no grandparents to show us how. When we were small, Mother taught us all music. That was how it all began, this playing."

The O'Neill lodgings had something of home about them. They were on permanent rental, and many of the family's belongings were left there during the summer touring. Unlike our lodgings, their rooms contained more than simply essential items. At the O'Neills there was a bookcase full of leather-bound volumes. I was drawn to these books and the smell of fresh-cut pages. I would stand staring, overwhelmed, unable to select one to read, for it would mean leaving the others. There were many great novels on those shelves, the works of Sir Walter Scott, Henry Fielding, and Jane Austen. I would run my fingers along their spines, confirming for myself that the objects were real and not merely conjured by my imagination.

"Where's your friend, Eliza?" I would hear Mr. O'Neill asking.

"At the bookcase, I expect," Eliza would say, herself looking up from *The Lady of the Lake*.

"Too much book learning be not good for a lady!" he would say and laugh. And then I would see Eliza appear in the doorway. "She is just dreaming, Father."

Eliza had her own bedchamber and a large collection of trinkets from Ireland.

"This is my memory stone," she told me once, holding out a piece of slate perfectly smooth and round. She had a tiny stoppered bottle that contained a sprig of lavender from her grandmother's garden. Eliza woke me with its sweet scent one morning, removing the stopper and holding it under my nose while I dreamed of walking among sweet flowers. There was also a lace handkerchief that had her initials embroidered in pink silk.

"My sister Kate made this for me when she was ill," she said solemnly. "For my twelfth birthday. Before she died of the fever."

At the O'Neills there was a large drawing room with a piano. It contained a number of heavy armchairs laden with cushions. It was here that we spent our evenings, Eliza and I curled up in the chairs reading to each other one of the latest serials. She had a particular fondness for the novels of Jane Austen. She would read a chapter, savoring the suspense, even though we both knew how the books would end. Then she would yawn and stretch.

"Oh, how sleepy I am!" and then, taking a moment to draw breath, she would begin to sing. Eliza's songs were unlike anything I had ever heard before. Even now sometimes I fancy I hear those soaring high notes. A bird call is enough to bring Eliza back to me, her awkward features, that thick blond hair that took hours to wash and comb, and her smile so warm, so unafraid, so full of love.

Eliza's haunting song had something ancient about it. The vowels meandered in her upper register, wordless but full of beauty. And this call stirred her family so that soon her brother John would be taking up his fiddle and tapping his foot, eyes closed, the very strands of his red beard vibrating with sound. After a few seconds of their duet, her other brother, Marcus, would be trilling on his uilleann pipes, that breathy Irish sound weaving over and under Eliza's melody. If I closed my eyes, I could almost see their threads snaking around each other, separate lines of melody so much in tune with one another.

Mrs. O'Neill would sit through her children's performances perched on her piano stool the wrong way around and swaying back and forth, animated joy on her face while her husband tapped his right thigh to the beat. The three O'Neill musicians could play like this for hours. In the warm evenings, with the window open, they entertained the street and we would hear shouts of all kinds from down below. Occasionally one of the neighbors thumped a protest on the wall over the noise, and Mrs. O'Neill would look briefly worried, tell her children to quieten their playing. But within moments they were back to their usual volume. John took over as leader of the band, since he only required his hands and not his voice to make music. And he would call out to others of us to join in. I would shake my head, laughing.

"No, John. I cannot sing."

"Dance then. Come on, Harriet. Dance!"

The rhythm burst from me, and within seconds I was dancing what could only be seen as some kind of ancestral dance, my feet stepping rhythmically back and forth, my arms curved in a swan-like gesture of grace, weaving around my head and body. Mr. and Mrs. O'Neill cheered as I circled the musicians; there was hot sweetness inside me, and my head felt light as though I were floating in the air. And all the time I was looking at John, his bow flying up and down the fiddle, with his smiling clear blue eyes and his encouraging words.

"Harriet," Eliza whispered to me one night as my mind began to slip into sleep. "Jane Austen has not married. Can you believe that?"

"Hmmm. . . ."

"All those stories about love. Do you think she simply invented them?"

"I don't know."

"Or perhaps she almost married. Maybe she had a secret suitor."

My mind was becoming more alert. "There are enough love stories around, Eliza. Enough for all of us to have one to tell if not to live."

"What if there aren't? I mean, what if we use them up by talking about them—or acting them—and then there are none left for us to live?"

"Now you're being silly."

She was silent for a while. I opened my eyes. The glow from the fire showed the shadow of Eliza sitting up, her hair falling around her shoulders.

"Harriet, if I were Caroline Bingley, would you be Lizzie or Jane?"

"Jane," I said. "But I'm glad you're not Miss Bingley."

"Shall I tell John?" she whispered.

"No."

Waterford: 1817

*I*N THE SUMMER OF 1817 I visited the Castle Cootes. I had been longing to see the family once more, and while I had had little time for letters, during my three years in Dublin I had been collecting tales with which to entertain them. But this was a visit unlike the others. When Lady Castle Coote asked after my father, she did not seem to listen to my response. I was most disappointed to discover that none of her sons were home during the period of my visit.

"The boys are all so busy now," she said. "Preparing their careers. I'm sorry we didn't have the opportunity to attend your season in Dublin." Her words had an air of falseness about them. Although I had been caught up in the excitement of our capital and the new friends I had there, there was not one night when I did not wonder hopefully whether a Castle Coote might be in the audience, and when I did not remember them in my prayers.

Lady Castle Coote had a letter for me from Mr. Elliston of England. A well-known stage manager and a friend of the Castle Cootes, he had written requesting my services for the Birmingham Theatre Royal in the following season. I confess this news did not please me as much as it should have.

"Harriet, you should accept Mr. Elliston's offer. You will be safer in England, and there are far more opportunities for a young lady with talent." She lowered her voice. "Irish theater managers have the reputation for buying more services from their actresses than they wish to sell. The custom in England is different; you would be well advised to go."

In spite of the significant event that had befallen me, I was in melancholy spirits that afternoon. I found a quiet place in the garden where I wept from loneliness. For the first time I realized I did not belong with the Castle Cootes and that, in fact, there was nowhere for me to belong at all. I had no home. My belongings were few and scattered wide. Many were with the Castle Cootes, but I knew that I could not take them with me, since I did not know where I was going or for how long. It was difficult enough to manage my trunk and my costumes without carrying unnecessary luxuries such as books and letters. My mother still carried some of my belongings with her; my childhood possessions had been left with charities in Ennis. Nothing reminded me of all that had been. Nothing proved the truth of my memories. And I remembered this when I saw the Castle Coote home and how it contained objects belonging to all the boys and even to myself. Other people did not live as I did. There in the garden under a peach tree where I could imagine the peach juice dripping from the chin of a young Charles, I wept for all that was not mine and for the home I did not have.

Mme Harriet Berlioz
Rue de Londres
Paris, 23 October 1840

My dear Louis,

It is some months since your father took you away to school. I kissed you and held you out from me so I could see your six-year-old face, for it will change again before we next meet.

"Dieu te bénise," I whispered, hoping you would not see my tears. You stood straight and tall, but I could see the quiver in your lip. As you grow you will be surrounded by people who are not your family. My childhood and yours are not so very different.

My papers occupy me as I recover. You are reading your mother's cure.

You wrote to me from school that you were studying Shakespeare. What could your father and I not teach you about Shakespeare! I shall expect a little Hamlet when you return in the summer. Learn it well, my son. To Shakespeare you owe your entire existence.

If I cannot speak with you about Desdemona, Lady Anne, Ophelia, and Juliet, at least I can remember them for you. Love them, Louis, as your father did. Donning a black gown in place of all those pure white robes, I could have played a witch in Macbeth. *I should have liked to perform a character with less purity.*

Most of all I was Ophelia and Juliet. Sometimes I think I am them still—one, then the other, even both at once. There was a time when all of Paris was under my spell. I will show you how Providence carried me there.

Your loving mother,
Harriet

Birmingham, England: 1817

I CROSSED THE IRISH SEA alone. The fresh air lifted my spirits, though the heavy rocking of the ship churned up my insides so heavily that I felt I was going to die. A gentleman whose name I cannot recall assisted me to a seat but did not stay long; I expect I was not very good company. The vessel was not crowded, and I found a post against which I could lean my head. White sleep relieved me from my illness, and when I next opened my eyes I was in England.

There was not much green or pleasant about this land; it was all black smoke and manufactories. It was disappointing to learn that there was still a long journey ahead. I awoke to an unshaven man shaking my arm and saying, "Birmingham, miss." In the dark I stepped down from the carriage somewhat shakily and was surprised to discover a man lifting my trunk. "Well, Miss Smithson. I trust you had a pleasant journey," he said in a clear voice. "I am Mr. Elliston." I nodded my head. My eyelids ached, and it took all my strength to keep them open.

"I have arranged lodgings for you," he said.

ALTHOUGH I WAS there an entire summer, I did not see much of Birmingham. I walked through the town square and past the town hall with its clock tower on my way to the theater every morning. This was a great meeting place for many shopkeepers and workers; some would doff their caps to me as I passed, and I would wonder whether this was from recognition or other interest. A lady walking in town on her own always occasioned speculation. Directly outside the town were many of the new manufactories, and in the distance you could see black smoke pumping up into the sky.

My days in Birmingham were long. While it was still dark I woke and began memory work on my lines by candlelight. I did not play leading roles during this time. The company was strong and featured Miss Somerville and Miss Brunton, both of whom were more accomplished and older than me. Since my roles were quite small, there was plenty of time when I was not required at rehearsal, and during this time I commenced my training.

Miss Brunton's mother was in charge of training young actresses. There were two or three other girls, though I no longer remember their names. Mrs. Brunton used to say, "An actress must perform with her whole person," and slowly I came to understand what this meant. At the beginning of each session we simply stood still. I remember Mrs. Brunton peering at me through her eyeglass, gripping the end of her rod while leaning it against the boards. Sometimes she would hold the rod against my limbs to examine their straightness, and she would rub her hands up and down my back, examining its curve and pushing down on my hips. My biggest difficulty was always in straightening my shoulders for I had developed a slight hunch during all those years of trying not to be noticed. At Madame Tournier's school I had begun the habit of retreating into myself; this had involved leaning forward and allowing wisps of hair to fall over my face like a curtain. Mrs. Brunton would stamp her rod on the boards, glare at me, and say with stern, clear vowels, "Miss Smithson, your *shoulders*!" And I would blush in front of the other girls, pushing my shoulders as far back as they would go.

All I lacked in deportment I made up for in dancing. I was frequently asked to demonstrate the steps for the other girls.

"Dancing is of particular importance to an actress," Mrs. Brunton would say. "Even if you err in gesture, all will be forgiven if you turn a pretty step."

Then there was the art of ordinary movement: Mrs. Brunton made even walking seem a chore. We learned to walk gracefully with a heavy blanket tied around our waists, trailing behind us on the floor. Our feet had to point straight in front of us at all times. We walked miles and miles up and down a plank which had been placed on the stage for our benefit. The elevation filled me with dread. While it was not very high, it seemed like a mountain when dressed in a long gown with satin shoes, so I practiced whenever I had an hour or two between rehearsals and performances when there was no one about. The exercise of walking the plank began with slow walking in a perfectly straight line. Then it had to be done with eyes closed; more than once my feet missed the plank or my knees buckled beneath me and I tumbled to the boards. I was glad of stockings and flowing gowns for they covered my bruises. Then there was fast walking with attention to be paid always to straightness of direction and uprightness of carriage.

As we progressed though our training, there was more and more work on gesture. Mrs. Brunton lectured us on the principles of the art of gesture; how it must always seem natural and refined. In spite of this, it was not natural at all but learned. I came to walk to and from the theater with my third and fourth fingers held together, my other fingers slightly curled. I learned about prone and supine palms, that an open hand can be seen to represent an open mind, while a palm facing downward can reveal conviction. She told us about beginning gestures in a downward position and working our way up with the drama of the play until our hands were held high above our heads. Mrs. Brunton frequently reminded us that too little gesture was always better than too much, especially for a lady. She showed us how, together with voice, gesture could add emphasis and meaning to our words.

Mrs. Brunton worked endlessly on my pronunciation. She said my Irishness should not be apparent through my speech, but I am quite sure that it always was. Sometimes she had me repeating vowel sounds until I cried. She emphasized the clarity and distinctness of the sounds.

"The English lack patience for foreigners, and you will be received harshly in London if you do not learn to speak like a lady, Miss Smithson," she said.

And through these private classes I came to realize that Mrs. Brunton had great faith in my abilities and high hopes for my success.

MR. ELLISTON WAS far more strict than my previous manager, Mr. Jones, had been during rehearsal. For Elliston, all was performance. He said himself that he was the same person on the stage as off. Mr. Lamb wrote that wherever Elliston was, the theater was there with him. He was known among actors as the Napoleon of the Stage. I believe he was flattered by the title.

There were times when I had to practice my mere entrance ten times while other actors sighed and shifted their weight from one foot to the other. He remembered my parts in such detail that I could be fooled into thinking he had attention for me alone. If I so much as misremembered a word or stepped too far to one side during performance, he would recall it the next day. Most days he would tell me that my voice had been barely audible during the previous evening's performance. But there was not much that could be done to help this during rehearsal when we were all trying to save our voices. Elliston advised me to imagine that the audience members were deaf, as they often seemed to be. Gradually I began to make more use of gesture. During this summer season I learned to survive on very little sleep, my body continuing long after my mind no longer could. I met and performed with many of the most successful actors of the day, including Liston, whose comic powers were increased by a missing front tooth, and Charles Matthews, who would later marry Madame Vestris. The two actors were great friends and assisted me in learning my craft. The older Mr. Liston relied on the comedy of situation and costume. He was one of the few great actors still prepared to play minor roles. In one such role he welcomed me to the stage offering warm wishes to my mother to such applause that he was quite overcome. He gave a particularly lively rendition of a broomgirl singing "Buy a Broom" in falsetto. Where Elliston performed on stage as well as off, Charles Matthews appeared to perform nowhere and was equally relaxed on the stage as he was off. He was known for a brown coat he wore at all times. More than any other actor, he remained himself upon the stage and employed few gestures or variations in intonation. Yet his performances were powerful.

"Miss Smithson, you have no need to force your hair into such ringlets. It is quite lovely of its own accord," Mr. Matthews would say as we waited in the greenroom. "And what an elegant gown. But surely it is too fine for Lydia Languish to be wearing at home in the drawing room with Mrs. Malaprop?"

I became accustomed to his teasing and soon learned to reply. "Why, Mr. Matthews, surely it is time your coat was cleaned? Should you not wear a cravat if you are dining in such elegant surrounds?"

I relished evenings without performances. On these occasions I would take my supper early in my room and retire just after nightfall, sleeping deeply through the night.

Friday evenings were most memorable at the Theatre Royal. Elliston had deemed them "fashionable nights." When I peered out at the audience I saw gowns in deep blues, reds, and greens. Sweet scents wafted around me. Audience chatter was polite, and round vowels echoed in the foyer. In the greenroom afterward we came to know many members of Birmingham society. Despite encouragement from my mother in her letters, I rarely attended the society dinners and dances to which I was invited, preferring instead to retire to my lodgings and read. I found it exhausting to spend days completely surrounded by people. I felt it important to guard my own reputation. In the greenroom I would sometimes stand like a statue in a corner, smiling to myself and wondering if one day I would come to see the stage habitually from its other side.

I was always at my most awake when returning from performance in the evening. Eleanor, the Irish maid from Limerick, often left some supper in my bedchamber and occasionally she would knock on my door before going to bed, to see if there was anything else I wanted. I would ask her to join me in the evenings, and we would speak for hours, remembering home and our friends there until the early morning. When I was alone, I took to writing letters to my mother and to Eliza O'Neill. In this manner I could forget my growing loneliness.

At the end of the season I earned my first benefit concert. Mr.

Elliston and Mrs. Brunton instructed me on the selling of tickets, and I began work composing letters to the ladies of Birmingham to request their patronage. I could no longer suppress my longing for a flattering gown of my own, an alternative to the white muslin dresses I wore in my performances. I decided to sew myself a new gown in anticipation of the funds I would gain. My only time for sewing was after returning from performance and eating supper. I was grateful for the thimble from Charles Castle Coote, which prevented many injuries. Still my hands were red raw, and I spent a number of tearful evenings realizing I had made errors in cutting or stitching, the thought of unpicking or recutting more than I could bear. I sewed in the early hours of several mornings and survived on even less sleep than usual. Although I had sewn previously, it had always been under the eye of my mother, and so it was with great satisfaction that I finally viewed my new gown. The dress was blue satin, displaying my shoulders and neck with short puffed sleeves. It flowed out from my growing hips. The fabric was the softest I had ever touched.

I was trying on my new gown when Eleanor knocked on my door. She frowned as she handed me a letter. "This arrived for you, Miss Smithson." She remained as I opened the letter.

"Thank you, Eleanor. That is all," I said with unaccustomed formality.

The letter was written in Joseph's childish scrawl. He had never written to me before, and I guessed what it must contain. Word of my father's death drew my thoughts from my upcoming performance and plunged me into a deep melancholy. There was nothing to be done, for the funeral had already taken place. My mother had taken it very badly, he wrote, and had not left her bed since the funeral. Joseph asked me to send any money I could spare. I know not how long I lay still and silent in my room.

The morning before the concert I awoke with a dry, aching throat. I forced myself to dress and attend the theater. On arriving at rehearsal I was sent immediately home to rest by Elliston himself, who did not want to have to alter the playbills or inform the public of the changes that would occur if I were ill. I barely made it back to Lichfield Street on foot. My knees shook as I pulled myself up the stairs. I was so relieved to see my bed that I fell asleep wearing my rehearsal gown. That afternoon I dreamed in vivid pictures. I heard symphonies of sound, I saw nymphs, fairies, and witches. I awoke with a start once, feeling that my spirit had left my body and been drawn back down to earth. I could hear drums, growing louder and more rapid, and then suddenly I heard someone call, "Are you ill, miss?" I groaned and the door opened. Eleanor stood before me.

"Good lord," she said. "I will find a compress."

She returned a few minutes later and helped me into my nightgown. Then she sang to me as she sponged my forehead. How tender were her fingers! How long it was since I had felt a human touch! I fancy I heard her sing one of Moore's Irish Melodies before I fell once again into a deep sleep.

Next morning I was still weak but sent word that, although I would not attend rehearsal, I would be performing that evening. I gave the maid two tickets for herself and two for my housekeeper.

"Thank you, Miss Smithson," Eleanor said, smiling. "I have never been to the theater before."

That afternoon I sponged myself down and dressed. I sat at my table and read through my parts. The Bruntons had been selling tickets for me, and at three they arrived. My quarters seemed quite small once they contained the woman and her daughter. They did not hesitate to sit upon my bed as though they had done so every day of their lives.

"Sorry to hear about your father, Miss Smithson," Miss Brunton said. "You will be performing tonight, then?" I nodded and she exchanged looks with her mother. "We have sold a great many tickets on your behalf."

Mr. Elliston sent a carriage to collect me that evening. I traveled alone; my hands could not keep still, and my limbs were weak. As I crossed and uncrossed them, my lines ran through my mind from beginning to end. It was nearing the end of the season. I needed to make a good impression if I was to secure work somewhere next season.

I arrived at the stage door to find a crowd waiting for me.

"Miss Smithson!" they all shouted, crowding around me. One man handed me red roses, and I know I soon imitated their glow in my cheeks. I did not see his face, only the flowers. And suddenly all manner of objects were being thrust in my direction. I felt enclosed, and the stage door seemed a mile away. I began to quiver and gasped for air. Suddenly I heard a very loud voice, "Clear the way, clear the way! Miss Smithson has been unwell, clear the way!" At the word *unwell* there was a gasp and the crowd cleared, allowing me just enough room to scamper to the door like a rabbit.

Mr. Elliston was uncommonly kind to me that evening. He bowed and kissed my hand, leading me to the seat in the green-room known as Garrick's Chair for the great actor who had once worked there. He brought water and enquired after my health. He offered smelling salts which he said would help clear my head. I must confess I could smell nothing at all, and my voice sounded as deep and rasping as Mrs. Brunton's.

"You have quite a remarkable resonance this evening, Miss Smithson," Mr. Elliston said. "I believe you will be quite audible." This, from Mr. Elliston, was high praise indeed, and I was pleased something good had come of my fever.

Either the smelling salts or the fever itself gave me great ease of mind so that I did not mind adjusting my gown or my hair in front of the other actors. Behind my own reflection I saw their eyes wide with admiration. I turned one way and then the other to examine the folds at the back, I whisked some unrequired eyebrows from my forehead, I adjusted a curl on each side of my temples with an index finger. The gown rustled as I walked, it flowed behind me like a bridal train. In the glass I noted my upright carriage and my straight step.

As I entered the stage, I heard cheering and plaudits. On that night it did not matter what I did, the audience was mine. The crowd cried when I mimed sadness, they laughed when I lifted my arms with joy. In the greenroom, Mr. Elliston was in a great state of excitement. He begged me to speak to the audience at the close of the evening. I no longer remember what I said, but I was showered in rose petals like a bride.

AFTER MY BENEFIT concert in Birmingham, Mr. Elliston gave me a week to recover my strength. I slept almost all the time, waking only to eat the cook's chicken broth. And while I slept, it was as though I still performed on the stage. I could smell the oil from the lamps and hear its faint sizzling sound. I could see faces in the audience smiling, throwing roses, weeping. I could feel the boards under my feet, and I fancy my hands made gestures while I slept.

On the final morning before my return to the stage, I was woken by sunlight warming my chin. I smelled chicken broth and saw a white teapot and a letter on the table. I sat and looked around the room. Someone had put my clothes away, and my scripts were in a neat pile. Several vases of fresh flowers decorated the room. I drew the curtains completely and looked down into Birmingham. I felt strong once more. That morning the maid found me sitting at the table reading the letter. I had bathed and dressed and tied my hair into a bun.

The letter was from London, and it informed me that, on the commendation of a Mr. Henry Johnston from the Scottish Roscius, I had been accepted into the company of Drury Lane commencing the following season, January 1818. I told myself that from heaven my father had seen me perform in Birmingham and he was pleased with what he saw. I would return to Dublin to tell my mother the news.

Ennis: 1806

HARRIET'S EYELIDS, in the morning, were glued down. She wondered if this was what it meant to be dead. She straightened out her back and lay flat. Her eyelids were smooth as marble, she knew that. She wondered whether perhaps someone had come during the night and transformed her into a statue. She would be a beautiful statue. Harriet imagined being laid stiffly on top of a carriage, tied down with rope, and carried all the way to Paris. She hoped someone would open her eyes when she arrived.

"Harriet?" Bridie's voice shrieked. "Harriet, child, why are you lying there like a dishrag?" Deflated, Harriet curled into a shape as close to that of a cat as she could manage and opened her mouth. The same thing that had glued her eyelids had also glued something in her throat. Harriet could not speak. An itch began in her toes and worked its way through her belly and then into her lungs. Her whole body began to shake with the cough that expelled a large green lump onto her pillow. The force of the cough shook the walls and unstuck her eyelids. Her large gray eyes began to drip something sticky.

Bridie's hand was cold lead on her forehead. Even for the few seconds she held it there, it weighed Harriet down so that she longed to push the woman away. But her body was too limp to move. Although Bridie did not sing loudly, Harriet could make out the words.

How dear to me the hour when daylight dies,
And sunbeams melt along the silent sea,
For then sweet dreams of other days arise,
And memory breathes her vesper sigh to thee.

Harriet imagined a Bridie who was not Bridie the maid. The Bridie Harriet saw with her eyes closed had a plump face above a heavy satin gown with a ruby teardrop like blood on a golden chain around her neck. Her lips were not tight and stern. The Bridie that Harriet saw with her eyelids glued down was pale and stared wistfully out of large windows.

"Who do you love, Bridie?" Harriet meant to ask. But the words got lost somewhere in the quietness of her room.

Harriet had heard about love. It was one of the things Molly whispered about. Before Molly's father died, whenever Molly was feeling bold she used to stare Harriet in the eye and say, "I love my mother and my father and Jacob who helps father with the cows."

Molly said that because she loved Jacob, and because her mother and her father also loved Jacob, one day she and Jacob would get married. This meant that everyone from the town would come and have a feast at their house and play music. Harriet could be one of her bridesmaids, and this meant that Harriet would also be allowed to wear a pretty dress. Afterward, Molly would have to leave her mother and father to live with Jacob.

"Who are you going to marry, Harriet?"

"No one."

"But you have to marry someone."

"Why?"

"You can't live by yourself."

"Why not?"

"You'll have no one to look after." Harriet thought of Bridie clearing away Father Barrett's dirty dishes splattered with gravy and cough. She remembered Bridie finding Father Barrett's jacket in the library on cold mornings and wiping his shoes before he came in the front door. She recalled Bridie pulling silver coiled hairs out of the brush in Father Barrett's room when she thought Harriet was not there, and muttering to herself about how she ought to give the hair back to cover Father Barrett's balding head.

"That doesn't matter," Harriet said.

But Harriet was fascinated by the idea of love. She and Molly crept around the cowshed trying to spot Jacob. The first time they passed him, he lifted his cap, nodded gruffly, and said, "Hello, Miss Molly." Molly beamed and Harriet felt a greater understanding. It was the way he had savored her name in his mouth, his politeness, the angle of the cap in his right hand, that showed how much he loved Molly. But as Harriet and Molly walked past the cowshed again, arms hooked together, they spotted Jacob coming out the other side and he said nothing. Molly did not want to talk about love anymore so they went to climb the apple tree.

Bridie scrubbed at Harriet's face with a rough cloth. She picked crumbly dry grains from around Harriet's eyes with jagged fingernails that caught in her skin. Harriet wondered whether she was dead after all and Bridie was preparing her to be a beautiful corpse. Once Bridie had finished with her face, Harriet let her eyelids droop again and felt warm stickiness from somewhere inside her head ooze outward. Bridie unbuttoned the nightdress and rubbed a coarse sponge over Harriet's body, pummeling the skin until she ached all over. After she had been still for a few minutes, her skin tingled and then burned. Harriet thought she mustn't be dead after all.

During the night Harriet met the ghost of Aunt Ellen who snarled with black teeth and clutched her wrists until they ached. "Come with me, child, and we shall steal!" Harriet knew that she had to follow. They wound their way through the cellars of Ennis. "A penny for the child!" Aunt Ellen shouted to strangers. When Harriet wept from loneliness, people showered her with coins.

"It's bed for you, from now on, Miss Harriet," Bridie told her, tugging at the sheets that tied Harriet so tightly into bed that she could not imagine ever moving again.

"No more climbing into cold dark places with Miss Molly."

Harriet could hear logs being dragged from the corridor and arranged in the fireplace. She smelled hot smoke and heard crackling. The tiny woodsprites were being burned from the wood, she could tell from the popping sounds. While her eyes were glued down, it was difficult to know where the fire was coming from. There was heat drying out her skin and making her cough, drying her out from the inside. Harriet could only hope that someone was containing the fire to make sure it did not creep out from the fireplace and climb her bedclothes.

Harriet drifted in the colors inside her head. She knew time passed from the sound of logs being thrown into the fireplace. Sometimes there was whispering. Sometimes there were cold hands on her forehead making her shiver and try to wriggle deeper under the bedclothes. Only Harriet was not strong enough to move under Bridie's bed-linen knot. The most frightening thing was the cold water. It was sponged into her hair, and it dripped into the crevices of her closed eyes. It trickled down her face and collected on her neck, making her feel as though she were drowning. It gave her icy dreams.

Harriet was becoming accustomed to the vivid hues of the

world underneath her eyelids. She knew morning by the deep orange light and by the heaviness of the smoke from the freshly revived fire. It was in the morning that her eyes oozed the most. Harriet imagined fat worms wriggling out of her head. When she lifted her fingers to her face, she felt throbbing hotness and bulging skin. Warm salty liquid should be poured into her mouth to bring her voice back, someone said. Harriet doubted that this would work. She knew that her voice preferred cocoa sweetness and warm milk. But since her voice had not yet returned, she was unable to explain.

She knew lunchtime by the paler yellow light and the quickness of Bridie's step. By lunchtime, Bridie had many important things to do before evening. Sometimes Harriet would be given treacle at lunchtime, and the sticky sweetness would make her see rainbows. By lunchtime the fire was quieter and did not need as much wood. Harriet's favorite colors were those of evening. These were the coolest and the easiest to look at. They did not hurt her eyes or make them ooze water. The dusty blue of evening made her feel cool and strong. In the world beneath her eyelids she could drift in a cool lake. Sometimes Harriet even saw the grayness of the ocean.

On the day the whispering stopped, it was time for Harriet to open her eyes. When Bridie came into the room, she pulled back her bed-linen knot and told Harriet her fever was subsiding. "I'm going to clean your face, Miss Harriet. Then I want you to try to open your eyes."

Harriet nodded because her voice had still not returned. She felt wetness and coarse grains making her face sting. She smelled something that made her feel as though she were floating above clouds. Fat fingers tugged at her eyelashes. Harriet pushed them away with her own hands and heard someone sniff. She pressed her eyelids and pushed them gently up toward her forehead. Slowly, her eyelids began to peel away from her eyeballs. Harriet took a deep breath. The world was blurred and creamy. The hues of her room were pale. Bridie revealed her teeth, and for the first time Harriet noticed that one of them was missing. She turned away.

"There, now. Can you see?"

Now that Harriet was allowed to sit up, she felt liquid quivering deep in her chest whenever she breathed. She was pleased to see that her coughs were green and yellow and that they made Bridie wince as though she had swallowed something bitter. Harriet liked coughing because it made her feel as though she was digging deep inside herself to find her voice again. The first lunchtime after Harriet could see again, Bridie brought her thick liquid the color of her coughs. Harriet pushed it away.

"'Tis broth!"

Harriet shook her head. She knew there was quite enough thick greenness inside her without adding more. Bridie pointed her nose to the ceiling and left the room. Harriet felt a hole growing in her belly.

She heard thumping and voices coming from downstairs. Bridie was arguing with a man who had a strong bass voice. The walls shook as something heavy moved up the stairs. Harriet curled her legs underneath her and hoped the heavy object would not come to her room. The door flew open and hit the wall with a thump. The Man Who Was Her Father took up almost the whole doorway. His gray eyes were almost round, and his thick eyebrows seemed to be climbing his forehead. His two coarse hands clutched a small red apple as though it were a baby bird.

"What have they done to you, Harriet?" His voice was quiet,

and Harriet had already opened her mouth to answer when she remembered that she had not yet found her voice. He placed a forefinger on her forehead and stood over her.

"Your mother will sit with you a while," he said. Harriet looked behind him and saw the Woman Who Was Her Mother. There were lines on her face, and Harriet thought she cradled a child that looked old enough to walk. The Man Who Was Her Father turned, took something from the Woman Who Was Her Mother, and left the room.

Dublin: 1817

I ARRIVED AT MY MOTHER'S lodgings by coach; my limbs felt heavy, and I did not want to leave the carriage. The driver had begun to remove my small case when Mrs. Cooney stepped outside and informed us that my mother had moved unexpectedly two days previously. Her face was stern as she said this. I thanked her, and we continued on through Dublin toward Kilmainham Jail which was the area in which my mother now lived. The streets became grayer and dirtier as we progressed, and I wondered why it was that my mother had moved such a great distance. We arrived at a greengrocer's, and the driver stopped. He offered to carry my case, but I preferred to make my own way. The shop was dark but I could make out withering lettuces stacked like so many skulls, and the air was thick with something rotting. A man missing many of his teeth nodded at me.

"I am seeking Mrs. Smithson," I told him. He pointed to a staircase around the back of the shop.

The stairs themselves were dark and dusty. They wound around in an untidy spiral. The man left me and my case outside a door on the landing. I knocked.

I almost did not recognize my mother when she stood in the doorway. Her hair was greasy and knotted and had been pulled back behind her ears. She wore an apron which was stained and threadbare. I noticed her stockings underneath were torn and her shoes scuffed. The room behind her was gloomy and airless.

"Harriet!"

"Hello, Mouse!" I kissed my younger sister's pale face and saw that it was lined. She smiled.

"You're back," she said, smiling as though I had handed her a gift.

"We were not expecting you!" my mother sniffed. "Have you lost your position?"

"I finished the summer season. I will be going to London in the new year."

"London? Where?"

"Drury Lane."

"That is grand, Harriet, grand." She stared at me in silence. "Your father would have been proud." As she said this her tears began.

Some moments later I saw her running her eyes up and down the fabric of my dress, and I was ashamed.

"You were a success in Birmingham, then?" she sniffed.

"I have enough to last until London. Where is Joseph?"

"He is working at the theater."

"And you? I thought you had a position at the Crow."

"Mrs. West is here from London. I am not required. Were you—safe—in Birmingham?"

I blushed. "Yes, Mama."

"We did not wish to disturb you on your father's death." After a pause she asked, "What has happened to your speech?"

"I was taught elocution so I can perform in London. They say the English don't like foreigners."

"London is a grand city. And a dangerous one. I cannot allow you there alone. We will come with you." As she said this she looked at the purse in my lap. Slowly I stood. I untied my purse from my wrist and opened it. I handed my mother half my coins.

"I will go by coach to Moore Street and fetch us some food," I told her.

I had to walk a long way before coming across a carriage. As we trundled toward the market it was difficult to keep my eyes open. I dreamed I was returning to Ennis where I would visit Father Barrett's chapel and say the rosary by his grave at Drumcliffe. I would visit the building of my father's theater in Cooke's Lane. I would find Molly, and we would talk for hours about the people of Ennis and all we did when we were children. I was awakened from my reverie by the words "All right, miss?" I handed him the fare and, clutching my skirts, stepped down to the street.

I had never been to the market before. When I first worked at the Old Crow, my mother had been wary to spare me domestic duties so I could concentrate on learning my lines. This was nothing like Market Square in Ennis where I had played as a child. This market was like an untidy chorus, people shouting long discords while others punctuated with staccato cries. It was full of disheveled women with dull eyes; I fancied it was themselves they were selling. The men were large with calloused hands; they stared at my gown which was not one of my best, merely one in good repair. There were no well-dressed ladies here. This was a place visited by their maids, and the few to be seen this late in the day had their heads down and scurried quickly. Shopping was clearly a task to be completed in haste. I bought a large leg of lamb; the meat had a green sheen, and I hoped it was not bad. The man wrapped it, staring at me all the while so that I was most relieved when the transaction was over. It remained for me to find a few small muddy potatoes and some shriveled carrots; I was glad the meal would be well roasted before we ate it.

After the Carmichael family had retired for the evening, they gave my mother permission to use the kitchen providing she left it as she had found it. My mother would leave the kitchen better than she had found it. Before she even started cooking she scrubbed the pots and pans and stoked the fire. A lifetime in the theater had accustomed us all to late meals, and so there was no hurry as I followed my mother's instructions. Joseph's eyes were wide when he appeared, slow from sleep with dark smudges around his eyes, in Mrs. Carmichael's kitchen. My mother sent him to fetch Anne, and he returned with her in his arms.

"There you go, princess," he set her down and bowed to her. She dismissed him with a playful nod. It was then that I saw he had grown and was almost a man.

We all ate until we clutched our bellies and felt so weighed down we thought we would never move again. My mother's spirits had lifted with the smell of roasting meat, and now she spoke about the lodgings we would have in London and what a vast city it was.

That night I shared a bed with my mother. It took all my effort to keep still. In Birmingham I had grown accustomed to my own sleeping space, and now I found it impossible to calm myself. As I lay there listening to the wheezing of my sister in the next bed, I wondered at the profession which had once so lauded my mother and now left her for dead in poor lodgings on the wrong side of Dublin.

Next morning I was woken by Anne speaking as my mother dressed her.

"The dress is grown too tight."

"We cannot afford to buy you another. You shall have to wait a few more weeks."

"Morning," I said to them. My mother tightened her lips as she tugged at my sister's dress.

"Your brother is gone for a walk. There are errands to be run. Will you watch your sister?" my mother said. "There's some bread for your breakfast." The air smelled of stale cooking fat, and with four of us and our belongings there was very little floor space.

"How do you spend your days?" I asked Anne after my mother had gone.

"I sew a little. Do you like being upon the stage, Harriet?"

"Some nights I do. There is a lot of life to be had in the theater. One meets all manner of people there."

"I wish I were strong enough to be upon the stage."

I stared at her hunched back and noticed her watching me. I looked away. "Shall I read to you?"

There was the hint of a smile on her cracked lips. "I can read," she said. "But it hurts my eyes."

Anne was now thirteen years old, and I realized that my parents had probably not had an opportunity to furnish her with reading. I knelt on the floor and dug beneath the underclothes in my trunk. Down at the bottom I discovered my copy of Lamb's *Tales from Shakespeare*. Some of the pages were now loose, and others had tears like tiny cracks around the edges. It was a book I still used to remind myself of Shakespearean plots before I commenced work on a new drama. And now I read from the beginning of the book, from a play I knew well but had never performed.

"The two chief families in Verona were the rich Capulets and the Montagues. There had been an old quarrel between these families, which was grown to such a height, and so deadly was the enmity between them, that it extended to the remotest kindred, to the followers and retainers of both sides, insomuch that a servant of the house of Montague could not meet a servant of the house of Capulet, nor a Capulet encounter a Montague by chance, but fierce words and sometimes bloodshed ensued; and frequent were the brawls, from such accidental meetings, which disturbed the happy quiet of Verona's estate. . . ."

Anne sat perfectly still, her eyes closed.

When Joseph returned, he found me halfway through *Twelfth Night*. Anne was lying upon a bed. She was not asleep; every now and then her brown eyes stared starkly into my face as I read. He sat down on a chair and listened silently. I kept reading until the end and then closed the book. Anne opened her eyes.

"That's enough for today," I said. "You can read some more if you like." I handed her the book and she took it quickly, pulling her feet up onto the bed and arranging herself upon some blankets.

"It is nice out," Joseph said.

"I would not care to go wandering about this vicinity on my own," I told him.

"Aye."

"Joseph, why have you moved here?"

"Mother couldn't pay the rent. Mrs. Cooney bade us leave."

"I see. And you are working now."

He grinned. "Aye, at the Crow. Just like you did."

"Are you acting?"

"Sometimes in the chorus. Mostly I help with the sets."

"Joseph," I looked at his face and noticed his bristles. "What are your plans?"

"I want to be a manager. Like Father."

"Joseph, you are a gentleman's son."

"Father was no gentleman. And I do not have the education that you have. I was born for the theater. I know nothing else."

I thought of the strolling player's life, the endless trudging from one town to another, the frowns from members of society when one encountered them and one's profession was made clear. I remembered my father's debts and the pressures these had placed on my mother. It seemed the theater would always be our lifeblood and our curse. I sighed.

"You must learn to be an actor first and learn all you can from the other managers. You must pay attention to all that occurs in the theater. Oh, you are a gambler, Joseph," I smiled, trying to hide my tears.

TWO MONTHS OF LIVING above the greengrocer's near the jail stretched before me as a prospect near imprisonment. It was only during the night when I was left to my own thoughts that I could plan and dream of other possibilities. I would visit Ennis and take up lodgings there with or without my family, until it was time to go to London.

After three weeks in Dublin I received a letter from Elliston informing me that he had taken the liberty of booking lodgings for my family in London. They would be available at the beginning of December. There would be one large room with a bed and table and a smaller room with a further two beds.

One morning, when my mother was taking the rare opportunity to read some old scripts for pleasure, I broached the subject of travel with her.

"Mother, I am thinking to go to Ennis next week."

"To Ennis? Next week? Is it mad you be? How am I to pack

up our lodgings in a week? And we have paid rental until the end of the month."

"I am thinking to go on my own."

"On your own? A young girl like you does not travel on your own if she doesn't have to. And what is to become of us while you are gone? You expect me to take care of your brother and sister alone again? Your brother barely makes enough money to feed us."

"I could leave you some money. Our lodgings in London will be ready in a month."

"London? Aye, that gives us enough time to pack up and give notice. That is grand, Harriet. What would you want to go to Ennis for when you can go to London?"

And so it came about that I only ever returned to Ennis in my dreams.

Ennis: 1807

*H*ARRIET KNEW SHE WAS almost grown up. Father Barrett joked she had grown taller than his cane, and that was why she needed to go with him to the charity school and the infirmary. Her eyes were growing larger, the women remarked when they saw her in the street. And Harriet knew this was because she had to see for Father Barrett as well as for herself.

Her lessons with him were becoming short and irregular. He would sit in his favorite green chair, a balding gray spot at the place where he rested his head. His right hand would support his chin, and his eyes would close. As he grew older, Harriet noticed that it was becoming increasingly difficult to tell whether or not he was awake. He could discuss the same matters in his sleep as he would when he was awake, and indeed, he did not seem to notice that he frequently walked about with his eyes closed.

"Harriet, my child, you know almost as much as I do," he would say during their lessons. "It is nearly time for you to go to boarding school."

"Tell me about France," she would say quickly.

"Ah, oui. J'étais jeune en France. . . ."

Harriet had learned a little French from him and a little more Latin. If pushed, she could conjugate verbs aloud or on a piece of brown packaging. But she found that if she did not think about grammar, she could understand his French as well as she understood his English. The meaning flowed between them.

Now Harriet also closed her eyes. She saw a younger, taller version of Father Barrett. His eyes were no longer misty but clear and dark. His hair was thick and framed his face in gentle waves. She saw him walking along a country road by a field in Bordeaux with a group of young men. They were adequately, though not elegantly, dressed. What struck Harriet most about them was their joviality. It was difficult to make out their words. It seemed they muttered quickly to one another, and their words were not for her ears. She was not sure what language they were speaking. It may have been French with an Irish lilt or English with a French sharpness. But their speech was heavily punctuated with laughter.

And Harriet saw the young men breaking bread and taking wine at a large dining table in a room full of light. After the meal they wandered one by one toward a large salon with heavy maroon curtains and thick carpets. Some sat in thickset armchairs to continue their discussions. Musicians gathered around the piano to sing and play their instruments.

"It is all gone now, that world," Father Barrett whispered. "Harangued and burned to a crisp during that revolution of theirs. All those starving people and barely a potato to eat. It will be a century before France has regained her dignity and culture. Remember that, Harriet. You will never know the France I knew. For all their *égalité* it is no longer a safe place for the education of Irish Catholics. Shame. A terrible shame. . . ."

Harriet nodded, knowing he could not see her, and wondered whether she was supposed to ask him a question now. But he seemed to have forgotten she was there.

It was time for them to attend the charity school in the chapel. Father Barrett had established the school himself in 1785. In recent years he had engaged the assistance of a schoolmaster. Harriet

remembered when, as a very small child, she had not been permitted to go to school with Father Barrett in the mornings. She
had clung to a leg of his trousers as though he was her mother,
sobbing, "School! Please, school!" It had been Bridie who dragged
her away from him as he wandered vaguely toward the door
clutching his books. It was not until she was seven that he had
allowed her into the building during classes. And then, he told
her, after three years of private tuition, she was too far advanced
to participate.

The day after her seventh birthday, Harriet had pulled on her
new dress and laced the boots that Bridie had polished for her. She
had brushed her own hair until it shone and tied a navy blue satin
ribbon in it. With the reverend she had left the house and stepped
into the stone chapel next door. A young man stood at the front of
the schoolroom.

"Harriet, this is Master Godfrey," Father Barrett said.

Harriet had looked around and seen fifteen ragged children.
Many had bare feet with blackened toenails. Large, hopeful eyes
stared out of their bony faces. Harriet could see that these children
were not used to bathing; their skin was tinted the brown of the
River Shannon during the muddy winter. She remembered her
blue satin ribbon and felt ashamed.

Harriet visited the school every morning now. The children
would call out her name as she walked down the aisle. She often
helped them with their spelling or their Latin. Sometimes she
taught them songs. Occasionally the schoolmaster let them have
morning tea. Harriet would knock furiously on the back door of
the house until Bridie opened it in exasperation. She would beg for
a little food, some bread and butter or bun, to feed the hungry children. Bridie would roll her eyes, but she would always return with

something. "Benevolence," Harriet would whisper after Bridie had made her delivery. Harriet taught the children the games she had learned from Molly and her other friends. Father Barrett's words were always on the tip of her tongue when she visited the charity school. She would say them at the slightest provocation. "Learning. Love. Harmony." The children would run up and down Chapel Lane, so that the reverend, if he happened by, would beam at the joy on their faces.

While she came to enjoy visiting the charity school, Harriet never grew used to visiting the infirmary. Bridie could have gone with him, but Father Barrett insisted that he wished for Harriet's company.

"He is mad, to be sure," Bridie said one day, wondering why the reverend, limping, hard of hearing, and almost blind, would insist on visiting the infirmary every day.

Harriet would shuffle silently by his side, not knowing where to look as they entered the building. There was a line of beds, each one with a horrible tale to tell. There were the three-minute amputations done after a large dose of laudanum or whisky. Harriet was grateful that the stumps were bandaged tightly and covered by a sheet, although occasionally the reverend would time his visit so that the dressings were being changed as they arrived. There were numerous bad-tempered, cursing men with head injuries. Father Barrett would shake his head at these and click his tongue.

"The Irish do like their drink too much, and it be not good for their heads," he would say. It had been necessary for the infirmary to procure a copy of Dr. O'Halloran's *A New Treatise on Different Disorders Arising from External Injuries of the Head with Eighty Five Illustrations.* Only in Limerick could there be found more head injuries per capita.

If Harriet lowered her eyes she could avoid the gazes of these gray, unshaven men. But it was the women's room that frightened her the most. While occasionally a good-natured Irish wife could be seen visiting in the men's accommodation, there was never a visitor in the women's room. Even Sister Rose avoided going there, Harriet sensed.

"Benevolence: We must bring peace to the troubled," Father Barrett would say, crossing himself to the invisible altar at the far end of the room. "Hysteria is a female tragedy we must try to understand." And Harriet wondered what hysteria was and why it was a female tragedy. Was it a disease men could not catch? Had no men ever lived with women so afflicted?

"Father Barrett?" she spoke loudly and clearly, not wanting to shout in case any of the women heard her.

"Harriet."

"What is hysteria?"

"It is an unhealthy mental state caused by the deprivation of love. This is why we must visit these women, Harriet. So that they know they are not alone."

It seemed to Harriet that the women were afflicted with a great sadness. From the day she first encountered them, they haunted her days and her nights. She dreamed that she spoke with them and they told her their stories. There was a woman from France who could not understand the foreign world around her. Another woman whose husband had left her for his mistress. A third woman who had been paralyzed by drink and loneliness. They wept, and she could offer no consolation.

There was old Ruth, usually restrained in a straight waistcoat, her eyes bulging as she screamed, "They have murdered my son!" And Harriet would wonder who her son was, and why anyone would have murdered him. Most of all she wanted to know why they had tied up his mother after his death.

Then there was Aurora, who sat staring out the small window and waving her arms peacefully up and down. Ellen sobbed periodically, whining, "Bring back my husband from that witch. Oh, please, God, bring him home." And this would bring tears to Harriet's eyes.

The youngest woman was Louisa, with long, blond, tangled hair. Harriet sometimes fancied she could see wisps of straw in it. Harriet had never seen a more beautiful woman than Louisa, with her pale, smooth face and high forehead. Louisa spent her days staring at a white wall and muttering about flowers and lost love. Sometimes she would skip about the room laughing, but since she never tried to leave, she was not restrained. At other times she held her arms to her chest; Harriet imagined her to be holding a child. Harriet and Louisa never spoke. Yet Harriet felt as though she understood the woman's grief. She wondered if she could be that lost child, and feared that she would become that lonely, pining woman. Occasionally a woman would disappear from the room with no explanation. None of them was ever cured.

As the reverend grew more tired, it became Harriet's task to make these visits alone. In the mornings she sat at the breakfast table, waiting for Bridie. As Bridie brought tea, she would say quietly to Harriet, "Father Barrett is not coming down this morning. You best make his visits alone." Harriet would sigh as she put on her cloak and stepped slowly out the front door.

Visiting with the reverend always offered a distraction. Harriet could concentrate on whether or not he understood what people said to him, watching that he did not trip, and offering explanations when people handed him things he did not understand. On one occasion, Father Barrett had sneezed, and not long after, one of the patient's wives in the infirmary had handed him a gift of a small embroidered tablecloth. It had only been Harriet's quickly spoken loud words of praise for the fine work on the *tablecloth* that had prevented him from blowing his nose in it.

In a strange way, Father Barrett had offered her some kind of protection. Harriet already knew that her own contented existence was as perilous as theirs. That with each rasping breath Father Barrett took, her own situation was threatened with extinction. If it were not for his attentions, Harriet might have been one of the ragged children in the charity school. Or worse still, like her own siblings, Harriet might not have been educated in Sound Knowledge and Moral Principles at all. And without the reverend's continuing help, what would become of her?

Bridie had told Harriet that Father Barrett was not to be disturbed. It was not proper, she said, for a small girl to be seeing an old man in his nightgown, unless he was her own father. Nonetheless, Harriet visited him every day. She would knock quietly and then enter the room. He would be propped up by some fat cushions, sitting and silently beaming with his eyes closed. In his hands, Harriet would always notice his Bible with the worn binding and gilt pages. It had belonged to his mother, Harriet knew. He had told her that one day it would belong to her. Harriet did not like to think about that day. The reverend held on to his mother's Bible as though it were the hand of an old friend. Harriet knew he could no longer read the pages, even with his eyes open. Yet he could find the correct page for almost any verse and then recite it from heart. Harriet wondered if the script was written in the innermost chamber of his heart.

"How are the children?" he would ask her, loudly, without opening his eyes.

"Well, Father. Little Johnny poured ink on his trousers today."

"Tut, tut!"

"And Kathleen recited Luke chapter 17 from beginning to end."

"Very good. And how are the patients?"

"Mr. McIntosh seems to be recovering from his head wound, and Mr. Barnes's appetite has returned."

"How pleasing."

Whenever he stopped asking questions, Harriet knew it was time to go. She would shut the door quietly behind her.

Sometimes Harriet would return to hear voices in the drawing room. Each visitor had their own favorite time to visit. The brethren occasionally arrived at lunchtime but usually preferred the evenings. Mr. Owen often came on Wednesdays when his wife was visiting her sister. On Thursdays, it was usually Mrs. Baird. Sometimes Harriet would be surprised and delighted to discover Molly waiting in the nursery. They would take skipping ropes out into Chapel Lane. They made up songs and dance steps. Harriet particularly liked jumping in when Molly had already started skipping. Together they would perform a complicated dance, and sometimes the men in the Carpenter's Arms over the road would cheer. Harriet taught Molly how to curtsy politely.

Mondays were always a quiet day for visitors. It was too close to Sundays, Harriet thought, and most people would have seen Father Barrett in church. So on the Monday afternoon when Harriet returned from the infirmary to voices in the drawing room, she knew something was wrong. She stood outside the room for some minutes.

"So you see, Father," a man's voice was saying loudly, "he decided to use a nine-pound shot in a wheelbarrow to make stage thunder in *King Lear*. An original idea, wouldn't you say? During the play, the stage carpenter was employed behind the scenes trundling the barrow backward and forward. At first, the thunder was powerful and Lear braved the storm. But suddenly the thunderer slipped, and the stage being on a decline, the balls made their way toward the orchestra and laid the scene flat." The man tried not to laugh, and Harriet sensed drama in his voice.

"This storm was more difficult for Lear to encounter than the tempest of which he so loudly complained. The balls rolling in every direction, he was obliged to skip about like the man who dances the egg hornpipe!" There was raucous laughter, and Harriet thought she could detect the reverend weakly joining in.

Just as Harriet was coming to the nervous conclusion that this must be the voice of her father, a woman's voice spoke her name. Her mother stood quietly, in front of the closed door to the drawing room.

"Mother." Harriet crossed her arms in front of her chest and stared at her shoes.

"You be taller than when we last saw you. Is Father Barrett looking after you well?"

"Yes," she mumbled.

"Come see your brother and sister."

Father Barrett was sitting in his favorite armchair, eyes open, smiling dimly with a blanket over his knees. Harriet's father, larger and more red faced than before, sat in the chair next to him, holding a glass of dark brown liquid in his right hand and clutching a bundle of rags to his left shoulder. Harriet thought that this was probably her younger sister, though she was so small and silent that she could well have been a doll.

"Be ye my beautiful daughter Harriet?" he asked her. Harriet said nothing and stared at the vein bulging on his forehead. She noted with some satisfaction that little Joseph was looking very thin and had a hole in the knee of his trousers.

"Hello, Harriet." The boy walked formally to his sister and held out his right hand, touching his cap. Harriet blushed, taking his sticky hand. The grown-ups laughed.

"Joseph," she muttered.

"Hetta." Harriet thought her father winked at her mother. "Why don't you take the children for a walk in Ennis?"

Harriet's mother exchanged her glass of clear liquid for the small bundle of rags and took Joseph's hand with her empty one. Harriet opened the door, barely lifting her eyes from the floor, and led her family back out into the stone pavement of Chapel Lane.

I DO NOT KNOW exactly what took place between James Barrett and my father during those last months of Father Barrett's life.

I do know that my mother sensed he was going to die all the way from Galway. She said that a dark and ominous feeling came over her during *Macbeth* and that it was still with her a week later when the actors were playing *As You Like It*. She told my father they had to leave. But moving my father from one town to another was a complicated business. It involved tired horses and carriages overflowing with actors and their properties and the scene painters. A special coach was required for the scenes alone.

My mother did not mention her own worries for little Joseph, who at five saw more of the acting troupe than he did of his mother. Nor did she ever admit to concerns over Anne, who at three still waddled like a fragile bird recently hatched from its shell and unsure of its footing. I can imagine what that poor sister of mine looked like at three. When I first knew her properly at the age of ten, she still had the air of a very young child about her. My mother had never been firm with her. She pitied Anne for being born.

And so my father sent word to Brother Foster Parsons at the *Ennis Chronicle*, who published the following tribute on October 7:

Theatricals

The inhabitants of Ennis and vicinity will be glad to learn that the gloom of the approaching season will, in a great degree, be dispelled by the timely interference of their old friend SMITHSON, who, with excellent company, intend commencing operations here in the course of the present month.

Foster Parsons looked to my father as though he alone could melt a townful of ice. Mother always said that Father saw himself as the center of Ennis cultural life. She said he would never have left the town to tour if the local theater-going public had not been so fickle. There were only so many times you could call upon the brothers in their full regalia to parade down Cooke's Lane singing before the performance. My father relied upon the interest his periodical reappearance would cause, and Foster Parsons's glowing tones.

I did not get a chance to say good-bye to him. I cannot be sure of any last words, any wisdom to carry with me throughout my life. Bridie, my mother, and even my father all seemed to have an opinion as to what was best for me. I came, I went, I played half-heartedly with my siblings. The sobs of grown-ups were bouts of thunder and lightning followed by gentle rain. Change hung over me like fog.

He would have held my hand and stared beyond me in his vague manner. He would have repeated his favorite words to me like a lesson, one last time. He would have asked if I was listening and told me to close my eyes. "Benevolence," he would have said. "Learning. Love. Harmony."

Part Three

LOVE

Why should I think that man will do for me,
What yet he never did for wretches like me?
Mark by what partial justice we are judg'd;
Such is the fate unhappy women find,
And such the curse entail'd upon our kind,
That man, the lawless libertine, may rave,
Free and unquestioned through the wilds of love;
While woman, sense and nature's easy fool,
Let poor, weak woman swerve from virtue's rule;
If, strongly charm'd, she leave the thorny way,
And in the softer paths of pleasure stray,
Ruin ensues, reproach and endless shame,
And one false step entirely damns her fame;
In vain with tears the loss she may deplore,
In vain look back on what she was before;
She sets, like stars that fall to rise no more.

—NICHOLAS ROWE, *JANE SHORE: A TRAGEDY*

Hamlet: I did love you once.
Ophelia: Indeed, my lord, you made me believe so.

—WILLIAM SHAKESPEARE, *HAMLET: A TRAGEDY*

Mme Harriet Berlioz
Rue de Londres
Paris, 21 February 18

My dear Louis,

In all the time I have known your father he has had his favorite stories. And although I never said so, I watched those stories wind and grow; he would grin with satisfaction at a well-timed exaggeration. For your father liked to think of himself as a writer, and when there was no other place for his stories, they filled his letters. Music was merely one of his languages. Your aunt, Adèle, once wrote to me that Hector saw his life as a "very interesting novel"; indeed, it revealed itself in neat chapters.

And although I know you have grown up with his stories, as you have grown up with his music, and that they, like the music, have formed the fabric of your own dreams, I feel it is important that I record the stories for you here. Through knowing your father and watching you grow, I have absorbed the truth of his history more honestly than I could have learned it through words. I knew those moments you were most like him, I remember your dreaminess and those times when I shouted and shouted, trying to draw you back to me. And then I saw your father looking with such sympathy—those moments broke my heart for I could see that you shared things I could never hope to understand. When Hector and I still shared a bed, his stories drifted to me through the rhythm of his breathing.

Your father was taught in his early years by your grandfather, the doctor Louis Berlioz after whom you and he were named. In fact, I recall that Hector named you after his father in a hope that it would make peace between us all. As it happened, you were embraced as the only grandson. Packages of jam and linen began arriving from La Côte Saint André almost immediately. As you know, I never met your grandfather. He did not approve of our marriage due to my profession. In these later years I have forgiven him. I can understand why a respectable country doctor would not wish his eldest son to marry an actress, for even I would be wary if you were to one day announce your connection with such a woman. Many in the profession have marred the reputation of all within it. And since your grandfather did not meet me, he did not ever discover who I was.

However, I still harbor some disappointment over this, and sometimes I imagine a meeting in which both Madame and Monsieur are so surprised at my humbleness, my ordinariness, my very respectability that they sob with joy. And I dream of a past in which we travel to see them each Christmas time. I dream that we are there to watch all our nieces grow and that I become very close to Adèle and Nanci. And that you are a boy always surrounded by aunts, uncles, and cousins, which is how life should be and how it never was for you or your poor mother, and that this makes you a happier person for feeling so loved by so many.

I believe Dr. Louis cannot blame your father for embracing the arts, for as a boy these interests were encouraged in him. It was Dr. Louis himself who first taught your father to play the flute and the guitar and then later employed a music teacher for all the children in the village. Dr. Louis gave him the great novels, smiled to himself as Hector wandered in the fields and read Virgil lying in the grass under the oak tree. And it was Dr. Louis, somewhat stunned at his son's sen-

sitivity, who discussed this poet with Hector while Hector sobbed with overwhelming emotion. But I also believe that if Dr. Louis had done nothing but encourage an interest in mathematics and human biology, Hector would still have come to music in the end.

It cannot be disputed that there were some years when relations between Hector and his parents were difficult. This began when Hector abandoned his medical studies to devote himself to music and ended when you were born. Hector claims things were never the same after he declared his desire to compose, but I recall moments when the family responded with great pride to his musical successes. I do believe Hector was partially to blame for this difficult situation. For he went in always fighting for what he believed. Life has been difficult for us, trying to survive on Hector's income from music, supplemented by money made from music articles he wrote for the papers, which made him angry and frustrated. Louis, I think this is partially responsible for our troubles because your father was never at home, and when he was, he was exhausted and anxious. This is no way to live year after year. I would have lived in greater poverty for his art if it would have made him a happier man. I would have slept on straw rather than bear his anger and my increasing solitude, but your father felt he had no choice. And so your grandfather's fears were partially justified. And had your father not been so hot-headed in his youth, I imagine he could have approached his parents at the crucial moments in a calmer, more reasoned manner which would not have alarmed them so.

I was not the first woman your father had wanted to marry, and I am sure your grandfather was unnerved by Hector's apparently sudden change of heart. The story of Camille was so important in his history that it was one of the first things Hector told me about himself during our early weeks together. I remember my surprise at his openness, for he confessed it as though it had been an infidelity, although it happened before we met.

For two years Hector had taught guitar at a large school in Paris. After our marriage I frequently asked would he not return to teaching, and he would glare at me as though I had just suggested he dive naked into the Seine in the middle of winter. He lacked patience for lazy children whose parents wished them more musical. "Not one ounce of talent among twenty students," he would shake his head sadly and then proceed with tales of their various pranks. Rats and mice were frequently released into the lesson room. Guitar strings broken to avoid practice. There were days when almost all students failed to appear for their lessons and Hector was left alone in the tiny room, as cold as a cellar. After some weeks he was introduced to a young German, also teaching music at the school. Hiller began using the adjoining room, allowing them frequent opportunity for discussion in between students.

This happened after your father had seen me on the stage, and he says he already possessed strong feelings for me. He has often said that every waking thought and most dreams have centered upon my existence since he first saw me as Ophelia. I can certainly imagine that the foolish young man he was at twenty-four would have told the world about me as though I were his life's great passion, in spite of the fact that he had only ever seen me on stage or running, to avoid him, between my carriage and the stage door for rehearsal. And so it is hardly surprising that his young friend Hiller did not hesitate in confessing his own passion for a female piano teacher known as Camille. He beguiled Hector with tales of secret nightly rendezvous and elegant

Sunday outings. Suffice to say he had far more to confess than Hector himself. And your father never liked to be outdone.

Hiller did not wish the news of his affair with Camille to be publicly known and thus employed your father as a messenger. Your father has never been able to follow instructions impassively. I imagine he was fascinated by a woman who appeared to give herself so freely. His curiosity was whetted as he walked into Camille's classroom that first day clutching one of Hiller's letters. And he saw instantly that she was beautiful. Camille was very slender with a pale, still face like a classical bust, and large blue eyes. She would sit at the piano, fingers poised and curved over the keys, wrists as fine as a dancer's and back straight. But within her there was something like lightning that could burst forth into laughter or rage.

I imagine that Camille took the letter from Hector and placed it unopened on top of the piano. Then she would have turned her back to him, his hair ruffled and wild, and begged him to sit. Camille Moke was already gaining a reputation as a virtuoso concert pianist at that time. She would have heard about Hector's impassioned performances, his fiery successes and failures. And Hiller had told her about your father's fascination with the young Irish actress at the Odéon, thus arousing her interest. But she would have awaited his own explanations, giving nothing away.

Your father says Camille had a deep unblinking stare that drew information from him almost against his will. I find this difficult to believe for I have never known your father to desire to withhold information from any interested parties. In a strong clear voice, Camille began to ask Hector questions. And bit by bit his story spilled forth. He would have told her about his parents, their disapproval of his chosen profession, his difficulties with the musical establishment. For these were the things that preoccupied him then and that preoccupy him still. In Camille he would have discovered a sympathetic audience.

The next day Hiller sent Hector forth with another letter to his beloved. It was only as he began making his way up the stairs to the piano room that Hector realized Camille had not replied to his previous day's delivery. He knocked and opened the door, shocked to see a young girl at the piano struggling through a slow movement of a Beethoven piano sonata. The girl looked up, startled by the sound. Camille touched her shoulder. "Keep going, Odile. This is Monsieur Berlioz, the composer. I am sure he would like to hear your Beethoven."

And so your father tried to hide himself unobtrusively in the corner, where he stood like a disgraced child, for there were no spare chairs. And rather than simply handing over his delivery, he suffered through one of his life's worst audiences of Beethoven. I am sure he made his presence felt; Hector has never been any good at standing still.

After the lesson had finished, Hector continued his interview with Camille, and on this occasion he noticed a softness in her eyes as she listened to him, wiping the occasional tear from her cheek. I have always believed Camille was as good an actress as she was a musician. However, your father was moved by her sympathy.

By the third day, Hector did not need to await Hiller's instructions. He began and ended his working day in Camille's piano room. That afternoon, Camille confessed her attachment to him. Later he wandered the dark streets of Paris in an overwrought state, unable to sleep. It was time to tell Hiller of his feelings for Camille.

Your father always claimed Hiller was very charitable under the circumstances. That he shook Hector's hand, wished him well, warned him of Camille's fickleness, and left the country. But I know the situation caused your father some grief. That he had to find new employment and burn the letters Hiller sent in the following few weeks. Male friendship was not yet more important to your father than the love of a beautiful woman. The School for Girls stopped employing passionate and talented young musicians and instead hired elderly ladies who could barely keep time but whose minds and hands did not wander.

Hector wooed Camille with great fervor, and I believe she dragged him behind her like a kitten pouncing upon string. Whichever way she turned he would follow, and Camille soon grew tired of her own games. That was when she began to tell stories. She told such tales about me which made your father turn pale and feel faint. He could live with my supposed rejection of his affections, but he could not bear the thought that I was not what I had seemed. I begged him for years to tell me what Camille said, but years later, even when he was most furious with me, this is the only part of his story that he never revealed. Hector was shocked that the woman he had loved and admired with such passion could have a reputation so black, that her supposed image of purity could be so false. He disappeared from Paris, and during this time Camille sent people searching for him all over the city. One of the manservants was seen enquiring at the morgue. I believe Camille paid dearly for her sins.

Although Hector never wished to live farther from Paris than Montmartre, it was always to the countryside that he disappeared during times of greatest grief. He would wander out his front door carrying nothing at all and walk until he was too exhausted to continue. He would find a barn or a field and lie sleeplessly in the hay while all man-

ner of horrible images flickered through his mind. On this occasion, the bells of grazing animals began the melody that became my symphony. Your father came to his senses one morning in a gutter in Sceaux, poked by the staff of a curious shepherd. He decided it was time to return to Paris.

The combined excitement of the previous months, of Shakespeare, Ophelia, Juliet, and then Camille, as well as the shock of my apparent downfall, sowed the seed of your father's most famous work. Your father has always referred to this symphony as mine, and I was quite happy to claim its success as partly my own. (Though I must confess its title had nothing to do with me, and "Fantastique" as the name of a symphony has always seemed to me to be lacking in imagination.) But when you hear that symphony, Louis, listen carefully to the first three movements. In them you will hear the music of realized passion. For almost ten years I have called this symphony my own. But in my heart I know all the sweetness of it belongs to Camille. For this alone I cannot forgive her.

Harriet

London: 1818

*A*T THE BEGINNING of the new season I must see Mr. Elliston to be given my play list. I know he is fond of me and puts particular thought into the roles I am given. He calls me his "Irish lass." Yet I prefer to be invisible when he speaks, to slip into the backstage shadows. For to be noticed by Elliston is to hear your name shouted out loud. I am wary of meetings with Elliston for there have been times when his breath smelled deeply sweet and his words slurred and his eyes were unable to focus upon my face. Whenever he has not been happy with my performances he did not hesitate to tell me so. My knees quiver as I stand before his desk.

"Miss Smithson," he declaims as though he wants everyone in the building to hear. "This shall be an important season for you." Today his voice is clear and his eyes sharp. And when he sees that I am writing hastily, he begins to list names and dates. There are so many of them that I can scarce keep up.

"Adelaide, *The Prisoner at Large*, January 9; Lady Ellen in *Children of the Wood*, commencing January 22." And then there are no more dates, just roles. "Adeline in *The Victim of Seduction*, Lavinia in *The Fair Penitent*, Signora Francesca in *Sleeping Draught*, Margaret in *A New Way to Pay Old Debts*." I relax in my chair thinking of the monotony of it all. Is there to be no Shakespeare? Then suddenly I hear "Anne Boleyn." I look up.

"You will enjoy Anne Boleyn, Miss Smithson. And you will learn a great deal in preparing for a role in Shakespeare's *Henry VIII.*" He pauses on the name *Shakespeare.*

The bedroom I share with Anne and my mother has white curtains so infused with dust that they have turned brown. The two single beds take up almost all the floor space. During the nights I have to retreat far inside myself to forget Anne's bony limbs against my body in the bed we share. That afternoon I find rags to tie the curtains. I rub the window with some old underclothes. I stand back in the doorway; there is more light in this room than I have seen before. I lie on the bed. In this position I hope to read all my plays. I will learn my lines practicing with my mother after lunchtime. There are old plays to revise and new plays to learn. But I know before I have finished reading them that I will be playing almost the same character in each. I will require the same collection of delicate hand gestures for the countless maidens I will play before the season is over. I relish the thought of Anne Boleyn. She is to be my reward. I shall savor her and spend hours on each of her lines. I shall endeavor to become Anne Boleyn herself.

London is gray and dusty beneath me.

"It is too light. I cannot possibly sleep with those curtains ajar."

I pull off the rags tying the curtains and drop them to the floor. The room is instantly in shadows once more. My fingers are rough from all the dust. I feel my way between the beds and walk out into the living room where my mother sits sewing. She is crouched over white satin, and I realize she must be sewing me a new costume since my old satin gowns are becoming dull and worn.

"She has not been well these past weeks," my mother says without looking up.

"She is never well, Mother."

"Anne suffers terribly."

"She has too little with which to occupy herself."

My mother glares and says nothing.

"Are we to have no peace?" I mutter.

"It is my punishment," my mother whispers.

"What punishment?"

"For leaving you."

"Nonsense. I was perfectly happy." I stand and pull on my cloak. "I am going to learn my lines in my dressing room."

Almost all my roles are in comedy. In order to amuse the audience I must exaggerate, appearing more stupid and more naïve than I am. Most importantly, I must never laugh on stage for my ignorance of the comedy is part of the joke. The nights are very long: we begin at six with drama for the upper classes; later, tickets are available at half price. Any seats that were previously empty are now filled with raucous crowds, and we must try to keep them appeased. There are songs, pantomimes, dances, singing dogs, prancing horses, and tightrope walkers. These performers occupy the second-rate greenroom, and I am thus spared their company.

I stand in my dressing room and wave my arms about. There is very little space here, yet it is my own for the purposes of work. Here I am an actress. The room is little more than a closet with a mirror, dressing table, and chair. Candles are to be used sparingly, but I light one all the same. The dressing table is sprinkled with rose petals like confetti, fallen from a bunch that was thrown to me from the audience some months ago. I never saw who threw them, but I imagine sometimes that it was a prince who will appear backstage one evening and propose marriage, whisking me away from this life forever. I have a piece of tinted silk given to me by one of my admirers in Dublin. It hangs over the mirror, and I fancy that it brings more light into the room.

I sit down in my chair and breathe deeply. In the mirror I see a smooth and pale face with sharp gray eyes. My nose is triangular, my lips small, and my forehead high. During the day I always wear my hair in a bun on top of my head. It is impossible to prevent those dark brown wisps hanging down, curling around my cheekbones. The girl in the mirror looks Irish without even having to open her mouth. Some days I long for the smallness of Dublin and the laughter one hears when walking the streets. I yearn for the lilting music of Irish voices while knowing that my own voice is becoming harsher in this cold city. But I am pleased with the success of London. Mine is not a huge success, to be sure, but it is something to be able to say one plays at Drury Lane and has done so for quite some months. An apprenticeship at Drury Lane is the best training in the world. My father would be proud.

I begin copying out my lines again, trying to concentrate on their meaning for I will remember them better this way. The ink is of poor quality, and I know it will soon fade. As the words steady to a rhythm, I hear a knocking on the door. It is one of the call boys, Will. He curtsies and says, "A letter for you, miss." I thank him and he leaves. The letter is in an unfamiliar hand; the writing is uneven and appears to quiver on the page. Thinking it from a member of the public, I put it to one side until I have finished reading through *The Victim of Seduction.*

Eventually my head aches and I close my eyes, resting my face on the page. My fingers find the envelope and I open it carefully.

Dear Miss Smithson,

You may not remember me for it is long since I wrote. My name was Molly Baird and has been Molly O'Brien these three years since I married David, you may remember him from Father Barrett's church. You will be forgiven if you do not reply to this, for I have not been a good friend to you. Please believe that I have thought of you often and that I remember those years of our childhood when you lived with Father Barrett and we played in the fields together. I have heard that you are in the London theater now. What is it like to live in such a grand city? I cannot see myself ever finding my way there now what with four mouths to feed and blighted crops. It is with shame that I write to tell you such misfortunes as ours. Even those in Ennis with money have no food to buy. Even Father Barrett, God rest his soul, would need more than God's help to fix our troubles now. And so, I do not wish to beg, but would like you to know that if you have even a little to spare, it would help us greatly and that my little ones would remember you in their prayers.

Yours,
Molly

It is not done for ladies to be too well acquainted with the goings on in the world. The newspapers are intended to be read by gentlemen in their libraries and coffeehouses, not by ladies in their parlors. The newspaper should certainly not be read by people of the theater; I have heard it said that some managers demand their actors sign that they will not read the newspaper while they are engaged at the theaters, for fear an unfavorable review will affect their willingness to perform. Having lost touch with all those I knew in Ireland, the letter I receive from Molly O'Brien is a shock.

In my mind I begin calculating sums. There must be something

I can spare. But then I remember that I give all my money to my mother, and by the time I am paid each month we are eating stale bread once more and drinking weak tea from reused tea leaves. She saves for months to buy fabrics to clothe us. I think of Molly and of all the time we spent together playing in the sunshine as children.

I still have two hours before I need to be in the greenroom. I can no longer concentrate on my lines. Tonight's play is *Venice Preserved*, and I know it well. I walk with heavy steps out to Brydges Street. Outside there is rare sunlight. I stretch my legs and take large steps. I walk so far that I feel as though I can walk away.

Three days later it is with a great sense of foreboding that I learn Mr. Elliston wishes to see me again. I have not missed a single line, the prompter could find no fault with my performance. But I know I have not played well the previous few evenings. And although I trust Mr. Elliston, I often wonder what it would take for him to dismiss one of his players.

"Miss Smithson, please sit down. You seem fatigued. Are you ill?"

"No, sir." I stare at my hands.

"Is something the matter?"

"No, sir."

"You see, Miss Smithson, Belvedira has been rather gloomy this last week."

"I see, sir."

"I think you should tell me what is wrong."

Before I know what is happening I am sobbing. I tell him all about my childhood in Ireland and about Father Barrett's death being mourned by all of Ennis and my crippled sister and my father's passing and all my mother's troubles. Finally I tell him about the letter I received from Molly O'Brien.

"I see," he says, handing me an enormous handkerchief. I wipe my eyes and blow my nose as gently as I can manage, ashamed at making such a spectacle of myself in front of Mr. Elliston himself.

In my dressing room I work on the shapes of my curved fingers and keep my feet in fifth position, remembering the importance of opposition between hands and feet. Gestures with the right hand should be accompanied by the weight on the left foot. My body remembers the actions, and I feel consoled by their familiarity. I clear my mind of everything but work. I remember to begin with low gestures and work up toward a climax. I will be natural and graceful.

I reexamine the text of *Henry VIII* and copy out my lines. I close my eyes and envisage the stage and where everyone will be situated. I first enter in scene 4, the ball scene in the presence chamber in York Place. I push bottles and petals aside and take the envelope from Molly's letter. With my pen I draw the stage. I draw a small table for Cardinal Wolsey and a longer table for the guests. Cardinal Wolsey will enter stage left and proceed to his table on the same side. The guests will do the same on the other side and will be seated around the back of the table so they may all be seen by the audience. I must be next to Lord Sands and seen to greatest advantage since my speech is most important. I draw chairs around the table and write my name. The table is at a slight angle. I seat Sands at the head stage right and myself on the other side of the corner. But then I keep reading and see that this is wrong. Sands must be between two ladies, and I must leave room at the front of the stage for the king's procession.

Finally my drawing is correct. I sit at the end of the length of the table, Sands to my right with another lady on his other side. We will all rise and the tables will be removed in time for the masquers, habited like shepherds and including the king, to enter from the same side as the cardinal previously. They will walk across the front of the stage, to be seen by all, and then around to where we are standing. Each man will select a lady for the dance. The oboe player and other musicians will stand just behind the dancers, where they can occasionally be seen and the sound heard throughout the theater. This is my plan, and it may not be the plan that is devised by Elliston. But it gives me a place to begin.

I hold the diagram upside down in my hand and imagine I am entering stage right. I walk almost straight ahead, slightly to the right, and sit in my chair. I try this again, imagining other ladies, dressed elegantly, following, chattering behind me. The third time I know where to go and where all the other characters should be. I work on the gestures. Both hands are lowered and prone, at slightly different angles; the fingers are curved slightly, elegantly. There is something missing, and I know I want to hold something in my right hand. A kerchief, a fan. I will see what Elliston decides for the ladies at rehearsal.

I learn Sands's few lines preceding mine. "By my faith, And thank your lordship." [*Seats himself between Anne Boleyn and another lady.*] "If I chance to talk a little wild, forgive me; I had it from my father."

I raise my left hand just slightly as I speak, holding the position from the word *mad*: "Was he *mad*, sir?"

"Oh! Very mad, exceedingly mad, in love too: But he would bite none; just as I do now, He would kiss you twenty with a breath." [*Kisses her.*]

At this, I lift my already raised hand to my right cheek and lower my eyes. The second time, I imagine the kiss itself and I do not have to feign the blush that strokes my cheek.

And as Anne Boleyn I grow playful with this man after his jokes of red wine rising to our cheeks and making us merry. I point elegantly, not with a tight fist but with loose fingers, at the word *you* when I say, " *You* are a merry gamester, My Lord Sands."

"Yes, if I make my play. Here's to our ladyship; and pledge it, madam, For 'tis to such a thing—"

I do not let him finish. "You cannot show me."

"I told your grace they would talk." This time he is interrupted by drums and trumpets heralding the arrival of the parade. At first we do not know who these new arrivals are; the servant describes them as "a noble troop of strangers . . . great ambassadors from foreign princes." And as the visitors arrive, we rise and the tables are removed. We must be sure to watch the new arrivals lest the audience be distracted by the removal of furniture. And then each of us ladies is taken to dance by one of the gentlemen. I imagine the king taking my left hand with his right. His thumb is over my fingers, his fingers support mine from underneath. But as Anne Boleyn I do not know he is the king, just that he is a masked man.

"The fairest hand I ever touch'd! O beauty, Till now I never knew thee!"

I hold my skirts with my right hand, and we each bow.

At this point I pause, trying to imagine the dance steps. I have been taught a great many dances: some are old, some are more modern, and I cannot begin to guess what would be Mr. Elliston's preference. I decide to wait until rehearsal, for I can learn new dances in almost no time at all.

I commence work on scene 3 of act 2 and am pleased I have already learned the lines, for there are many. In it I discuss the fate of the poor queen whose king wishes to divorce her. I speak with an old lady who wishes to discover whether I would ever be queen.

And I insist that I would not. The discussion is lengthy, I unlace and remove my boots, drawing my stockinged feet underneath my limbs. I begin underlining the important word in each phrase and creating gestures. Above each underlined word I write tiny letters, notating gestures in Austin's code to assist my memory.

WHAT A STRANGE life this is! My mornings in the madness of rehearsal, led from one stage door to another while Elliston grumbles at those who are late and those who have failed to appear, threatening fines but delivering few. And then whispering with other actors at the dark back of the theater when not required, hearing enough tales to fill volumes. Not one actor is above suspicion of some sort of scandal, and I can only wonder what they say about me at the rehearsals when I am not present. One day I am told about Edmund Kean's weakness for the drink and how, during his summer tour, he had to be dragged to the town square and cold water poured on his head before he was put on stage. At this, many eyes light up and someone else says that Mr. Kean was once not conscious enough to perform and the entire play of *Hamlet* was played without the leading role. Apparently Sir Walter Scott pronounced this version an improvement.

The afternoons are my favorite time of day, spent in gentle contemplation of words and action, locked in my tiny closet, my mind in a different world. My evenings are a more concentrated and exciting version of the mornings. Only this time we are all far more vain, examining the fall of robes in the full-length glass, straightening hair, checking teeth. Mr. Elliston says we should be assuming character when not on stage, but only beginning actors comply with this rule. The rest of us wait until we stand behind the wings, minutes before we are to make an entrance. We spend the time when not on stage informing those not at the morning's rehearsal of the news exchanged. And every now and again the call boy enters the room, threatening to blow his whistle if we are too slow to respond, calling actors by their characters. For the purposes of *Henry VIII* I am Anne Boleyn and will be called to the stage with Cardinal Wolsey, Lord Sands, ladies and gentlemen, and the king.

One morning I am called to rehearsal. I arrive early in spite of a bad previous night with my sister keeping me awake after I returned from performing. I take my seat, and before long Elliston announces he will begin with the king and his men. I am left sitting in the dark theater with Mrs. Bland. The theater is much like a family, for where else would one be thrown together with all manner of people of different ages and characters?

Now I have heard many stories of Mrs. Bland. That she does not wash nor brush her hair. That her husband left her and that she works on the streets after our evening performance. That her children have left and no longer speak with her. I believe it is true that Mrs. Bland cannot be relied upon to attend rehearsals and that Mr. Elliston has lowered her pay so he will no longer have to impose fines. When I sit next to her I smell the sourness of soiled linen. Her hair hangs down her back in a long silver plait that is oily and stiff as horse hair. But when I look into her face, I see unbearable sadness.

"Miss Smithson," she nods her head to me.

"Good morning, Mrs. Bland."

"Miss Smithson . . . I was young once," she says. And I do not know how to reply.

"But now I am old and my day is done. I will work 'til I am dead, Miss Smithson." And at that she clutches her chest and a loud wail emanates from her mouth. Briefly, the men on stage pause and look in our direction. Then they return to their work. I wait for Mrs. Bland to stop sobbing but she does not. After some time, I touch her arm and the skin is all oil like lard.

"Mrs. Bland, may I take you home?" I ask.

"Much obliged," she sobs.

Mrs. Bland's lodgings are in Cheapside, a part of London I have never been before and quite far from the center of town. Fares are expensive and it is more usual for me to walk, but with Mrs. Bland's frail state I pray I have enough coins to pay our journey. In the carriage I try to calculate how much it will cost and whether or not I will have enough money to pay the fare back. If I miss the rehearsal of any of my scenes, I will be fined. Our driver raises his eyebrow when Mrs. Bland gives directions. As we set off, she sobs and moans, "Oh, my pretty. Oh, my pretty." I wonder what she means and if she remembers I am there. Mrs. Bland reminds me of the ladies I used to visit in Father Barrett's poorhouse. I tell myself she is not to be feared.

I pay the driver, and he tips his cap in my direction. I jump down the steps to the dusty street and help Mrs. Bland wobble down tentatively, gripping my hands as though I am a piece of wrought iron railing. "Much obliged, much obliged," she says, and I wonder if it is me she speaks to. Her hands shake so hard that she cannot unlock the door; I take her key and force it to turn. With a great creak I push the door open and we are inside a house that is dark and damp. And then she is making her way up some stairs, gripping the banister and pausing after each step.

"This is the last time I take the likes of you." I can make out the sharp features of a woman standing in the doorway.

"A quarter's rent, you owe. And still no thanks. One more month, and if you don't pay your bed is on the street. If you'd so much as mentioned your profession you would never've set foot in my house."

"Oh, my pretty. Oh, my pretty," she replies, breathlessly pulling herself up the stairs.

I am struck by the horror of Mrs. Bland's room. The sheets are gray and crumpled, and when I pull them back to make her bed I see bloodstains like rust. On the carpets there are rotting apple cores, flakes of paint off the walls, and clumps of hair. Large cracks creep down the walls.

"Respect, Miss Smithson," Mrs. Bland says, remembering my presence and forgetting her own grief.

"If you respect your profession, it will respect you. If not, marry a nobleman and be done with the stage to keep an eye on him. Men must be watched. Mrs. Jordan was a cousin of mine, you know. The great Mrs. Jordan, Queen of Comedy." She grins as though she has said something clever, and I remember my father speaking of Mrs. Jordan of Drury Lane. "Gave the king ten children and still he would not marry her. One babe a year for ten years and still worked. Paid her own way and more, never met the king's family. She died alone, you know. In France, hiding from her creditors. Gave her children all she had. Gave her life for those children."

She sits on her bed and begins undressing. I do not know what more to do for her. I look around the room once more. I wonder whether Mrs. Jordan was ever happy.

"Good afternoon to you, Mrs. Bland."

"Yes," she says.

The next morning when I arrive for rehearsal, Elliston hands me a playbill:

On Saturday next
Will Occur
A Variety of Popular Entertainments
THE PROFITS
Of which will be appropriated to the FUND
Now faring for the immediate Assistance of the
EXTREME TEMPORARY DISTRESS
Of several
Provinces of Districts
of
IRELAND

I smile but cannot speak on account of my tears.

For the rest of the week, Molly O'Brien is in my dreams. It is as though she herself arrived in the envelope with her words. At first I dream that I am a child again. We run past Bridie and Mrs. Baird, and they smile and wave to us. Everywhere I look there are familiar faces whose names I have not spoken for ten years. Then I dream of traveling back to Ireland. For days I travel by coach toward Wales, and then I take a sailing ship from Holyhead to Dublin and another mail coach through Limerick to Ennis. After all that traveling I feel as though I have been beaten. Ireland must be the farthest place on earth. And there is Molly, standing in a long cloak, thin hair pulled back and face covered in summer freckles. She is thin with fine bones. She smiles and runs toward me.

I do not perform in the Irish benefit concert. At first when Elliston informs me, I cannot hold back my disappointment. But then he tells me I am to rest that evening and may attend the performance if I wish. I think to myself that the English will give more easily to the poor Irish if they do not have to see one paraded before their very eyes.

There is great excitement at our lodgings as we prepare for the concert. I have two weeks without upcoming performances and feel at liberty to take an afternoon to visit Oxford Street with my mother. I wear one of my white satin gowns for performing and lend a muslin one to my mother. And though it is long since she performed, my mother gives a very good performance of a Lady on a Shopping Expedition, and together we examine the fine shades of satin and the latest styles. Then we find a small fabric shop, dark and dingy, and turn up our noses at the seamstresses there. I select a gold satin and my mother chooses bottle green, which she says is more becoming to a lady of her age. Somehow she has managed to save a few pennies each month, denying herself tea and butter, for an occasion such as this. For five days and as many nights my mother is bent over her sewing until we have beautiful gowns to wear lest anyone accuse us of being poor Irish at the benefit concert.

"Harriet, will you help me dress?" Anne asks.

She has a gown in pale pink that must have been mine once, and I manage to button and pin it tight enough to fit. I wipe her face with a wet cloth, and the coolness brings color to her cheeks. I ask her to keep still as I pull the rags from her hair. I can feel her softening, warming to my touch.

"Will you try a new style?" she asks. I am inexperienced at arranging the hair of another. I smile. "I cannot be trusted, Anne, but I will try!"

I separate the thick curls into thinner wisps and pin them around her face. The curls framing her face soften her hard and pinched appearance which comes from being so thin. She smiles, and I step back in surprise for I glimpse a woman's beauty within.

When Joseph arrives home from work there are damp round patches where he has tried to remove the stains from his doublet. My mother refrains from asking him about his recent ventures, and I know this means she intends to enjoy the evening. It is with great lightness that we step from Mrs. Simpson's lodgings above the apothecary into our awaiting carriage.

It is not often that I am in the audience during an evening performance at Drury Lane. At dress rehearsals we are permitted to sit at the back of the dress circle and observe the entire play, making sure to enter during our own scenes. It is at such moments that the drama really comes to life and we see the play in its entirety, all the pieces slotted together to form a whole. But during dress rehearsals we do not always have the benefit of the full lighting. On nights when I am not required at the theater I prefer to lose myself in a book rather than be reminded of my everyday toil by watching my friends.

We arrive early to avoid the crowds and make our way up the stairs to our box for the evening. I nod to the ushers as we pass. In our box, Joseph and my mother discuss news of Ireland, and before long I am lost. The first play for the evening tells the story of the heroic John Bull. I read on my playbill that this is to be followed by "By way of Epilogue—The Birth, Parentage, Christening, Marriage, and other Family Misfortunes of Denis Brulgruddery, by Mr. Johnstone." This is a grand epic, complicated and full of characters. The men are rough and stupid, the women whine. It seems that the English will not resist the temptation to laugh at our expense. During this performance I notice that the house is only half full. They will barely cover costs. The poor Irish will receive nothing from this empty gesture.

I close my eyes and fancy that Father Barrett sits next to me, laughing at my father on the stage and holding my hand to make sure I am still there. I do not know if I ever attended the theater as a child. But suddenly I am a small girl again, sitting as tall as I can in Smithson's theater in Ennis. And there is my father in front of me, clutching his belly in the role of Autolycus the Ballad Singing Peddler in *The Sheep Shearing*, singing about "the pretty, ugly, black-haired, red-haired, six-feet, three-feet pale-faced, plump-faced, dainty, dowdy ladies that were smitten with his person" to a roaring crowd. And then I am only half present at Drury Lane when someone on the stage begins to sing some of Moore's Irish Melodies. These take me back to Bridie's kitchen, and I remember those days when my biggest decision was whether or not I would break off a piece of cake when she turned her back. I know that I have a weak singing voice, and I have never been trained in any other music. I could not read a note if my life depended on it. But as the words to "Believe Me, If All Those Endearing Young Charms" flow around the theater, I cannot stop my tears. I wonder if anyone will ever love me as the man in Moore's song loves his wife. And whether, by then, I will still be young enough to have any charms at all.

TRAVELING TO LONDON presents an opportunity to renew my friendship with Eliza O'Neill. After a number of messages back and forth, my mother and Mrs. O'Neill manage to arrange a Sunday evening for us to visit the O'Neills.

"What is Eliza O'Neill really like?" Anne asks shyly in the carriage that afternoon.

"She is very kind, Anne. You shall like her."

"But—is she not conceited at all? All of London is in love with her."

We are greeted by Mrs. O'Neill who first kisses my mother.

"Marvellous to see you again, Hetta. And Anne, how much you have grown. Harriet, you have become even more lovely. Please do come in."

The moment I step in the door it is as though I have traveled back to Dublin. The O'Neills have transported everything of home with them, and I note the same reading chairs and piano, the same bookcase.

"Sit down," Mrs. O'Neill says. "The two Johns and Marcus will be in later. Eliza is in her room. Eliza! Your friends are here."

When Eliza emerges from the corridor, I know immediately that something is wrong. She has grown pale and thin, she walks slowly and unsteadily.

"Harriet! It is so good to see you!" She smiles and leans over to embrace me. I am afraid that when I let her go she will fall.

"Eliza. What has happened? Is something—"

"I have been ill, but I am much better now. The doctor says I shall be able to return to the stage in a week or two. I am much stronger. Really."

"She is better for seeing you folk," her mother grins. "Will you take tea?"

After the meal, my mother remains talking with Mr. and Mrs. O'Neill in the kitchen while the rest of us retire to play charades by firelight. John and Marcus are particularly accomplished at this game. John wears a dour expression while Marcus shows a look of joy; they join their arms together in a frame. Eliza laughs and shouts, "The masks of tragedy and comedy!"

It is late in the evening when we return to our lodgings. With a little difficulty, for she is growing heavier, I carry my sister to bed and kiss her. "Good night, Mouse. See you in the morning," I whisper.

I find my mother boiling the kettle over the coals.

"Mother, what has happened to Eliza? Did they tell you?"

"Harriet, it was a tragedy. A real tragedy. She fell in love with a young Englishman, an earl living in London. A very handsome young man, according to her mother. They became engaged to marry, and the young man's father insisted on a year-long engagement while the man traveled abroad. During this time they were not permitted to correspond."

"Not even letters?"

"No. And after some time, Eliza began to hear rumors about the earl's behavior. Marcus and John accompanied her to Paris where they discovered him living a debauched life. Women, drink, gambling. Well, Eliza took to her bed immediately, and it was all they could do to get her home. For some days she was delirious with fever. Now she is slowly regaining her strength. Mrs. O'Neill said she had to lock her husband in the house to prevent him traveling to Paris with a knife. At least they discovered what that man was, Harriet, before it was too late. Breeding cannot buy propriety, remember that."

SOME MONTHS LATER, Eliza returns to the stage at Covent Garden and I visit her there. I am young and quiet enough not to arouse suspicion, and the chaos backstage during performance is such that my presence remains largely unnoticed. Sometimes we have the entire first comedy during which to share our news or play cards. On one such evening a number of ladies of the company receive an invitation to perform with some of the local gentlemen.

Acting is a very fashionable pastime with gentlemen of the upper classes. The performances are strictly amateur, but since they do not wish their women to be exposed to the lower echelons of the acting world, actresses are frequently required to act along-side the gentlemen. They are usually well rewarded for their efforts and provided with a lively audience consisting mainly of the actors' friends. The audience also includes wives of the less trustworthy gentlemen.

On one of these evenings Eliza O'Neill performs with Lord Wrixon Becher, MP of Mallow, County Cork. The play is the comedy *The Belle's Stratagem* by Mrs. H. Cowley. The role of Letitia Hardy, one I have frequently had occasion to play myself, allows Eliza O'Neill to display her varied powers. Mrs. Cowley's play gives the young woman the opportunity to woo the man of her choice, an unusual state of affairs. And I wonder whether it is Lord Becher's decision that Eliza O'Neill should play Letitia Hardy to his Doricourt, thus allowing him the pleasure of danc-ing with the foremost tragedienne of our time.

I observe the weakness of Lord Becher's performance during one of the early rehearsals. I confess I take some pleasure in real-izing that fortune cannot buy genius, and I wonder at Eliza's patience as he forgets lines, makes gestures at the wrong moments, shows his back to the spectators, and trips over his bootlaces. Yet Eliza is tender with him as though he is a small child, smiling all the while and offering the gentlest advice. And while Eliza never says so, I wonder whether her treatment of Lord Becher is motivated by something other than loyalty to her profession, for her father is getting old and she herself is stiffer than she was in earlier youth. She is nearing thirty, and I believe her family is growing anxious about her future. I have heard rumors that John O'Neill asks a high price for the professional services of his daughter, and he is highly skilled at making the most of every opportunity.

It is some time before I am in a position to discuss Lord Becher with Eliza; I long for the intimacy we enjoyed in Dublin. I watch him garland her with flowers and small gifts. It is near impossible to guess Eliza's interest for she is a very good actress with a genuinely kind heart. I stop attending backstage at Covent Garden for my presence is little noticed even by Eliza herself.

I tell my mother about Lord Becher on a gloomy Sunday afternoon. I grieve for the impending loss of my closest friend. But my mother tells me I must maintain my friendship with Eliza even if she leaves the stage. "For Eliza has a thing or two to teach you, Harriet," she winks.

All through Lord Becher's courting, Eliza O'Neill maintains the utmost propriety. If she sees him outside the theater, she keeps this to herself. Mr. O'Neill, John, or Marcus continue to accompany her to and from the theater. She still attends church every Sunday with her family, and not a black word about her appears in the newspapers.

After some weeks, she sends a note inviting me to supper after a Saturday night performance. We shall each play at our respective playhouses that evening and should meet at the O'Neill family lodgings afterward. The invitation includes my mother.

"I wonder if Lord Becher will be present?" she asks more than once. "I long to meet him."

On the evening of our visit, John and Marcus are absent. After supper, Eliza and I retire to the drawing room. While I have been expecting Eliza to be longing for an opportunity to discuss Lord Becher, she begins, instead, to speak of Ireland.

"Harriet, I have been away four years and how I ache to return there!" she says. And although she has perfected her English accent, the Irish lilt I first heard in Dublin begins to return. Her words bring pangs of homesickness.

"But—you are loved here, you are successful here."

"Yes, yes. But there are only so many times one wants to be— Belvedira, Lady Macbeth, or Jane Shore. I have just refused the part of Imogen, for I will not be seen by the public in breeches. And I am getting older. What shall I do when I am too old to play such roles? Where is the King Lear for a woman?"

"There is always Queen Gertrude and—and—"

"Queen Gertrude is not enough, Harriet."

I clasp my hands together in my lap. What else is there for me who may never have her success? What shall I do if it comes time to retire and there is no one for me to marry?

"Eliza?" I begin shyly.

"Harriet?"

"Are you fond of Lord Becher?"

For some moments she does not answer, and I fear I have offended her.

"He is a very kind man, and he holds great admiration for our profession. I think I should like to spend more time with him. But Harriet—I will not come under his protection. It is sometimes expected of us, you know. You must never do such a thing either.

For if a man wishes to keep you, then he must do so in a respectable manner. You must not take on debts you can never repay."

I NEXT VISIT ELIZA in June 1819. I notice her mother watching her at all times, correcting her enunciation, commenting on her deportment and on her manner of eating. It is as though Eliza is undergoing a second apprenticeship. She quivers slightly while sitting at the dining table.

"Harriet," she says later. "This may be the last time you visit me here. Lord Becher," she swallows and holds her right hand to her mouth. "Lord Becher has asked me to marry him and—his family wishes to make sure that I am suitable. It seems I am to go to their estate and live there with my father for three months, and then, if all goes well, we will be married."

"That is wonderful news."

"Harriet, it has been so hard. My mother is quite offended at the thought that perhaps I may not be suitable to marry into the Becher family. So you see she has fallen to correcting me all the time. And my father looks for faults in Lord Becher. He has been waiting for me to make a good marriage these ten years, and now that it might possibly take place he cannot bear the thought of my career ending. It has quite occupied him since I was fifteen years old, and he must wonder what else there is to do. And Marcus teases me about Lord Becher's fondness for ladies in breeches parts. And then there is the question of what is to be done and said. For it would be too hasty for me to retire from the stage now, when my marriage is uncertain. But the Becher family will not accept me if I am still working as an actress. There is little hope of my slipping away quietly from London. You know what the newspapers can be. And yet if Mrs. Haller in July is to be my last role, I feel it would be most hard on the London public were I to deny them a farewell performance."

"But Eliza, do you wish to marry Lord Becher?"

"Oh, yes! I am becoming very—attached to him. He is attentive and wishes only the best for me. And after we are married we shall return to Ireland. I shall no longer have to perform when I am tired or unwell, or travel to the provinces in the summer. And after all, I have had as much success as I would wish. I do not want to travel in order to perform elsewhere. If I travel it shall be to see the world, not to be a strolling player. I am tired of performing. There is no joy for me any longer in being someone other than myself. Before long this monotony will show in my playing and the public will no longer flock to see me. But if I marry Lord Becher I will be able to perform whenever I wish, we shall have parties, and I shall play for our guests. You will come to visit, won't you Harriet?"

THE THOUGHT OF ELIZA leaving the stage fills me with dread for my own situation. She grew up in Ireland as I did. She drank the stage with her mother's milk, and her education was on the boards and not in the church or schoolroom. She has had ten years more performing than I and has grasped the public's affection. I may follow Eliza O'Neill into some of her roles. I can speak to her about gesture and feeling. But how can I expect to follow her by making a similarly prudent marriage?

It is not through me that the rumors begin circulating. Indeed my friendship with Eliza is little known even in acting circles. But a week before her performance as Mrs. Haller in *The Stranger*, people are saying it will be her last. For one thing, it is described on the playbills as her "last appearance at this theater before Christmas," and it is only July. We know she will not be joining us at Drury Lane in the new season, and no actress in her right mind would leave the two main London theaters for any other theater in England. There is some talk of work on the Continent, but since no one has the particulars this idea is soon dismissed. Then there is a rumor that she has fallen ill. But it is the idea of marriage which most fascinates the actors at Drury Lane. Who is the man in question, they wonder. And why is Eliza not taking a farewell from the stage when it would clearly be in her financial interest? It is not like the O'Neill family to miss such an opportunity. The anonymous speculative article in the *Times* is somewhat damaging. The public waits for a reply, but none comes. And on the night of Eliza O'Neill's last performance at Covent Garden, our theater at Drury Lane is empty.

Eliza writes me afterward that the Becher family prevented her taking a formal farewell from the stage. They believed the entire business in bad taste and best forgotten. The public hears no more about her, and attendances at Drury Lane soon return to normal.

TWO OF THE MOST popular actresses of the day are my colleagues at Drury Lane. The best known of these is Madame Vestris, who speaks fluent Italian and French and sings like a bird. Although she made her name in opera, she takes roles in theater when it pleases her. I believe her acting is somewhat overdone and her method more suited to opera. Madame Vestris is frequently the subject of scandalous gossip in the greenroom. She married at only fifteen, and her bankrupt, and by all accounts ugly, husband fled to Paris, leaving her free to behave as she chooses. She has appeared before the public in breeches on a number of occasions. Fanny Kelly, by contrast, is extremely careful to behave with propriety, and her mother is frequently seen in the greenroom. Fanny plays with sensitivity. Her mother is unable to prevent the friendship between the two women, and they are frequently to be seen gossiping in a corner of the greenroom.

One day I overhear Madame Vestris discussing Eliza's departure and what a loss this will be to Covent Garden.

"Not that she was a particularly fine actress," Madame Vestris says, "but the public was very fond of her."

"I was fond of her Juliet," Fanny says. "Do you think the management is seeking to replace her?"

"That depends," Madame Vestris says, "on the precise circumstances of her departure." She glares at me as though daring me to inform her of all I know.

I read about Eliza's marriage to Lord Becher in the *Times*. Joseph points out the article to me, and I cannot speak for a full ten minutes.

"Harriet, what is it?" my mother asks finally.

"It's Eliza. It says here she's married."

"Show me!" She takes the paper from my hands. "And you were not invited. Well. Well."

I cover my eyes with my hands.

"It seems we're not good enough for them now. That is the end of your friendship with Eliza O'Neill. I expect you'll not write to her again."

A few days later I write to her at her parents' home. Within a month she replies, begging my forgiveness. The wedding was small from her side; only a few relatives attended. Lord Becher's mother refused to allow any stage persons to attend unless they were immediate family. They are living at Lord Becher's London residence but hope soon to move to his estate in the south of Ireland.

It is some time before I recover from the loss of Eliza's presence. As I went about my daily business in London I always had at the back of my mind the fact that Eliza was nearby. Whenever I received rehearsal schedules I would look to see if there was an opportunity to visit backstage at Covent Garden when Eliza would be there. It was often the thought of Eliza's friendship that propelled me through the weeks. Now there is no one who understands my homesickness for Ireland or lives as close to their family as I do. No one with whom I can feel so much at ease. For months I feel lost, and it is my mother shaking me at half seven that forces me out of bed each morning.

Liverpool: 1819

*I*N ALL THOSE YEARS of traveling to and fro in the off-season, Liverpool was my favorite town. Though my mother turned up her nose when I first said we would go there.

"Liverpool!" she exclaimed. "That town that spews so much smoke into the clouds! Who is there in Liverpool to watch you play?"

But as it happened, there was quite a crowd. For it was not just the workers who lived there, but the people who owned the manufactories and the merchants who breathed the money into the town. These people lived a little farther out on their country estates which employed many servants. There was a good deal of society to be had in Liverpool. And soon my mother had no desire to leave.

In that town I played Letitia Hardy, Lydia Languish, Lavinia, Mariette, and Adeline. So many foolish maidens, one after the other. It awakened my yearning to love.

My mother was always quick to learn who was worth knowing in a town, and thus she was very pleased on the evening a steward appeared from the Heywood estate with an invitation to dinner.

"Mr. Heywood!" she whispered to me after he had gone. "His father was in the Africa trade and earned his fortune. That was how he established Heywood's Bank! They are the first family in Liverpool." Her voice grew louder. "I hear he has never married."

On my way to and from the theater I could not help but notice the stone building of Heywood's Bank with its archways and barred windows as my carriage bumped over the cobblestones.

It was with some trepidation that we traveled to Larkhill Estate. Only a tradesman's entrance had been built, and thus we passed by the outbuildings and stables before reaching the front of the house. Yet how quaint it was! I had been expecting a mansion, imposing and proud, but there was something gently welcoming about this house. It had but two floors, and the main building was separated by a corridor from the servants' quarters. Wrought ironwork framed the entrance to the mansion, and although it was summer, a chimney puffed gray into the sky.

I had anticipated the occasion to be a gathering with guests and was surprised to see that Sir Arthur awaited us alone. He was a kindly silver-haired gentleman, and after we had taken tea with him he stood.

"Miss Smithson, would you like to see my fishpond?" he asked.

"Of course," I smiled, trying to hide my surprise.

My mother said she would take a turn around the rose garden while we walked to the pond. Sir Arthur took my left arm in his right and used his left arm for his cane. Occasionally he paused and leaned upon it thoughtfully. Mostly he used his cane to point out aspects of his garden. A good number of the garden beds formed a formal arrangement with trimmed and shaped hedges. But as we neared the pond, we passed a garden like a painting, with a perfect blend of flowers and shades. Sir Arthur paused, noting my interest. And he lifted his cane to point to the flowers.

"Foxgloves," he said. "Forget-me-nots, daisies . . . ," he coughed. "Miss Smithson, each season I design one garden bed, and then Mr. Warley executes the design." He frowned. "Next season I shall try a little more silver foliage in this bed." As we continued along the path, we reached a wooded area and I could not help but think what adventures could be had by children in such a place.

Sir Arthur had three fishponds; each contained a different type of fish. There were large white ones with black spots like some sort of malformed dog. The others were orange or yellow, with gaping mouths. And long after I had tired of them, he stood bent over a pond, watching keenly his underwater theater—the gaping mouths, the garish colors—until I feared he would fall in.

We took supper in the dining hall which did not feel vast although it could have seated forty people. Sir Arthur discussed Shakespeare and Lord Byron and other things he had read. And then he turned to me sternly.

"Miss Smithson, it is my wish that you should read to me this evening. If you would be so kind."

The gentleman smiled in spite of his drooping eyelids, and my mother's snoring did not stir him. And the words lost their meaning to me as I thought that I should be very happy to spend more evenings in this manner. When I could no longer read sentences forward, Sir Arthur stood and took my hand.

"Miss Smithson, I must allow you to leave. Forgive me for putting you to such work."

"Not at all," I said, nudging my mother's foot with my shoe to wake her.

"I hope you will come and read to me again."

As I slept that evening I saw the Castle Cootes' estate. Sir Arthur was an old man, and though I could never love him as I could love someone younger, I knew I was already developing a deep fondness for him. And this could sustain me the rest of my days.

Twice a week I read to him, and on our last evening together he said he had a gift for me. My mother left the room discreetly, and I stood. It was as though the following moment would change my life. He asked me to close my eyes and hold out my hands like a child. I cupped my hands, anticipating a small box or the coldness of metal. But instead, he handed me a finely leatherbound volume of poetry by Keats.

"This shall keep you company as you continue your journey, Miss Smithson. And do let me know when you next visit Liverpool."

London: 1820

*O*NE HAD TO WONDER, of course, whether one was deliberately excluded from performing during the king's visit due to one's "provincial" manner. By 1820 I was very much involved with Drury Lane, and my salary had been slightly augmented. Thus it was with great disappointment I learned I would not be seen by King George IV. By this time I had been performing on a regular basis in Shakespeare's histories: I had been Lady Percy in *Henry IV* and was soon to play Lady Anne in *Richard III*. I was coming to see myself as a member of the nobility.

There was great excitement in the greenroom the week leading up to the play. Fanny Kelly and Madame Vestris put much attention into slight alterations of hair and costume. The men shaved even before rehearsals, and I do believe one of them was wearing a new scent. Although Elliston did not require my presence, I decided to attend nonetheless. I knew what people said about the Royal Family. I knew that it was the taxpayers with barely enough to eat who kept them in the manner to which they were accustomed. Yet meeting King George and his attendants could only be of benefit in my observation of the upper classes. And there was always the chance, slight though it may be, that I would meet someone who would prove an advantageous acquaintance.

On the night before the king's visit my mother washed my hair carefully. She guided my head backward so my hair soaked in the basin. The ends were heavy. She lifted my hair out of the water in a towel. I closed my eyes while she rubbed gently at my scalp with her fingertips.

"You will be beautiful, Harriet," she said. "We will tie your hair in rags so you have perfect curls." Her hands left my hair, and I could hear her rubbing soap between palm and fingers.

"You will be noticed by dukes and officers," she said.

In fact, it was a great pleasure to attend the theater without having to perform. I had the liberty of going simply as myself. I wore my newest gown, and my curls did indeed fall neatly around my face. Since I had not been required at rehearsal that morning, I was well rested. I had so much energy in my limbs that my mother had trouble keeping up with me on our way to the theater. Eventually we linked arms. We were like two girls on their way to their first ball.

I was pleased to arrive early at the theater for the crowds that evening were immense. The chatter was almost deafening, and I hoped it would die down in time for the performance. I knew how hard it was to shout lines over so many voices. As I led my mother in through one of the doors, people smiled as though they had seen me before. I thought I spotted Charles Lamb through the crowd.

My mother and I had a box for the evening, and I fancy we looked just like ladies as we sat there politely conversing. We all stood for the king's entrance and "God Save the King." By the time the chorus was halfway through "Rule Britannia," many audience members, including my mother, had joined in and were clapping their hands. I noticed she had tears in her eyes. This performance was encored, and by the second time there was barely a self-composed person in the house. After *Measure for Measure* the doors were opened to those with half-price tickets. They stumbled in, many of them staring distractedly upward, tripping over their own feet, gasping and pointing at the king. And the king himself sat there serenely smiling as though oblivious to the commotion he had caused.

At the end of the evening, my mother feigned tiredness and said she would go home. "You join your friends for supper in the greenroom, Harriet," she said, patting my arm. "Mind you travel home safely. I shan't wait up for you."

She opened the door of our box and joined the surging crowd snaking down the stairs and out into the street. For some time I sat completely still, savoring the peace. I was free to do as I chose and imagined fleeing to Paris in the dead of night. What a strange place the theater was after a performance. I fancied I could hear lost lines and peals of laughter like bells floating about in the air. The air was dim and smoky. I looked down into the pit where men from the laboring classes elbowed each other and laughed. Some of them tipped their heads back with bottles. It would take some time for the crowd to clear. Most people within a mile of this building had spent at least part of the evening transported to another place.

There was tea, coffee, cucumber sandwiches, and scones in the greenroom; I had never experienced such a feast backstage previously. I was pleased to be acquainted with so many of the actors; I could imagine great stage fright if the place had been new and the faces unfamiliar. For the greenroom was gilded with lush flowers in crystal vases and filled with people who looked like nobility. The ladies wore flowing silks and shining satins. One or two were in warmer muted velvets. The greenroom held every hue of the rainbow and all possible variations. To melt down all the gold within would have been to hold a fortune.

Madame Vestris was surrounded by ladies and gentlemen and was most easily accessible to the doorway, so after pausing briefly I sought her out.

"Miss Smithson," she grinned with every muscle in her face. "Please meet Lord and Lady Meredith, Lord Simons, the Duke of Wells, the Duke of Suffolk, Lord and Lady Sawyer."

I curtsied quickly and smiled, looking around the group. After some time I noticed they were still staring at me. I looked to Madame Vestris, who was no longer smiling.

"Miss Smithson, we were just discussing the orchestra's playing of 'Rule Britannia.'"

"I see," I said, earnestly.

Madame Vestris, due to the strength of her voice, was practiced at commanding attention. It was not long before she conducted the conversation once more, the guests nodding politely. I slipped into a reverie. In my mind this was no longer London but Paris, and I was playing a tragic heroine in one of Mrs. Siddons's best roles. I was Lady Macbeth. I looked up and saw the Duke of Wells peering into my face. As I tried to prevent myself from blushing, he stepped out of the circle and walked around to my left side.

"Miss Smithson," he said, "can you tell me where I may find the sugar?"

Madame Vestris paused in her sentence, looked to him, and then turned back to the group. "But of course," I said, leading him to the table in the center of the room. I handed him the silver sugar bowl and spoon, which I had never seen before, wondering who had provided them. The duke held the sugar bowl, peered inside it with green eyes, turned it around in his long fingers, and put it back on the table. He lowered his voice. "You know, from the balcony one does not get the impression of Madame Vestris so outspoken," he said. I laughed and prayed I would be able to stop.

"I saw you play Anne Boleyn last year. Very good, very good. And soon you will play Lady Anne in *Richard III* with the riotous Mr. Kean. Many *Annes*." I looked away, somewhat anxious to be reminded that I was to play opposite Kean so soon after the very public trial in which his mistress's husband had taken him to court.

"My sister is also *Anne*," I said quickly, wondering how he knew about my forthcoming roles.

"You have quite an unusual style. I should like to watch you play more often," he smiled. "Your strength is . . . ," he paused and I concentrated hard, wondering whether he had, in fact, seen me perform at all, "gesture I think. You have fine hands, and you move delicately. Your movements speak to a person's soul. Sometimes I fancy that you are a dancer. Are you a dancer? One does not need to hear your words." I had stopped laughing but began to feel very hot in my gown. One of my undergarments was causing me to itch.

"I hope you do not mind me speaking to you like this." The duke's head was bent toward mine. "Do forgive me, Miss Smithson. One forgets that one does not actually know you. Watching you perform convinces one that you are a very close friend. Forgive me."

"Not at all," my voice sounded unusually loud. "You are very kind."

That night I was not aware of darkened London streets as I walked home. I forgot to be afraid of deserted alleyways. I barely noticed the snarls of drunken men in the streets. Fallen women appeared to me like angels. In my mind the duke rowed a small boat on a vast lake. I sat under a parasol smiling, wearing a white dress of lace. Occasionally I looked up from my book to read him some Shakespeare. After a time he laid down the oars and moved closer to me. He stroked my face with a finger. Ever so gently he lifted my chin and kissed me. As I paced through London streets I imagined that I floated.

And then I saw myself perform Jane Shore, the duke waiting in the wings. Every time I came off stage he handed me water, encouraged me, praised my performance, kissed my cheek. In fact, he was there in my dressing room, straightening my hair, listening to my lines. He was friendly with other actors, but they all knew it was me he waited for. In summers he traveled to the provinces with me, introducing me to members of society and finding beautiful hotels for us to retire in at ease. During the day we frequently bathed or walked or took tea. The other actors looked on in envy. And he always escorted me to and from the theater in a carriage. I never again had to walk the distance alone.

My mother stirred when I entered the front door. I pretended not to hear her call my name for it intruded upon my thoughts. I yawned loudly so there would be no doubt as to my tiredness, though I feared a sleepless night. In my mind I explored a castle on vast grounds with sprawling gardens. I drank tea with ladies in a parlor. I had enough gowns to wear a different one each day and night for a month and to discard those worn thin.

As I undressed I saw my own bedchamber with fine wooden furniture imported from Denmark. A crackling fire kept me warm. I no longer heard the muffled breathing of my family but instead heard merely the rustling of wind through the trees. Outside my window there were no city lights but rather pure darkness. My pillows were fine duck down, my blankets lambs' wool. As I curled under the covers I knew I was safe for there were many people within the house with the task of watching over me. Oh, how practiced I was becoming at inhabiting different worlds.

The duke was not a patient man. The following morning I discovered a note and a bouquet on my dressing table at the theater. I was somewhat unnerved by the idea that a stranger had been in my private room while I slept, but if he had examined any of my belongings he had left no sign. I was quite sure the duke would not have made the delivery himself and expected that anyone in his employment would be completely trustworthy. For a duke would have more important secrets than my own to be uncovered. The note requested that my mother and I dine with him after the following Friday evening's performance at which he would be present.

That afternoon I found my mother sewing. She looked up at me as I entered the room. and I saw her eyes were bloodshot.

"It's no good." She threw her sewing into her lap. "My eyes are going. I will not be able to sew much longer."

I sat down on a chair in silence. Gently my mother placed the fabric and the needle on the small table at her feet.

"Mother, we have an invitation."

"That's grand, Harriet. I do not think I will be able to attend. There is so much to be done here. Take your brother."

"We are invited to the London residence of the Duke of Wells."

"The Duke of Wells?"

"Yes."

"Well, Harriet. Something good has come of all this after all. When shall we go?"

"Friday next."

My mother kept me awake every night that week with her chattering. How did I know the duke? What kind of person was he? Who else did I think would be at the gathering? I had no answers to any of her questions and thought I would lose my wits altogether. She spent her days adjusting one of my better gowns to fit her widening hips. She no longer complained about her eyes. Joseph grew more and more sullen.

"Why cannot I visit the duke?"

"Because the duke has not invited you and someone must look after your sister."

"Well, I shan't. I shall go and play cards with my friends."

"You will stay here," my mother glared.

In my dreams I wore rags, and ladies in fine dresses laughed at me. I lost my hair, and my fingernails fell out. I wished I had not been forced to tell my mother of my new acquaintance. For I had rather enjoyed having him to myself. And now she was going to direct me as though she were Elliston himself, telling me where to look and what to say, as though she knew.

All week I quivered during my performances, peering out from the stage to the boxes above, wondering if he was there watching me. I never saw his face, but twice more I received flowers in my dressing room. On one of these evenings as I was leaving with my bouquet, Elliston met me at the backstage door.

"Ah, Miss Smithson. You have an admirer."

"Yes," I willed myself not to blush. His breath smelled very sweet.

"Very good, very good. Encourage him, Miss Smithson. For you never know what the future will bring." He shifted his worn case from his left hand to his right.

"I have lived off the stage these twenty years. And there has not been one," he shook his left hand, pointing his index finger upward, "not one year when I have not wondered how I will sur‑ vive. If my daughter were on the stage, Miss Smithson, I would advise her to marry and leave it behind. Watch the stage from the other side, from a private box in the balcony. But never again from behind."

That Friday evening my mother met me in my dressing room. She found me slumped in front of the mirror wondering if I would ever walk again. I felt as though I had been on an exhaust‑ ing journey up a mountain but had not yet reached its peak. It was time to either summon the courage to continue or to retreat qui‑ etly. But my mother would not give me the choice. Without speaking, she unbuttoned my dress. She poured cold water from the pitcher into the basin and used it to sponge my armpits; my arms jerked violently. She rubbed soap into my skin and dabbed my underarms with a towel until they dried. She pulled a small jar out of her purse.

"Lavender water! Where did you find that?"

She winked and applied it behind my ears and on my chest. "Wherever you walk will be sweetness," she said, helping me push my arms into the short sleeves once more.

"Harriet, you do look a fright," she scolded a minute later as she stared at my face in the glass. She placed some rags around my neckline. Three times she squeezed the sponge into the cold water. Then she began to scrub at my face. She smudged the colors so that I turned gray and the water pale pink. I could no longer bear the sight or the stinging soap in my eyes. I closed them and emp‑ tied my mind. I sat still as a corpse while my mother worked at my skin. When she had finished I had a pale and gentle complexion. I noticed that my hair shone. My mother stood some feet away and squinted, turning her head on an angle.

"You are like a portrait," she said. "Now we must go."

We discovered one of the duke's carriages awaiting us outside the backstage door. At first I was alarmed that I would be faced with him before I had had the opportunity to prepare myself, but then the driver informed me that the duke's party had left immediately after the performance in another carriage. It was an immense relief to have a carriage for I could not have walked the distance and my mother feared my damaged appearance before the duke.

She knotted her hands tightly together in her lap, and by the silence I detected she had also clamped her jaw so hard that it was an effort to speak. My spirits were falling faster than usual after a performance on account of so many sleepless nights. The soft leather behind my head cushioned me against the jolts of the carriage, and I fell into a state that was close to sleep.

I was next aware of my mother gripping my arms hard and shaking me violently.

"What! What is it?" My first thought was that the carriage was on fire.

"We have arrived!" she whispered.

I peeled her fingers from my arms and pushed them away in my nervousness.

We alighted from the carriage before an imposing building; there was an air of unreality about it that made me feel as though I continued to dream. But as the butler took our coats and led us inside, the sound of voices grew louder and convinced me of their reality.

There was no hope of slipping into the dining room unnoticed. Our arrival was announced by the butler, and as we entered, people stood and applauded, shouting "Bravo! Bravo!" I curtsied to hide my blushes, and when I looked up the room was a mass of faces and it was as though I were on the stage once more. I stood still, not knowing what to do, and at that moment the duke came and took my hand.

"Mrs. Smithson and Miss Smithson," he bowed and my mother beamed. Normally I would not have had difficulty recalling the twenty names I learned that evening, but I was so concerned with keeping the smile upon my countenance and appearing polite that I did not hear a single one. The duke sat me by him at the head of the table, and my mother was on my other side. Thus I was freed any unpleasantness that may have come from the other ladies present.

It is known that women of the theater hold a strange fascination for well-bred ladies. Whenever I have met with such ladies, it has been clear that they believe us to have a certain freedom that is not allowed to them. I believe this idea to be wholly false for indeed we are seen to be fallen women whether we are so or not and must be three times as careful as one in a more respected profession. Indeed a woman with no profession at all is the most respected woman one can meet. As a result of these strange ideas as to our liberties, I have often met with hostility. I know that this is also because they fear that we will perform our way into the hearts and trousers of the better men.

The table was long, and there were too many people to conduct a single conversation. Guests spoke in small groups with those sitting around them. My mother and I were engaged in conversation with the duke and a couple sitting opposite us. When I say *engaged* I mean mainly that we listened and gave every appearance of being involved.

The duke was an excellent conversationalist, unafraid to speak his mind. "No modern writer has understood the *passions* to the same extent as Shakespeare. Wouldn't you agree, Miss Smithson?"

I drank a little wine, and this added to the warm contented feeling I had that evening. My mother was silent, and it was as though she weren't there. I noticed her watching me after the soup, to see which cutlery she ought to use with the roasted venison. After checking that no one was watching, I smiled and gestured to the larger knife and fork.

I was reminded of many such evenings with the Castle Cootes and wondered whether there would be play and poetry readings after the meal. I hoped I would not be expected to take part. When I viewed the duke over the top of my spoon he almost looked like Charles Castle Coote. The very name sent a stab of something cold through me, and I returned my thoughts to the present moment. Something like homesickness was spreading over me.

After the meal there was music in the drawing room. By this time it was early morning, and I longed for nothing more than sleep. I whispered this to my mother, and she glared at me.

"Leaving now would be most improper!" she whispered. "Besides, we may have to walk home and that would take all night. Keep your eyes open, Harriet. See how the duke pays you particular attention. When the other guests are leaving he may lend us a carriage."

I discovered a soft armchair upholstered in tapestry. It was behind the other guests and next to a wall. Although I could not see, I was certainly in a position to hear an excellent musician at the piano. I was asleep within minutes.

I awoke to discover the duke leaning over me in a most familiar way and touching my hand. The room was silent and almost dark. I sat up in alarm, wondering where my mother had gone.

"Miss Smithson, you must stay, I insist. I do apologize for not giving you a room earlier."

"But my mother. . . ."

"I am here, Harriet. The duke has kindly invited us to stay."

A young woman appeared wearing a bonnet from which a few dark hairs escaped untidily.

"Jane, please take Miss Smithson and Mrs. Smithson to their rooms and ensure that they have everything they need."

The young woman curtsied and I did the same, wondering whether keeping us here was somehow part of his plan.

I was pleased to see that the fire had been burning long enough to produce glowing coals and that it seemed the room had long been prepared for me. I kissed my mother and dismissed the maid, turned the key in the lock, and began to undress. I tried to recall whether I had to attend rehearsal the following morning and then realized that this was near the end of a long week. The following evening's play was one that did not require rehearsal. My morning would be free. The room was large with dark wooden furniture, heavy curtains, and a soft carpet beneath my bare feet. The bed was tall and large enough for two, I observed. I climbed on it in my underclothes and sank into a soft mattress and pillows. That night I dreamed I slept in clouds.

I confess that when I woke I wondered whether I had begun a new life and all our difficulties were behind us. I wondered what would happen if I simply stayed where I was rather than return to work. But although I had not told the other actors of my admirer, I knew that Fanny Kelly suspected. She had already asked who the flowers were from and was not convinced by the story of my uncle visiting. This was perhaps already enough for rumors to begin circulating. It was equally possible that one of the other guests the previous evening was closely connected with one of the newspapers and would circulate stories for his own amusement. Simply by spending an evening away from home I could turn into another Mrs. Jordan overnight. At best such a reputation could increase one's popularity and one's price. At worst it could ensure one was shunned by the theater and the public. One could be pelted with tomatoes and forced to make a public apology on the stage or in the newspapers. I could not bear such shame.

I had only ever heard the life and death of Mrs. Jordan in one telling with the hindsight of the teller. She was almost of the same age as my mother was now when she died. At that time I was sixteen and performing in Dublin. I remembered the other actors at the Old Crow bringing their Dublin newspapers with London news, two weeks late, telling us about the tragic circumstances of Mrs. Jordan's death. I wondered what she had been like in her youth. And what her hopes had been when she first met the then Duke of Clarence who would one day become king. Had she, like me, simply accepted a single invitation? Had she been flattered by royal attention? Had she seen the possibility of a way out of her situation, or had she been motivated by the idea of love itself? Would she have become so successful if not for her alliance with the duke?

I DREW THE CURTAINS and peered into the courtyard below. Light poured in through the window, and I returned to the bed. The light was that of late morning. I was free and completely alone. Before long there was knocking at the door, and Jane returned.

"Did you sleep well, miss?" she asked.

"Yes, very well thank you. What time is it?"

"About half nine, miss. The master asks if you would care to join him and your mother for breakfast."

There was something very intimate about the word *breakfast*, and I wondered at sharing this meal with a man I barely knew.

My mother seemed delighted with herself and her eggs in the dining room that morning. I was surprised to discover them both already eating, and I hoped my mother had not been discussing me in my absence. The duke got up from his chair to help me in to mine, and I bade him good morning.

"Miss Smithson, you appear well rested."

"I am, thank you."

A maid poured my tea and brought eggs before I had a chance to ask for them. I looked up from my plate to see the duke watching me intently.

"Miss Smithson, should you like to play the pianoforte or take a turn about the grounds after breakfast?" I chewed slowly, yearning for the peace of eating breakfast alone. My mother's eyebrows arched expectantly.

"I do not play, sir. And I would be happy to see the grounds, but we must leave soon after. I shall be performing again this evening." For a moment I imagined a life of leisurely walks and music, a duke by my side to bend to my every wish; dinners, parties, no performances to attend. I allowed myself the hint of a smile in his direction. I wondered if I imagined his wink in reply.

I BEGAN PREPARATION for my Lady Anne in earnest. My mother gave me the dress she had worn to mourn my father and altered it slightly to fit. We discovered some dark glass beads in the drawer of my dressing table at the theater, and my mother sewed these to the fabric, making patterns of flowers and stems. We hoped the beads would glimmer in the stage lights and help give an air of nobility to my performance. It was at this time that I bought my black veil. All day lines rushed through my mind. I came to think of myself as a pitiful widow. I perfected an expression of misery upon my countenance that caused my mother to ask what was wrong.

One morning I stayed with Anne while my mother ran errands. I gave her bread and tea.

"Harriet?" Her large eyes stared out from her tiny frame.

"Yes?"

"Will you marry the duke?"

"Marry him? Where did you get such an idea?"

"Mother says he will ask you to marry him. And then we will all go to live on his estate. And I shall be bought new dresses."

"Does she? This is news to me. Now, drink your tea."

Later, my mother offered her opinion, uncalled for though it was. "You will be safer with a man behind you, Harriet. We all will. Particularly a man of his standing. You will be free from the stage, free from all this hard work, free to go to church as often as you please," she said.

At times I was convinced of his love, and it was him I mourned, far in the future, as Lady Anne upon the stage. On other days I believed him indifferent. I would ask myself how he could possibly care for me when he knew so little of my life. He had not shown interest through the asking of questions. Yet when I saw him, he watched me intently and seemed at ease and open in my presence.

I composed letters to Eliza in my mind as I walked to and from the theater and whenever I was not required on the stage. The letters were never the same twice and depended on my mood. Sometimes I told of the duke lightly, embellishing to make it a fairytale. Some days it was a comedy and we all lived happily ever after. Other days the story I recounted to Eliza was a romance ending in tragedy.

Finally I sat down to write the letter at hand. I longed for her advice. I own I took pleasure in telling her of a romance of my own. And the man who paid me particular attention was not merely a lord, MP of Mallow, but a duke. If the duke should propose marriage, should I accept even though I did not know him well? What if he should ask to see me on my own? Was that safe? And what if he offered his protection? Was that not still better than being by myself? I yearned for someone to be there for me alone, to free me from the strange bonds I shared with my family. I did not want to be forced to give up the stage altogether but would have been happy to give up my dependence upon it.

One afternoon as I was rehearsing in my dressing room there came a knock at the door. I was somewhat surprised for I had thought I was alone in the building.

"Yes?"

"It's the Duke of Wells. May I come in?"

I wished I had been learning lines quietly rather than rehearsing stage movements. If only I had been silent enough to hide and convince him my room was empty. There had been no time to prepare myself.

"Just a moment," I said, snatching my mother's lavender water from the dressing table and dabbing spots on my wrists and neck. I smoothed my hair in the mirror and stood, straightening my skirts. "Come in," I said.

"Ah, Miss Smithson." He ducked under the doorway and stared around him as he came toward me, hand outstretched. His skin was warm as he clasped my hand.

"Thank you for sending the flowers. It was very kind of you." I looked up at him and then away, for I could not meet the intensity of that stare.

"Not at all, not at all. Sweets for the sweet," he added, smiling. "Miss Smithson, I must say you have been looking particularly beautiful of late."

"Thank you, sir." I felt myself growing hot and cursed myself for wearing such a worn and stained gown to rehearsal. I had been expecting solitude. I was as unkempt as one of Macbeth's witches.

"Would you like to spend an evening reading Shakespeare with me, Miss Smithson?"

"Oh, yes, that would be very pleasant. I shall have to ask my mother, though, and to consult my schedule."

"I think, Miss Smithson, that I should like to spend every evening with you and Shakespeare," he moved closer and slipped his arm about my waist. I prayed he could not sense my trembling. "Alone. You would be freed from the stage, Miss Smithson."

I looked up, confused. For I had not heard the word *marriage*.

"Miss Smithson, I propose to keep you in a very comfortable manner. There would be an allowance for your mother and sister, of course. In return you may accompany me whenever I desire it. You will not be seen with any other man."

I could hear footsteps outside my room and realized that the other actors must have arrived for rehearsal.

"Thank you, no. I am otherwise engaged, sir." I stepped around him and flung the door open, only to reveal a rather surprised Mr. Elliston.

"Do you require assistance, Miss Smithson?" he asked.

"No, thank you, sir. The duke is leaving; he has urgent business to attend to."

I WRAPPED MY CLOAK about my shoulders and ran from the theater, my head bowed, gasping for breath as tears flowed from my eyes.

"Harriet, dear God, what has happened to you?" My mother led me to a chair and knelt at my feet. "Are you hurt?"

I shook my head and sniffed. "It was the duke, Mother. He wanted me to come under his protection. He was very forward, he—" I took a deep breath to compose myself.

"His protection? What did you say?"

"I said—I said—no."

"I see."

"I could not, I wanted. . . ."

"I understand, Harriet. Surely there is something better waiting for you than to be mistress to a man of means and so easily cast aside."

"But he might not—perhaps I should have—"

"I could not have blamed you if you had accepted him. It might have made our lives a little easier. But it is better this way." My mother wiped my cheek and pushed a lock of hair behind my ear. "I am sorry I did not accompany you to rehearsal today; I should not have let you go alone." She kissed my cheek and stood. "I shall bring something to calm your nerves."

The weeks following were difficult. I had tried to keep his courting private for fear the newspapers would take an interest. At the same time, I had secretly wanted all London to know of the affair. It linked me with Mrs. Jordan and Eliza O'Neill more than any other performance could have. It would have granted me much attention from actors and public alike. Now, Fanny Kelly and Madame Vestris raised eyebrows and smiled knowingly whenever I passed. Elliston took to winking at me during rehearsal.

Privately I grieved. I knew I could have learned to love a man like the duke had I been given the opportunity. Eliza O'Neill's marriage had given me hope that I could have a similar fate. How naïve I was! There could only be one Lord Becher in all of England. And it was true that my virtue could not have been as carefully guarded as those of the idle classes. Even when absorbed in my role I could not help noticing shapely women with long hair parading the aisles looking for custom. But was it not the gentlemen who used their services? Was there nothing better for me to hope for than to be paid for my services off stage as well as on?

For some months I retreated within myself, barely opening my mouth except to utter my lines. My mother shook her head sadly at me and sighed as she said, "There will be other men, Harriet." That was exactly what I feared.

Anne Boleyn

I WONDER HOW LONG it will be before my end. It is dark here, and I am alone apart from the women who bring me bread and water. They barely speak a word and will not tell me who else resides here. I remember Henry describing the Tower of London as a fortress for the most villainous of criminals, built so that even the most agile are unable to escape. A cold dark building with thick stone walls where people are sent to await death. And now it is the place of abode for his own wife. Sometimes I hear the cries of gulls, and they sound like people fighting death. I shall not fight. I shall embrace it with all my heart. For in it I will find certainty.

I spend many hours thinking about my daughter Elizabeth. I pray she has not yet lost favor with her father and that she never shall. For the day my Elizabeth is queen of England will be the day I have my revenge.

She has always been a favorite with the king. If he could not have a son, at least he has a daughter who is strong willed and knows her own mind. He thinks that by denying him a son, God is punishing him for wrongly marrying Queen Katharine. I think God is punishing him for so desiring a son and so neglecting his women. Even though Elizabeth is only three years old, Henry already thinks she has the wit of a man. I consider her more like me than her father, yet she is more interested in learning. She has begun studying poetry, learning verses and music by heart. Only once have I been permitted to see her dressed in velvet gowns, her hair neatly tied back from her face, reciting sensitively with occasional gesture. She is King Henry's best exhibit whenever visitors come to the court.

Now I know his ways. King Henry tires of everything before long. He will tire of his court. He will tire of the woman he has after me. One day he will even tire of being king. He does not have the disposition to be king. In part I blame his mother for she gave him everything he asked for as a child. He never had to learn patience, restraint, or sacrifice. Now all of England must bow to his every wish. Born into a different family he would be a different kind of man. He would have made a great explorer searching for new lands yet to be discovered. When he tired of rivers he would have found lakes, and when he tired of lakes he would have traveled oceans and then mountains. And in each place he could have had a different companion and a different wife.

I ask my women whether he has taken a new wife. I long to hear news of any description to relieve the monotony of my days. But they ignore my pleas to such an extent that I wonder whether they understand me at all. I even tried speaking French to them but to no avail. Before long I shall lose my wits and the king will be right to have me locked up.

Often nights, as I sit in the darkness of this cold tower, I return to sunny days in France. I had a nurse who loved me as a mother should. It was only when my father visited that I spent my days at learning, my legs heavy with the burden of a lady's gowns, my shoulders and back stretching as straight as these walls, my head still and my hair pulled tight so that my head ached.

When my father was not present, in the mornings my nurse dressed me in a lighter gown, kissed my forehead, and sent me out into the grounds. I met the gardeners there, and sometimes gruff men at the tradesman's entrance where they dipped their caps at me and smiled. I learned a little lowly French from those men.

I passed many, many days among the summer greens and yellows of Burgundy, roses in my hair. I ordered about my many subjects, people of all sizes and accents, visible only to myself. I knew that I would one day be queen.

When I was fifteen, my father sent me to the court of King Henry VIII. I was maid to Queen Katharine at York Place. Father thought I would learn royal manners from her and that this would help me to make a good marriage.

I came to know the body of the queen almost as my own. In the mornings I helped her bathe with warm water in the royal porcelain, with soap smelling like roses. The queen liked to begin with a clean face and work downward; she said she was truly herself with her cheeks pink and sweet. I sponged softly but firmly, watching her lift first one arm and then the other so that I would know where to clean. I followed the queen's movements with my sponge, always watching only the skin I was cleaning and never allowing myself to stare. Queen Katharine was round and soft as are women who have borne many children.

She was always bright of mood in the mornings, and sometimes she would let me use some of her rose soap and warm water when she had finished. In this way I came to think that we almost had the same blood, sharing sweet water like communion wine. The queen was almost twice my age, but until the trouble with King Henry her skin was smooth and firm. After that her body lost its form as though it could no longer hold itself together. When the trouble with King Henry began we were most surprised for it was not anything that had ever happened before in the history of England. I heard that on her deathbed Queen Katharine still wept for him and said she feared our Lord would punish him on Judgement Day.

For two thousand nights I served my queen. After her toilette I shook out her skirts and tied them firmly around her waist. I did love the vivid reds, greens, and blues of her gowns. I could feel warmth in those shades that seemed to come straight from Queen Katharine's heart to my fingers. I loved to brush her hair. It was fine and silver, and as I brushed it would begin to shine so that I longed to take a lock and put it under my pillow and watch it glisten whenever I wished. I never asked the queen for a lock of her hair. It was only after she died that I remembered it had been my wish, and I had a maid cut some from her waxy forehead. But when it arrived in a paper package the hair was already as dull and lifeless as her own bones. I kept it in my bureau where the king would not find it. I have it with me still.

I only remember one night when King Henry came to Queen Katharine's rooms. He must have used the back entrance, the door that looked like a line cut into the wallpaper. He must have crept stealthily for it was not until he climbed to her bed that I was awoken by a rustling and a grunting breathlessness. I heard cries of surprise from her at first, and then it sounded like pain. It took all my strength to stay in my own bed for I wanted to soothe her cries. In those days I was still ignorant of the ways of men. I did not know how quick King Henry was to have his way with a woman. That she could be in the midst of sweet sleep and woken by a piercing hot sharpness inside her. That was the only time I knew the king to come to the queen in the night.

The queen passed her knowledge and wisdom to me. She warned me that beauty was a plaything of youth and that I must use it wisely. "Your face will not always be so fresh, nor your hair so dark," she said to me once. "But those who truly love you will always see your beauty." Queen Katharine was always beautiful to me.

She told me never to trust men. This seemed strange to me since her husband was king of England. She said that marriage is different for people of our station than for the common people and that I was not to have fanciful notions of it.

"Many days I do not even see my husband," she said.

I was already aware of this, spending all my days with the queen, but until that moment had not thought upon it.

"Does this not sadden you, my lady?"

"I have become accustomed to it," she said. "And there are many aspects of my life which bring me joy. My daughter, the flowers in the grounds. And visitors from my homeland in the summer. I have much time to spend however I choose."

There were times when noblemen would seek an audience with Queen Katharine, who would decide whether or not to pass on messages to the king. Sometimes she would let things pass, reassuring the messengers that she would take measures to assist them. On smaller matters she often wrote to kings and queens of other nations to spare the king the trouble and free his mind for higher thoughts. But when there was talk of rebellion over taxes, she met with His Majesty immediately. Queen Katharine was always well acquainted with all the noblemen in the court. She took pains to ensure the king heard their concerns and treated them with respect.

Before I was sent to King Henry's court I had many fanciful notions about what my new life would be like. I thought it would be like the estate in Burgundy where everyone kept to his or her own place but knew the goings on of everyone else. In Burgundy

I had been free to spend my mornings with the cook in the kitchen, or the gardener, though I did have to spend time at my lessons or with my father if he visited. And the nurse always kept me informed about the lives of her own daughters. There was no one there who would not smile at me or stop to say a word or two. And I wonder now whether this was all because I was a small child then, and no danger to anyone at all.

The court of King Henry VIII was a place of great secrecy. If you happened upon one of the lower servants, she would curtsy quickly and look to your feet. If a messenger or a noble chanced to meet you, he would rarely look you in the eye. In this way I never forgot my station. And whenever I went around a corner I knew there were whisperings in the air surrounding me. I always felt that I was being watched. The court of King Henry VIII was a place where stories grew from sentences left in unswept corners.

Until the day of the ball, I only ever saw King Henry from a distance. He was always heavily robed and surrounded by his men. His was a weathered face. He had bright eyes and thick hair; I fancied he was handsome to look at, though he had a large and round figure. I knew that I should never stare, but I do not think anyone ever saw me peer from afar into his face. I wondered at all the other kings and queens of England who had left a legacy in his face as well as his name. I wondered at the important matters that must fill his mind every minute of the day. And yet, as I was to discover, the king often played with great frivolity.

The first time I had any personal communication with His Majesty was the day I received my invitation card to the supper ball. Queen Katharine urged me to go; I would never have gone without her permission. And when I asked whether Her Majesty was coming, she shook her head and said she would be otherwise engaged that evening. But I must go, she said. And what would I wear? Many morning discussions were taken up with this subject until I almost thought Queen Katharine would even help me dress. And although she did not do so, she let me off early on the day to allow me time to prepare.

The presence chamber was all color and light on that evening. I cannot think how much all those candles must have cost. There were quite a number of guests, some of whom I had seen around the court, others I knew to be lords and ladies from the district. At first Sir Henry Guildford on behalf of Cardinal Wolsey greeted the ladies. Lord Sands sat next to me and commenced a conversation regarding the madness of his father. I do believe he himself is losing his wits for before I had time to draw breath he kissed me wetly on my left cheek. At that moment Cardinal Wolsey entered, and I was most pleased because it drew all eyes away from my fiery cheeks.

There was much wine and merry laughter that evening. After a while I could hear the faint echo of an oboe. It grew louder in its reedy mellowness, and then finally a musician entered the room with red and green silks flowing from his instrument. Following the musician was a line of men dressed as shepherds wearing all manner of masks. Each man took the hand of a lady. The man taking my hand was large with thick, dark hair. "The fairest hand I ever touch'd," he said to me. "O beauty, Till now I never knew thee!" And I curtsied to him as is the custom before dancing. He spoke little during the dance, but his feet moved gracefully and I fancied he was staring at my face all the while.

After one dance, the music stopped and a game was played. Cardinal Wolsey was set to discover which of the masked men was the king. And I was astonished to discover that it was in fact the

man I had been dancing with. The king bowed to me, and I curtsied once more. Then he led Cardinal Wolsey away and I saw
them whispering in the corner, their eyes looking in my direction.

It was after the ball that I first heard rumors of the queen's
plight. Betsy the kitchenhand stopped me one morning and asked
if the rumors were true.

"Which rumors?"

"That the king wishes to leave his wife!"

"I have not heard such tales," I told her.

And from then on I watched Queen Katharine carefully at all
times. I fancied she looked poorly. Her skin became too soft and
wrinkled like wilting petals. During the night it was hard for me
to sleep because her tossing and turning caused her bed to creak
like the masts of a ship.

It is true that some days after the dance I met with Lady
Oswald, an elderly lady of the court. This lady questioned me for
some time on whether or not I would ever be queen. I was frightened. I did not know who had sent her or why. No, I told her. I
would never be queen, not for all the money or jewels in the
world. And I swear, at that moment I would not have been queen.
For I had seen what it did to a woman to be locked up like that
under the pretense of freedom but really watched over by a husband who could do as he pleased. And I had seen what was being
done to her now that she was older and could bear no more children. I now knew that King Henry wished to divorce her, which
meant to cease to be married to her, and that this meant he would
be able to choose another wife under the law.

The ceremony could have been a wedding; I know not what
the ceremony for the ending of a marriage should be. There was
cheerful music which did not seem right. Many noblemen were

present as well as the Archbishop of Canterbury, several bishops, Cardinal Wolsey, and Cardinal Campeius. If God was ever present in a room it was that one. And there in front of all those people Queen Katharine knelt before the king and asked him why he wanted to be separated from her. And as she listed all she had done for him, I stared at the floor. Even the king could not find fault with her. But suddenly he revealed that they had never been truly married. He thought that God had punished him by denying him a son and male heir.

Life was very different for me from that day forward. Queen Katharine took to weeping and staring wistfully out of windows. Oftentimes she asked us to sing for her pleasure, but she failed to look pleased. She demanded that windows be left open in the night. Even I began to catch a slight chill. The queen grew weak and tired; when she breathed, a rasping sound came up from her chest. We were told that soon we would all have to leave the court.

I noticed that as I moved around York Place, people stared. The noblemen examined me as closely as they dared, while the lower servants peered at me as though I were the queen herself and would give them orders of my own. And then finally Betsy asked me whether I had caused the rift between the king and queen.

"Where did you get such an idea?"

"It is all over the palace. Everyone says so."

The next day the king summoned me. Heads turned as I walked through the antechamber where noblemen waited for an audience with His Majesty. I was led through the door and into the king's chamber. Suddenly I was alone with His Majesty for the first time. He sat back in his chair with a gilt oak table between us. I stared at my feet. He asked whether I understood what was happening between himself and Queen Katharine. I confessed I did. He stood and walked around the table until he was standing beside me. He took my hand, forcing me to look into his eyes. Then he asked if I would be his wife and the next queen of England.

Panic welled inside me, and I wanted to run from the room. I thought of Queen Katharine. She had been brought from Spain to be queen of England, and now she was being banished. And as though he saw me hesitate, King Henry told me that our marriage would be true, unlike his marriage with Queen Katharine. Until that day I had been someone who would one day be lost to the world. If I were queen of England in such important historical circumstances, I would always be remembered. I would have my own elegant rooms in York Place and my own attendants. And why had my father sent me to the court if not in the hope that I would make a suitable marriage? Who could be a more suitable husband than the king? I wondered if the difficult circumstances of my becoming queen would also be remembered, and whether I would only be seen as the second queen.

And suddenly I wondered what would happen to me if I did not obey the king's wishes. I realized that I would be banished from the court and that there was nowhere for me to go except back to my father in shame. No one would ever wish to marry a woman who had been banished from the court of King Henry VIII. I saw his weathered face with those bright eyes, and I imagined kissing his thin lips. I imagined his touch on my skin and shivered.

"I will think on it, my lord." I said. He kissed my cheek. I fled his chambers.

I could not face Queen Katharine and asked another of her attendants to tell her I was indisposed. I fled to the garden where

I walked; the spring grass was soft under my feet, and the flower beds were rich royal colors. I passed fountains and statues. Could all this be mine? I passed a gardener and saw Princess Mary in the distance. I wanted to sleep and wake some time in the future when decisions were made and difficult situations over. And then I heard someone call my name.

Queen Katharine had seen me through her window and wished to speak with me. I felt hot to my very core as I made my way up the stairs.

"My Lady Anne," Queen Katharine took my hand and pulled me close to where she lay. I fell to my knees and sobbed. She stroked my hair until I was calm. I lifted myself to a chair next to her and peered at her old face.

"There is nothing more to be done for me. I have fallen from His Majesty's favor. But you, you must marry him. For your own sake."

London: 1821

*I*T IS NOT SURPRISING that I am barely noticed at all when I perform beneath Madame Vestris and Fanny Kelly. Madame Vestris is a tall woman, and her voice is clear and strong. Even when speaking normally, her voice rises above the audience and can be heard over a certain amount of shouting and plaudits. And when she sings she commands silence. A crying infant would halt its wailing to hear the sweetness of that sound. People believe she has important things to say. Critics find only praises for her. I wonder if they are as afraid of her wrath as her husband is. Madame Vestris is the favorite with Elliston and has the power to demand whichever role she pleases. This is because Madame Vestris draws crowds. She frequently absents herself from rehearsal and feigns illness before a performance (illness is one of her most successful roles) yet she is never fined, and though Elliston mutters under his breath, I am certain he never complains to her directly.

Fanny Kelly's moods vary greatly. She is a particular favorite with Charles Lamb, and when I see him creeping about backstage I wonder whether he has been with her though I have never seen them together. She would do well to deny she knows him at all. Her popularity with Mr. Lamb has caused her to be much written of in the newspapers. This means Elliston ranks her highly. The papers speak of her *feeling*, her *bright eyes*, and her *fine figure*. They do not use such terms to describe me.

I know that Fanny Kelly is very thin and has not changed the size of her dresses since she was fifteen. I have never seen her eat. Compared to Fanny Kelly, I am large boned, rounded, and clumsy. There is none of that quick boyishness about me. And so it is Fanny Kelly who is the great favorite with the London crowd. I flit in and out of secondary scenes like a ghost. All Fanny need do is enter the stage and spectators roar and clap. She is barely required to act at all.

These women treat me like a younger sister. At times they are kind; Madame Vestris once consoled me after a difficult rehearsal where I had forgotten my lines. But there is always something artificial about their kindness, as though it is payment for some future demand. And more often than not I am running to them in the greenroom with glasses of water or cold compresses for their headaches. I am tying their corsets and arranging their curls. On occasion they bequeath me a carefully timed leading role when they decide they are too tired or too ill to perform. Only rarely does this occur in time for my name to be added to the playbills.

I have spent three years hanging about backstage, waiting for some new opportunity. I wonder whether Fanny Kelly may marry and retire from the stage, allowing me my own attempt at fame. If they would only let me have a season at her roles, I know I would have as much success as she. But how am I to be noticed when I am on the periphery of the company? As I grow older I long for the success that will lead me to love and something new in my life. I feel strongly that the man I am to marry is there among the smoke and laughter, his passions stirred by what he sees. If only I could capture his attention.

Mr. Elliston does not tell me personally of my demotion. He hands me a letter which I read later in my dressing room. My income is stated as three pounds. And when I return, my cheeks red from the cold water I have used to scrub away the salt, I notice Fanny Kelly beaming. Later I hear her salary has increased to twenty pounds a week.

It is 1821 and I am one of the lowest paid in the company. I wonder whether I have performed badly enough to deserve this. I imagine myself as a governess or a schoolmistress. Or tending the sick. But now that my career is marred by years on the stage, no other profession will have me, of that I am certain.

Anger swells my body like venom. If only my father were still alive. He would speak to Elliston and have him improve his treatment of me. Fanny Kelly has her father acting as her manager. Madame Vestris has her husband, Charles Matthews, though she is naturally in a far stronger position. I try to remember every mistake I have made. Every wrongly executed gesture or misremembered line. But the errors have been slight, and I know I have had favorable reviews in the newspapers. One day I will be successful and Elliston will blush at his error of judgment. My name will be on the lips of every worthy member of society. I will play Shakespeare to my heart's content. I will feign illness whenever I do not feel like working.

As I begin the journey back to the lodgings I share with my family, I feel ill. How will I provide for us all? I cannot bear the thought of telling my mother. I do not go home straightaway. I walk through unseemly London streets. I look at the loose women, their hair streaming around their faces, painted bright colors, their dresses revealing their figures. One woman grins at me, and I notice she is missing some teeth. Acid rises from my stomach and I am ill on the dirty cobblestones, my head swimming. Somewhere behind me I hear cackling laughter. The toothless woman touches my shoulder and asks if I require assistance. I shake my head, wipe my chin with a handkerchief, and continue walking.

I cannot think clearly what I ought to do. If I joined one of the illegitimate theaters, I would have no chance of ever truly succeeding. I would never again play Shakespeare or perform with the best actors in London. I would share my dressing room with horses, dogs, and dancers. And I would never earn more than three pounds a week. If I stay with Drury Lane, my fortunes may change. It is a fickle business. I can never know who will see me on stage and what will come of it. But at least I can observe the successes of others, if not share in them myself.

The next evening I realize I have been relegated to the second greenroom. Oh, the trials I must endure! I try to think of my father's strolling players and the conditions they must have lived through for months on end. They slept in coaches or under trees. They bathed in icy rivers during the cold northern summers. I fold my arms before my chest, lift my head, push back my shoulders, and enter. This room has no carpet or fire, and the air is chilled. It is not difficult to see how everyone else keeps warm. A tightrope walker is walking on her hands. A man in garish costume is juggling. In the corner I see a horse covered in ribbons and silks. It neighs, and I notice a bucket and shovel in the corner. There are lumps of dirt on the boards. The room smells like a barn. A dwarf sits on a bench, joking with a man holding a fire stick. Three ballerinas are shouting steps to each other by a bar before a mirror. I read through my script from the very first page. I tell myself one day I will be a great success and my experiences in the second greenroom will form an interesting anecdote in my remembrances.

The men in the company treat me with more interest now. I have seen the way some of them look at me, imagining they will have me at their mercy in their dressing rooms after the performance. I am always the first to leave opening night parties for fear of being taken advantage of. And my mother rarely offers advice or instruction, but her presence is enough to frighten any man. Yet they do not lose hope, and many of the younger men in particular come to speak with me in the quietness backstage during rehearsal when my mother is not there. They whisper gossip and news. They smile, and when they move too close I find a reason to move into the foyer and into the light.

One morning I arrive slightly early to rehearsal. I am on my way to my dressing room, which they have not yet taken away from me, weaving among properties, when I hear footsteps. They are light footsteps and sound unfamiliar. My heart begins to beat quickly, and I start to run. As I rush I trip over a plank, landing on my knees. I try to get up, pulling at my skirts. Suddenly a gloved hand is on my arm. I see a thin man with a bushy mustache in a heavy coat and wearing a hat. He helps me to my feet. I struggle for air as he says, "Can you tell me, please, where I can find Mr. Elliston? It is rather urgent." I try to speak but no sound comes, so I point to the location of Mr. Elliston's dressing room.

Once finally in my dressing room, I lock the door and fall into my chair. It is some minutes before I am calm again.

I first hear about John Howard Payne in the greenroom during rehearsal for *The School for Scandal* that morning. His name slips quietly from everyone's lips. Madame Vestris and Fanny Kelly look at their feet when he is mentioned. The men huddle together and speak of him with animated gestures and bright eyes. John Howard Payne is in jail.

Not only is he in prison, he is translating plays there. And Elliston is interested in staging them. In fact, theaters are fighting over his work. Somehow John Howard Payne was sent the latest plays from Paris. The very word glitters in my mind. No one will tell me what John Howard Payne was imprisoned for. I wonder if he has robbed a bank to support his craft. In the end I conclude he has stolen books and perhaps a French dictionary or two.

Next day Madame Vestris is absent. Mr. Elliston calls an important meeting. This meeting is so important he waits until we are all assembled before speaking. By this stage it is late morning and I feel faint with hunger on account of having missed break-fast. The thin man with the gloves and mustache is there. Elliston introduces him to Fanny Kelly and me.

"Ladies, this is Mr. Howard Payne. We will be performing his new drama in four days."

I tremble, and Fanny Kelly looks faint.

Elliston predicts it will be a huge success. It must be ready to perform quickly, he says, lest a rival version be brought out by another company.

When he has finished I notice Fanny Kelly trying to tell me something. I lean toward her. "He has escaped from prison. We are working with a criminal!"

She grows flushed and strides after Elliston while the other actors disperse.

"Mr. Elliston," she shouts. "I will not be playing tragedy num-ber two!"

Thus I become Mariette in Payne's drama *Thérèse*. Elliston is forced to add my name in bold to the playbills. I spend my time at rehearsal pondering John Howard Payne, who escapes from prison every day in disguise and returns there in the evening. His disguises become a matter of great interest. He is a difficult man to recognize in a bonnet, white curls escaping, and an apron. One day he arrives wearing a regal crimson jacket with brass buttons. He is always a little breathless on arrival; every day we actors slump around the stage waiting for him. I curl hair around my fingers, men tie knots in their bootlaces, Elliston paces up and down muttering. He has heavy shadows under his eyes, and I know he is not sleeping for fear that John Howard Payne will be recaptured and the staging of his masterpiece prevented. Elliston believes Mr. Howard Payne will save his theater. Eventually Elliston says, "We will give him ten more minutes," and we hear a scurrying backstage. The footsteps are as light as rats in a roof. And then he appears, his weathered face framed by some new sort of headpiece and wearing an anxious expression. Elliston beams as though we have all been having a fine time and Payne's appearance is an unexpected and pleasant surprise.

He plays well, if a little too dramatically, but Elliston does not give him much direction. I know that he is thinking of his good fortune in having an escaped prisoner on his stage. Of the criminal playwright and actor. Of the crowds it will draw.

I cannot help feeling a little frightened of him and endeavor not to be alone in his presence. For I have still not established the reasons for his imprisonment, and I do not know if he is a ravisher of women. When I believe he does not notice me, I stare into his face and wonder what it has seen. I imagine the cold darkness of a prison cell and the harsh words exchanged by inmates. I wonder whether he feels guilt. I see my own world through guilt. I feel guilt that Joseph was forced to work as a child, that Anne is made to suffer, that my mother is burdened with caring for us all on her own. I feel guilt that my position in the company has been lowered to such a degree that we can only eat meat once a month, that my mother feeds me more than she feeds herself. That I am the only one who has known real comfort and love and reading. But this guilt can be nothing compared to the guilt of a real criminal. One who has knowingly and deliberately defied the morals of society. I imagine his crimes. I see him wearing his mustache and gloves, breaking into a vault in the dead of night. I see him hitting a policeman with a metal bar. I see him snarling as he counts banknotes. But when I look into his face, I see only a man who believes he is right.

I am careful not to tell my mother about my latest performance. I fear she will be angry that I have been forced to associate with such a person. I spend little time at home in between rehearsing and performing, so it is easy to keep information from her.

Two nights before our first performance, I dream I am on stage with Payne, staring into the crowds. All of a sudden, a plump lady in a gray wig appears from behind the curtain. Then another and a third. They are brandishing swords and popping up from among the spectators. There is a long line of them shouting and running in through the door. One hundred policemen disguised as chorus ladies have stormed the theater. People scream and try to run. One plump lady knocks me to the ground in a dead faint. When I recover I am alone on the stage in the empty building. It is pitch dark, and I cannot see my way out.

Last rehearsal is desperate. Mr. Elliston is in a great state.

"What are we to do?" he is almost sobbing. "Covent Garden will release a version of *Thérèse* this evening. Who told Kemble about the play? Who gave him the plot? I will discover our betrayer." He is pulling at his hair, his face is swollen and red, and I notice part of his left eyebrow seems to have disappeared.

"This was going to save us, to *save us*! Oh, who could have done this to me?"

"Per'aps we could rehearse, Mr. Elliston?" John Howard Payne says.

"Not until I discover the culprit!" he growls. For two hours he paces, staring at us as though the information is written in our faces. One by one we are all questioned. I blush and stare at my feet.

"Miss Smithson, what have you to hide?"

"Nothing, sir."

"Why do you blush so?"

"Leave 'er alone," someone says. Elliston turns violently and begins to question another. When he has finished questioning the troupe, in a fit of madness he begins looking for spies. It is late afternoon, and he is searching all the corners backstage for someone hidden. One by one we slip out the backstage door.

There is time for me to return home, bathe, and eat some bread and a little cheese before opening night. I feel unprepared. One more rehearsal and I could have played Mariette with more certainty. I find my mother in a great state of excitement.

"Harriet, why didn't you tell me? Fancy performing with a prisoner. I saw Mrs. Pitchett at the greengrocer and she told me about *Thérèse*. All of London will be there. I don't know if I will be able to get a seat. And your name heading the playbills! Will you be paid more for this?"

"I don't imagine so, Mother. I am playing as it states in the contract."

"How can this be? The leading role and all!"

"I don't know." I take her hand. "All of London will see me, Mother. This is more important than money."

"What's 'e like?" Joseph asks.

"Quite ordinary, really," I reply.

"Does he wear chains? What does he look like?"

"Well," I stare him sternly in the eye. "He wears all manner of costumes to rehearsal. It is his disguise, you know, allowing him to escape from prison."

"What did he do? Why is he in prison? Will they let him out if he succeeds?"

"They say," I lower my voice. "They say he murdered a beautiful woman. No one would allow a man like that to run free."

That night the crowd warms the theater like so many embers. If a rival version has been launched, it is clear that it has failed. Elliston is walking about with a cold compress tied to his forehead. It is difficult to take him seriously as he shouts backstage orders.

Once I step onto the stage, I am Mariette. I see George before me, I am deaf to the audience, and I forget all that has led to his performance. It is not until the curtain call that I briefly become Harriet Smithson again, in time to hear the roar from the house, and to see John Howard Payne wink in my general direction.

Mr. Elliston seems to have recovered his spirits the following morning, though he still wears the cold compress—perhaps for a different reason. He makes one final change to the playbill before it goes to print. It seems we will be repeating *Thérèse* because "No piece, however successful, was ever received with such extraordinary applause. *Thérèse* is the most successful piece that has ever been produced."

After two nights, John Howard Payne disappears. As I walk home from rehearsal, I turn quickly and see him following me. I run into him backstage, I see him near my lodgings. I even see him winking in my dreams. I tell Joseph I believe John Howard Payne might have committed another crime. Two weeks later I overhear Elliston telling someone that Payne is collecting new drama in Paris.

Mr. Young takes over his role. Young is not a passionate performer; he is measured and controlled, his gestures perfectly timed, his elocution clear. His playing is as accurate as a clock, and I am at ease performing with him. I am buoyed by the crowds, and I notice Fanny Kelly's bitter glances, worth more than any possible increase in my salary, during other rehearsals. I fancy some of the audience members are coming to see me. One critic writes that I "lie fainting in the arms of [my] enemy, pale and lovely, with a reclined head, like a lily snapped by an ungentle hand." In my bed at night in the darkness, I practice lying pale and lovely. We play for an unprecedented thirty-one nights.

Mme Harriet Berlioz
Rue de Londres
Paris, May 1841

My dear Louis,

I remember when your father first told me about the symphony. I knew I had been its inspiration, and so I assumed the symphony was about love. I waited for him to tell me how I was represented in his music. I listened for his descriptions of my sweetness, modesty, and grace.

"L'idée fixe, the theme of the beloved, haunts the young musician's being," he said. "This is your theme." He closed his eyes and began to hum. At first his song was gentle and lilting, and he seemed to conduct himself in a dream. Soon he was trying to be an orchestra all by himself. Holding his nose, he did a fine imitation of an oboe; with his lips round and using his tongue, he was a plucking harp. His music grew in volume.

Hector seemed to think the kitchen table had a fine resonance, and this became his drum while he hummed a dirge-like minor melody.

"The young musician of morbid sensibility and fiery imagination poisons himself with opium in a fit of amorous despair.

"He dreams he has killed her," he said.

There was a coldness to his words, and I pulled my arms around myself.

"And then he dreams his own execution." He hummed something more violent. He clapped loudly and thumped the table four times. "That was his head falling after the guillotine!" he said.

I squirmed in my chair. "What happens in the end?"

I remembered an ominous version of the "Dies Irae"; the melancholy tolling of bells, a heaviness with an occasional high-pitched fluttering as though something was escaping. A triumphant conclusion. It alarmed me like some species of forbidden black magic.

"She turns into a witch."

This symphony, said to have sprung from our story, almost changed its course. Following his melancholy nights away from Paris, apparently haunted by my image, your father resolved to marry Camille. I have often wondered how it was that his parents gave their consent so readily to their union and so reticently to our own. Perhaps it was Hector's first request to marry and they felt him genuine. Or perhaps it was due to her reputation as a concert pianist that they falsely thought her too preoccupied with her work to have time to dally with other men and was therefore a suitable match. It is certainly true that there are far more musicians than actresses in the middle and upper classes for it is only those classes which can afford to educate their children in music, and this is thought to be a profession for which one must be groomed from childhood. Unlike acting, which, it is supposed, can be learned in the blink of an eye when one is a woman in need of an income.

But while Madame and Monsieur Berlioz readily gave their consent, the same cannot be said of Madame Moke. She did not dismiss Hector; however, she determined that he should prove himself a suitable match for her daughter. She was concerned at Hector's lack of fortune which would necessitate Camille continuing to perform after their marriage. And thus Hector resolved to demonstrate his ability to earn money as a composer.

During the July Revolution of 1830, your father sat for the Prix de Rome examination for the fourth time. On each of his previous three attempts Hector had been short-listed, but his refusal to follow given rules of composition had deemed him three times disqualified. The competition itself reflected everything Hector hated about the institute. But your father proved he could follow rules if the prize was big enough. As gunpowder fired around him and the walls shook, Hector dipped his pen in black ink and finished his cantata. I am grateful that the prize required your father to be locked up, for foolhardy as he was, he would have run out there with a gun and had himself shot within five minutes.

He handed in his score and ran out into the streets at five in the afternoon, rushing to see Camille. Once satisfied that she was unharmed, he searched for weapons, wanting to be able to claim a part in the revolution which would bring freedom to the arts. I believe it was fate that provided your father only with an empty handgun, then with bullets and nothing to shoot. The riot was over.

Your father says he was astonished, as he passed by the Palais Royal later that evening, to hear a group of over-excited though bedraggled men shouting his "Chant Guerrier" in the street. Among them were some of his friends. Hector joined in the singing which continued until nightfall when it ended with "La Marseillaise" which had previously been banned. They defied the Bourbons to shoot them.

The details of the 19th of August 1830 are still clear in your father's mind. He slept poorly the previous evening and brewed a powerful cup of coffee in the morning, not to waken his mind but to sharpen it. The meeting to decide his fate would not begin until midmorning, so Hector wandered the streets of Paris from seven until ten. He *planned to visit the Moke household to divulge the results at two for lunch. After arriving at the institute, it was difficult to find a place where he could be away from his rivals. Eventually he made his way to the library where he came upon one of Beethoven's earliest scores, which he examined with relish until he lost all sense of time.*

And it was there that Monsieur Pradier the sculptor discovered him at five in the afternoon. He was surprised at Hector's tears. The score shaking in his hands, Hector stood and Pradier shook his hands, gazing into his eyes for some moments.

"The prize is yours," he said.

Harriet

London: 1826

*E*ARLY IN THE YEAR a letter from Charles Castle Coote
arrived in my dressing room. He had not written to me since my
school days, and I had heard nothing from him since I left Waterford for the Dublin theater twelve years earlier. I wondered if his
interest in me had been rekindled by some favorable reviews in the
London newspapers.

The letter was formal in tone and informed me merely that he
was studying the law in Oxford and would be in London at
midterm hoping to see me. He had read of my successes in the
theater and was proud, he said. He remembered our early performances together at Waterford and hoped we could be friends
once more. I kept the news of his impending arrival from my
mother as long as I could. But a few days before, I had to tell her
for I knew I needed her presence. It would not do to spend too
much time with Charles Castle Coote alone.

My mother aired our lodgings and spent an entire day sweeping the floor and wiping away the dust. Our home was humble,
she said, but no Castle Coote could say it was not clean. She
scrubbed my sister until she screamed, and even Joseph was forced
to bathe in a basin of almost-cold brown water.

Charles appeared in the greenroom two days before I was
expecting him. I was alarmed at all the people who saw him and
could start rumors circulating again. From the other side of the
room I gestured to him as subtly as I could manage and left by a

side door. A few minutes later he was in my dressing room with the door closed. He was much taller than I remembered and had lost his thin raggedness. He seemed to have grown into himself and had turned into a very handsome man. I was unsure how to greet him. He took my hands and kissed them. He stood staring into my eyes for several moments. Energy and light surged through me and I felt as though I were in Waterford again, that all I had to do was open the door to find orchards and fields about me.

"You are looking very well," I smiled. "Please, sit down." I dragged a chair out from the corner and turned my own chair away from the mirror, glancing quickly at my face as I turned. I had been planning to change out of my costume. That would have to wait.

"My mother sends her love. She hopes to see you again soon." I smiled.

"George is in the navy, and Edmund is soon to be married."

"Please pass on my congratulations." After a brief silence I asked, "And you, Charles, are you married?"

"No, not married."

"My mother—my mother was expecting you to supper in two days' time. Is that convenient to you?"

"Yes," he nodded. "Yes, that would be lovely."

By the evening of Charles's visit, our lodgings were almost unrecognizable. I had bought some posies from a flower seller in Covent Garden, there was clean air and light and the smell of baked apples. My mother and sister wore freshly laundered gowns. Joseph had reluctantly changed into the clothes my mother had cleaned for him and sat with us as we waited. When the knock came, my mother hissed at us to stay where we were while she went to the door. She returned with Charles, and for a few seconds we all stood awkwardly looking at each other. Then Charles remembered himself and leaned over to me, kissing my cheek.

"Harriet, lovely to see you again." He turned his attention to my sister. "You must be Anne. You may not remember me. Charles. Charles Castle Coote. And Joseph, good evening. You do resemble your father."

"How is your mother, sir?" Mother asked, serving the vegetables.

"Well. They are well, thank you."

"Harriet says you are at Oxford."

"Yes. I am studying the law."

"Your father must be proud."

"I think so."

"Do you plan to return to Ireland?"

"Perhaps eventually. I shall see where my work takes me. And I should like to travel abroad." At this point, Charles paused and looked at me. I looked away and saw them all staring at me, my mother and siblings all waiting for me to speak. I took a deep breath.

"And where shall you go, Charles?" I asked.

I WAS SURPRISED at my own feelings upon seeing Charles once more. Age had only improved him, and he seemed a more spirited person than the boy I had known. I saw much of him during that week. He arrived always unexpectedly. One afternoon I was about to walk home after rehearsal when he appeared at my door. He handed me a bouquet, and I reached to kiss his cheek. That afternoon we walked arm in arm. I told him of my life in London with my family. I had not felt so free since childhood days and was pleased when he asked me to sit with him on a park bench. He toyed with some curls around my face with his right hand. I held his left.

"Harriet," he said, "I think I ought to tell you that I am engaged to be married." I dropped his hand and clapped my left hand to my face. I scanned the park to see if anyone had noticed me there with him.

"It is a good match. My father is very pleased." He reached for my curls again, and I swerved backward to avoid him.

"You and I could still—see each other. I do so miss you, Harriet."

Trembling, I put my hands to my face. He peeled my hands from my eyes and wiped the tears with his handkerchief. Gently he kissed my cheeks. After some moments, I summoned the energy to stand.

"You came all the way to London to tell me this? I'm sorry. I could not bear to see you again. You have said enough."

London: 1820–1827

*I*T IS IMPORTANT to remember that the business of the theater is precisely that, a business; and that Mr. Elliston has as much need to eat (and to feed his nine children) as the rest of us. In all my years at Drury Lane, Mr. Elliston made a number of grand attempts to appeal to a great audience and save that theater from extinction. I had frequent cause to wonder whether I had a future there. At times I hoped not. I recall my fury on the debut of Miss Mary Ann Wilson in January 1820. Miss Wilson's premier performance, only two years after my own, was announced on top of the playbills in red ink; the *Times* and the public lauded her simply because she could *sing*. For that was all she could do. The young woman was incapable of acting. Her beauty and tolerable voice drew large crowds, and within a few days Drury Lane had become an opera house three nights of the week. At this time I began to enquire after other theaters, knowing there would be no work for me if Drury Lane were to stage only opera. Aside from my inability to participate, I have always disliked opera for its falseness. It demands too much of an audience. Spectators are expected to suspend belief to such an extent that characters singing as a means of communication seem quite ordinary. It was therefore with some satisfaction that I noted the public seemed to tire of so much opera, and before long Drury Lane was primarily a theater for other entertainment once more. Miss Mary Ann Wilson disappeared after a very short season, and I never heard of her again.

In the summer I was not the only one who groaned on learning we were to stage an imitation of the coronation of King George IV. Elliston had drawings made of all the costumes, accoutrements, and paraphernalia. I cannot recall my own role in the spectacle, only that I wore a grand costume paid out of Elliston's own purse. It was an extremely tiresome performance, requiring no lines but merely gesture, color, and noise. I believe Mr. Elliston enjoyed it because he had the role of King George and carried it off with such aplomb that the king himself came to see him and applauded the performance with great enthusiasm. Real horses were brought in to draw his carriage, and I believe they would have tried cannon fire had it not been sure to burn the house down. The coronation ran for ninety-one nights.

In 1822 Mr. Elliston made alterations to the theater. I had been somewhat alarmed on learning he would be increasing the number of private boxes, for I recalled hearing of the Old Price Riots of 1809 when a similar undertaking had occurred at Covent Garden under John Kemble. The alterations would include increased room backstage, which was a great relief to us, although Mr. Elliston's primary motivation was not the comfort of his actors but increased room for staging spectacles. The renovations were a great success and led to the *Times* describing our theater as "the most furnished theatre in Europe."

Once he had the theater of his dreams, Mr. Elliston set about obtaining the most popular actors in London. There was much discontent at Covent Garden on account of Charles Kemble refusing to augment his actors' salaries. I believe Charles Kemble behaved honorably and thought that the name of Covent Garden would be enough to draw the best-known performers. He was already trying to create historically accurate costumes and properties for Shakespeare's plays. His work seemed new and interesting. Had he invited me to perform at that time, I would have left Drury Lane at an instant for barely any salary at all. However, his actors were soon wooed by Mr. Elliston promising them large sums. Mr. Elliston did not always think of the consequences of his actions and could be underhanded in his dealings. A fairer man would have increased the salaries of his current troupe before enticing others. But Mr. Elliston wanted the drawing power of the very best actors in the country. And so that season I had the pleasure of working once more with the precise tragedian Mr. Young and the soprano Kitty Stephens, and of becoming reacquainted with the comedian Mr. Liston. Although I did not much perform with these people, I learned a great deal from watching them rehearse. I took to attending rehearsal even when I was not required, just to observe the comic gesture of Liston or hear the sweetness of Kitty's voice. But the arrival of these stars at my theater made me worry for my own future opportunities.

Mr. Elliston was quick to take advantage of the refurbished theater in his staging of *The Chinese Sorcerer; Or, The Emperor and His Three Sons*. The scene painters worked long days and nights for an enormous series of scene paintings featuring the "Illuminated Marine Pavilion of the Princess and her Ladies by Moonlight," the "Rude and Terrific Passage to the Enchanted Valley of Lo-lo with a Peep at the Tremendous Necromantic Tower of Hi-hi," and finally, the "Magnificent Hall of Tien, Superbly Decorated for the Feast of Lanterns." I was far from delighted to learn that I would be playing the role of O-Me, niece of the emperor and princess of China. I do believe Fanny Kelly smirked upon hearing my name. For her presence was reserved for tragedy number one that evening. And so I was draped in a costume made from dyed silk sheets donated by an anonymous benefactor, my face painted white and my eyes outlined in black. In this ghoulish costume I appeared before the public for three months.

At the end of this time I had earned my benefit concert, and so, with a sigh of relief, I decided on a fine tragedy, *Adelgitha*. By this time I had come to know many of the London players of note, and although my own success was modest, I was respected and liked by my colleagues. I was honored with the presence of Mr. Kean and Mr. Young, those actors with such contrasting styles whose names attracted a large following. Mr. Kean was often seized by the moment in life and on the stage; his characters were never the same twice, while Mr. Young's characters plodded with great predictability. I was pleased that Madame Vestris and Fanny Kelly would not be playing that evening. Among my other friends was Miss Kitty Stephens singing "If a Body Meet a Body Comin' through the Rye" in fine voice. Kitty had been trained as a soprano since girlhood and considered herself a singer; she only ever took singing parts and did not try her hand at acting. Even though it was summer and London was quiet, the house was three-quarters full and I earned one hundred pounds, half of which I gave to my mother.

During the summer I learned that Charles Kemble was refurbishing Covent Garden. Kemble and Elliston were like two schoolboys competing in a soccer match, each trying always to better the other. Theater has always been a very bad business, and during those years it was not a question of profit but rather of somewhat reducing the size of the debt. Elliston in particular chose entertainments he hoped would draw crowds. In most cases he was right, though there were moments, such as the staging of Lord Byron's first play, which lasted only one night and caused him sincere regret. Charles Kemble usually kept his eye on a higher prize; he prided himself on his classical style of acting, for he was a well-read and intelligent man. All the Kemble family moved in respectable circles and upheld high moral standards. As my opportunities at Drury Lane continued to diminish, I allowed myself to take an interest in the rival theater. I attended plays there whenever possible. After some time I became known to the management and the troupe. By the time Charles Kemble made me an unusual offer in 1827, I was ready to follow him to Paris.

Mme Harriet Berlioz
Rue de Londres
Paris, October 1841

My dear Louis,

It was only years later that your father guessed what had passed between Camille and her mother the afternoon he learned he had won the Prix de Rome. He realized that Camille's weakness and anxiety had not been entirely the result of her desire for Hector's success. He discovered her that evening, languishing on her mother's sofa in a state equal to a dying Juliet. And if Hector arrived at the Mokes' that evening expecting their immediate consent to his marriage to their daughter, he was disappointed. One success was not enough. Hector needed to achieve prominent concert successes in Paris. I wonder that Hector did not see this ploy for what it was. The prize required him to spend three years in Rome, and if he could not be in Paris, how could he possibly achieve prominent success there? And if he renounced the prize, he would not have the income which was the first requirement for him to be permitted to marry Camille.

Sometimes I wonder what would have happened if Hector had married Camille that summer. Would he have taken her with him to Rome? Or would he, instead, have remained in Paris and pursued some other living to support the woman so accustomed to material comforts? Would Hector have forgotten my existence? When Hector first related this story to me, he cursed the dishonesty of Madame Moke. And I can see that she should have admitted that she was never going to consent to the marriage. But I can also see that she would have feared telling him this. For Hector's rage has always been something to be feared. And he is a rash man who could easily have made off with their daughter in the dark of night. Madame Moke probably thought distance would cool his romantic fervor.

Hector wrote proudly to his parents, telling them of his achievement in winning the prize. Instead of sending him praises, his mother reproached him for failing to visit them and their Parisian friends and for becoming involved in politics. His father did not write for some time. And so the winning of the Prix de Rome did not immediately alter Hector's life as he hoped it would. The judges at the institute complied unknowingly with Madame Moke's secret plan and forbade Hector from accepting the prize and remaining in Paris.

Hector set about organizing concerts of his music before he left. The first performance of his music composed for The Tempest was flooded out by the most violent storm to strike Paris in fifty years. On this night your father sensed his music would one day shake the world like thunder.

Hector has always said that the first performance of the Symphonie Fantastique was for me. It was his last attempt to attract my attention before he left France. But I believe it was for Camille, so that she would finally hear some of her lover's music. And for her mother, in case a successful performance would encourage her to give her consent to their union. I believe Hector would have traveled to Italy more gladly had Camille been permitted to travel with him. Although the music itself was happily received by the public and many critics, it failed on all other counts and Hector was forced to say farewell to Camille for the last time.

A new world opened up to your father during the voyage to Italy.

He befriended young Italian revolutionaries and experienced near death during a violent storm. His love of travel was born. For some months, Hector became an adventurer. He attracted the attention of Italian authorities wherever he went, exploring ruins and hills. All the time he waited to hear from Camille. In Florence he visited Il Duomo cathedral where a beautiful young woman was laid out for burial, having died in childbirth. Hector clutched her hand and wept.

When he could bear the solitude no longer, Hector resolved to forfeit his prize—his five years of income to compose—to leave Italy and return to Camille. It was on his return journey that he received the letter from Madame Moke. It seems she had been waiting until he left Paris to match her daughter with the wealthy Monsieur Pleyel. Your father has never repeated to me the derogatory remarks contained in the letter, but he says that Madame Moke had the forethought to ask him not to take his own life. I wonder whether it was this reference to death that inspired your father with his plan. In his state of extreme fury, your father devised to arrive at the Moke household in disguise and kill the entire family before shooting himself.

Hector had himself measured for a lady's maid's outfit and packed his bags with vials of strychnine and two loaded pistols. With a strange clarity of mind, he scribbled a note on the revised ball scene from my symphony and left it with his other belongings in a trunk to be sent to La Côte St-André.

In Genoa he realized with great disappointment that he had left his disguise in a previous coach and resolved to have another made. He was staring into the sea from a low-lying cliff that afternoon, weak and exhausted, when dizziness overcame him and swept him into the sea. It was not the first time he had resigned himself to death by drowning, and he was lucky he did not hit rocks as he fell. A passing fishermen dragged him from the sea with a boat hook. Fear and salt water had made him ill, and he lay in the sun until his clothes were dried and stiff with salt.

For four weeks Hector reworked movements from my symphony and composed its sequel, "The Return to Life," in which music proved a purer mistress. He breathed sea air and sunshine until his fever for Camille passed.

Harriet

London: 1826

 ot long after the visit from Charles Castle Coote,
Joseph moved away from us. He was secretive about his where-
abouts but continued to come for Sunday dinner.

In the evenings my mother sometimes stayed up late washing
the clothes in near darkness. Occasionally I returned in the evening
to the sound of sloshing and dripping. When there was no work
to be done, Mother retired for the evening at the earliest opportunity after dark. I have always been drawn to the still of darkness,
where I can capture time and hold it greedily to myself. And so
with those parts of my wages that remained mine, I would save for
months to buy the cheapest candles I could find. There were some
alleyways I occasionally slipped to in secret, in a break from
rehearsal, always in daylight, and a Chinaman with a toothless
grin would sell those shapeless waxy lumps with enough wick to
read a book by.

And at night when the house was still, after a performance or
earlier if I had not been required to work, I would sit by the fireplace with its glowing embers, and a single candle lighting my
pages, not worrying that it would hurt my eyes. And there I would
become Lady Anne, Portia, Cordelia, whoever took my fancy.

On one such evening I heard a faint scuttling and drew my
knees up to my chest, thinking some animal might have come to
warm itself by the fire. Then I heard my name, whispered from
behind the door.

"Harriet!"

"Who is it?" I whispered back, clutching my book to myself like a shield.

"It's Joseph!"

I fumbled with the heavy key in the lock and stepped aside for him to enter. Once in the room, he swung me up in the air.

"My fair sister!"

"Joseph!" I laughed. "Where have you been?"

There was a saltiness about his skin and the smell of smoke in his hair.

"About London," he said.

"Sit down."

"Are Mother and Anne. . . ."

"Asleep. There is a little hot water left. Will you have tea?"

"Not tea," he said, pulling a small flask from his pocket. "Will you have some of this?"

"What is it?"

"Try."

The liquid burned my throat and brought tears to my eyes. But it sent heat through me like fire.

We sat, staring into the glow of the fire. Then he leaned to one side and pulled something out of his pocket. He began shuffling cards. "Do you know how to play Black Magic?" he asked.

"Black Magic? But isn't that—"

"It's a game, Harriet. That's all."

And so he showed me, in the dimness, and we played until it was too dark to read the cards.

"Joseph, you know we will soon be leaving for Paris?"

"Mother sent word."

"Will you come with us?"

He shook his head. "I have friends here now. And work."

"Where are you living?"

"I have a room. They know how to find me at the Coburg."

I said nothing, for I could not blame Joseph for taking work at London's illegitimate theaters. But he had made a choice that could not easily be undone.

Mme Harriet Berlioz
Rue de Londres
Paris, December 1841

My dear Louis,
My mother gave me some papers before she left France. I still have
in my possession an article from the Clare Journal and Ennis Advertiser. *February 1808. Its edges have been hurriedly cut. The paper is*
brown and spotted. I try to imagine my mother snipping quickly, hush-
ing children, a sense of heaviness in her heart. The weight of decision
bearing upon her shoulders.

THE REV. DEAN BARRETT

About six o'clock, on Tuesday morning last, departed
this life, at his house, in Chapel-Lane, after an illness
of only a few days, the Rev. Doctor JAMES BAR-
RETT, Titular Dean of Killaloe.

The task of portraying in language of appropri-
ate energy, the truly Christian career of this exem-
plary man, must devolve on abler pens than ours:
claiming only to ourselves the right of paying a last
tribute of esteem to departed excellence—to vener-
ated worth and piety the most adorned.

The unwearied vigilance of this reverend pas-
tor, to the duties of a sacred and arduous function,
has only been equalled by the "spirit and the truth"

with which he performed them; during a period of 46 years, he combined in every sense, the earnest Christian with the man of feeling and philanthropy; to the poor of this populous town, he has ever been a sedulous benefactor—a benefactor whose finances never kept pace with the munificence of a soul illumined by the sacred fire of real charity: In truth, he loved his neighbour as himself—sought the cheerless abode of wretchedness and want—of sickness and despair. Sorrow fled from his benignant smile, and the before hapless wretch felt the influence of his ministering hand. Heaven has blessed his deeds, and registered the reward in another and a better world.

Your loving mother,
Harriet

Ennis: 1808

W HEN HARRIET STOOD in Father Barrett's dark room with her family, the old man lying death white with closed eyes was no longer someone she knew. Her mother sniffed and heaved her shoulders. Her father looked grimly and respectfully downward. Bridie twitched sadly from the doorway, not wanting to tell them it was time to leave. They had had their turn. Harriet thought she heard her mother whisper "Thank you" before someone took her hands and led her away.

There was whispering in the stairwell, and a line of people snaked down the stairs and all the way out into Chapel Lane. People began to arrive in the early hours of the morning, and Bridie sent them away at dark. Every day there would be a shout of "Doctor" and people would move respectfully aside while Dr. O'Brien wound his way carefully up the rickety stairs to the sickroom. Everyone who had ever seen Father Barrett administer the last rites to a family member came to pay their respects. People came by coach from Limerick. It was as though they wanted to give something back, Harriet thought. Only Father Barrett was probably too tired to notice.

Harriet wanted to stay in the house. She wanted to greet all those people who had come to visit. She wanted the women to pat her head and stroke her chin. She wanted the men to sing her songs. She wanted to run up and down the staircase in her boots with her hair flowing behind her as though nothing were wrong.

She was the one who lived with Father Barrett. She was the one who knew about his dirty dishes splattered with gravy and cough, the noises he made. She was the one who saw him sometimes in the mornings, silver stubble on his chin and tufts of hair on end. Harriet's mother took her arm and led her away.

She had only been allowed to pack her clothes and some of her books. Harriet's bedroom at Father Barrett's house still looked as though she might come back. In the small room where her parents lodged, she sat sullenly reading the *Tales from Shakespeare* that Father Barrett had so often read to her. Little Joseph tugged shyly at her hand. "Please, Harriet. Play with me?" and Harriet shrugged him off. In her mother's arms, Anne wept. The air smelled like rotting wool.

A gloom descended on the town on the day of Father Barrett's funeral. If Father Barrett wasn't dead, it could have been Easter the way all the shops were closed and everyone gathered on the streets. It was an icy but fine winter's day. Harriet trailed behind her father as they joined the crowd in Chapel Lane. And there was Father Barrett, inside his wooden box in a carriage drawn by six horses. The streets were slippery, and the sound of sobbing was heavy in her ears. Where had all these people been when he was alive? Harriet wondered. Why had they waited until he was dying to come? And who would say the eulogy now that Father Barrett could no longer speak?

The procession was made up of just about everyone Harriet had ever seen. There were Protestant and Catholic church elders in robes, scarves, and bands, the landowners and merchants, as well as many of the poor people from the district. Harriet waved to the children from the charity school and wondered how she would ever find Molly. It didn't matter whether she found Molly or not, she thought. On a day like this, her parents would never let her go and play.

It was a long walk to Drumcliffe. They went through Market Street, Jail Street, and Church Street, over the Lifford-Lysaght bridge. Harriet started to feel lighter as they moved through pastoral land. She stared at the cows, and some of them stared back. If she could just forget for a moment the fleshy hand so unlike Father Barrett's bony fingers gripping her wrist, she could imagine she was with him on their way to visit Molly and Mrs. Baird. Soon she would be able to take her shoes off and run in the fields. Harriet tripped on a stone and began to cry.

Her feet were tight inside her boots. As they neared the cemetery, her father let go of her hand. She ran from him, in through the metal gate. The grass smelled damp, and Harriet watched her feet leave footprints. The cemetery was crowded, and Harriet doubted she would be able to see what happened, let alone hear the eulogy.

A shy-looking man wearing a large hat and draped in a brown coat stood near the entrance to the cemetery, pointing upward with his spade. A man with a small notebook was asking him questions. Inside the cemetery were three black-and-white dairy cows with fat udders. They munched the wet grass thoughtfully. Harriet could hear the moaning of other cows in the distance.

The thing was to climb the hill. Father Barrett would have wanted to be buried up high, close to God and with a great view of the surrounding valley. He was going to be underneath an oak tree, near a fence backing onto some of the greatest dairy country in all of Ireland. And from there you could see Lake Ballyalla in the distance. Even with all the people clambering up the hill, she could still see robins, thrushes, and blackbirds flitting among the shrubs.

Harriet wished she could be here by herself. Father Barrett had not taken her to many funerals, but he had told her once that they were a time of "reflection." This helped her understand why he was being buried so close to the lake. And she knew that the service was not in Father Barrett's chapel because it was too small and the Protestants would not have been allowed in. She wondered if she would ever come back. One day, when she could make her own decisions.

"Harriet!" She stared behind her at all the grown-ups panting as they climbed the hill. Suddenly, Molly burst through and came running toward her. Harriet grinned to herself. She had hoped that somehow Molly would find her. Friends always had that sense of where you were. She and Molly had practiced sending secret messages to one another at a certain time each afternoon. It was like understanding Father Barrett when he spoke French.

"Let's visit the old chapel!"

Harriet looked around for someone to ask permission from. All around her was a mass of Irish faces. Some plump, others oval. All pale, with doughy skin and bright eyes. Wisps of black hair twitched in the wind like kites. Many people were blowing their noses on worn, stained handkerchiefs. Most were muttering to each other over the shame of it all. They were familiar faces, but they held no expectation. Harriet knew that she did not belong to them.

"All right."

Harriet had not noticed that a little farther up the hill was a small graystone chapel. Some stones were missing, and the roof was falling away in tufts. Around the side was a heavy wooden door with a hole just big enough for a small child to climb through. She scampered after Molly, and they slipped through the hole before anyone could notice.

Inside the chapel, Harriet could feel God. He shone in warm

shafts of light onto the stone floor. He touched the walls so that you could see their rough texture. He kept her warm and safe.

"This can be our secret place," Molly said. Harriet smiled. She thought she remembered Father Barrett telling her about the old church at Drumcliffe. It used to be the local church long before he built his own chapel. It was hundreds of years old but had now been left to ruin.

There was no trace of any of those people who had been here before them. The church was but a warm shell, and it did not tell stories. You would have to sit quietly and wait for stories to come to you. Among all the people and noise, the church was quiet apart from the twittering of a bird somewhere in the remaining roof and a scuttling in one of the dark corners.

Harriet wondered if there would come a time when no one would know where Father Barrett was buried. A thought came to her that some day a girl might come looking for traces of him, for traces of her own story. She saw someone standing in a long coat, staring toward one of the windows overlooking the lake beyond. And then the thought evaporated into the dark stillness.

"Molly?"

Molly stood in front of Harriet, her long hair coating her shoulders. "What?"

"Remember me? Remember me always?"

"Why? Are you going away?"

"I don't know." Harriet stood staring into Molly's face, sadness dripping from a cold place inside her. "I don't know what will happen next."

"Will you live with your ma and pa?"

Harriet tried to imagine her future. She saw herself in a cramped, damp room with her tired mother and her screaming sister. She saw her little brother tugging on her hand and want-ing her to play. In Harriet's mind there was nowhere to play. She could not see beyond the room. She could not see any books apart from her copy of *Tales from Shakespeare* from Father Bar-rett. She would have to read it over and over again for the rest of her life. She would know it by heart. She would be able to recite it in her father's theater. The word *theater* was sweet in her mouth, and when she spoke it Harriet saw lights and heard laughter. There was more world than she had ever even imag-ined in the theater.

"I will never forget you, Harriet. Can't you stay here? Mother wouldn't mind. You could come and live with us," Molly said solemnly.

"Can you ask?" This was a solution Harriet had not thought of. Endless days of playing on the Bairds' farm and eating Mrs. Baird's stew stretched before her like a summer's day. She and Molly would be sisters.

They pulled two flat stones over to one that was shaped a little like a table.

"Some Irish stew?" Molly broadened her accent to make it more like her mother's. "Don't be shy now," she screwed up her eyes as she tried to wink. Harriet watched Molly dip her fist as though reaching into a pot with a long ladle. She saw Molly's fist tip slightly, her eyes watching the invisible liquid dripping into a bowl. "Here you go then."

As they ate their stew, the girls talked quickly, fitting the rest of their childhoods into their last half hour together. In their minds, they climbed the apple tree, played in the cellar, ran down the hill to the house, watched Jacob milk the cows, and flew, all the way to Paris.

SHE STOOD NEAR the door of her family's lodgings, surrounded by torn cases and battered trunks. She could be a statue.
Harriet thought that if she stood still enough, perhaps her family
would forget to take her with them. Her mother was pulling stockings on Anne's bony limbs. Joseph was tracing a finger trail
through the dust on the windowsill. Her father was preparing to
pack the carriage. Someone knocked at the door. Harriet opened
the door a crack and saw Mrs. Baird, a twin on each hip. She pulled
the door wide open. Molly stood next to her holding Mikey's
hand. She had combed her hair until it shone, and Mrs. Baird had
taken her apron off. Suddenly, Harriet's father stood behind her.

"Joan Baird, a friend of Father Barrett's."

"Pleased to meet you." Harriet's father sounded quite English,
and he looked puzzled as he moved aside to allow them to enter.
Harriet's mother looked up from Anne and pushed a strand of
hair behind her ear.

"My daughter Molly here is a great friend of Harriet's."

Harriet's father nodded.

"The thing is, we were wondering. Well, if it would help
you—Harriet could come and live with us."

Harriet's mother sniffed loudly. She stared at the woman and
noticed that her dress was frayed along the hem. One of the twins
began to cry, and the woman started rocking up and down on her
feet.

"Mrs. Baird. Please sit down." The chair had uneven legs and
rocked slightly as she sat, pulling the twins on her lap. Harriet's
father did not sit down.

"You're very kind. It's just that—Father Barrett made

arrangements. His wish was—" he puffed out his chest like a fat bird. "He wanted Harriet to be ed-u-cated." He said the word slowly, savoring it like pudding. "She will be going to school in Waterford."

Harriet stared at Molly who stood behind her mother, perfectly still. She traced a line around Molly's figure with her eyes. Molly twitched and held her fingers to her lips. She began to blow slowly and opened out her hands, moving them wider and wider apart. Harriet knew that she was blowing a bubble. These invisible bubbles could travel great distances with secret messages inside. Molly mouthed "good-bye" and pushed the bubble gently toward Harriet. Harriet watched the space in the dingy room where she thought the bubble was. She held out her hands to catch it. She hardly noticed as Molly ran out the door, slamming it shut behind her. Harriet caught the bubble and followed Molly to the door. The last time Harriet saw Molly, Molly was running down Simms Lane, her dark hair streaming behind her. Harriet looked to her hands, which still cupped the large bubble. She felt as though Molly had handed her the world.

Part four

HARMONY

At length, after having refused the hands of several Dukes, Princes and an innumerable number of commoners, after having caused a dozen suicides and about twice as many duels; after having drawn tears from the Dutchmen's eyes, fast as the medicinal gum flows from the Arabian trees . . . Miss Smithson has appeared.

—*DRAMATIC MAGAZINE*, 11 MAY 1829

The impression made on my heart and mind by her extraordinary talent, nay her dramatic genius, was equalled only by the havoc wrought in me by the poet she so nobly interpreted.

—HECTOR BERLIOZ, ON FIRST SEEING HARRIET SMITHSON IN 1827

The tide of mutual passion in their breasts is seen mingling and flowing on, making sweet music as it flows to immortal raptures. . . .

—OXBERRY'S PREFATORY REMARKS TO *ROMEO AND JULIET: A TRAGEDY* BY DAVID GARRICK

Mme Harriet Berlioz
Rue de Londres
Paris, 24 November 1842

My dear Louis,

These last days have been among my worst. For months Hector and I have been arguing over whether or not he should travel. I begged him to stay with me for I am not well enough to journey and the thought of him going to London was more than I could bear. How different my life should have been had I been lauded there as I was in Paris.

Then I woke to find him gone. By the time I dressed there was nothing but the solemn face of Joséphine and a hastily scrawled note to tell me he had left. I have little memory of the intervening days. I believe I took to my bed in hysteria and a clear liquid was administered to me. A death-like sleep deprived me of my affliction.

Every morning Joséphine brings my papers to me in a box with a cup of tea. Today I begin to write once more. I thank heaven I still have Joséphine. She sends her love to you. This morning I awoke more determined than ever that you should have my story.

I do not know how this will end, or indeed, how we came to this.

Your loving mother,
Harriet

In the Beginning

I MIGHT HAVE BEEN CONCEIVED at Kilkenny. My mother turned pink when I was bold enough to ask and said she does not remember such things. She asked where I had learned to ask such questions. I reminded her that she had sent me to work in the theater and that no amount of protection from licentiousness during the first fourteen years of my life could make up for that. In fact, it was my father who relayed to me every detail he could recall, late in his life during some of his less sober moments. In the absence of knowing his love, stories were all I could cling to. And when my father told me that I had always been his favorite child, the words had an air of emptiness about them. I was the one most like him. I was also the one he had left.

I have chosen to believe that I was conceived at Kilkenny, after a very successful performance of *A Cure for the Heart Ache: "An Excellent Lesson to Mankind."* My father had combined "Drama as may be found Moral and Instructive" with his love of comedy, the thought of which would light up his eyes. He would clutch his stomach absently at the memory of a good belly laugh. But my mother, during these early months of marriage, had instructed him on the purposes of drama. She always believed that people learned most quickly from watching other people's mistakes, even if they were merely a facade. Keeping in mind the instructional purposes of drama, my mother convinced my father, for the first time, that children should be admitted to the theater at half price.

The season had begun with the musical play *Every One Has His Fault*. And following this production, my father had moved on to matters more romantic. *A Cure for the Heart Ache* had filled all the players with a sense of frivolity, Father said. Even the apple sellers and the charwomen were buoyant. So they had all celebrated with an evening at The Rose and Crown. Father told me that there was an air of something new in the mild darkness that night.

I imagine my mother, warm and happy after a little whiskey, not long married and still a little shy, losing her timidity with him that evening.

Paris: 1827

M Y MOTHER DID NOT UNDERSTAND why I wanted to leave England. As a young actress herself, she had longed for England. She used to close her eyes and whisper "Drury Lane" as though it were Buckingham Palace. But the English are a riotous crowd. I remember one night when they could no longer contain their fury at some unknown offense. They pelted us with brass buttons and the remains from their dinners. An egg smashed on a pillar and dripped pungent brown ooze in my hair. I stood at the back of the stage, frozen, as orange peel flew in all directions and Elliston screamed his lines to a deaf crowd.

After that night I had felt directionless. London had always been my destination, and I had served my apprenticeship there. In London I was more beautiful than ever before. In the mirror I saw that I had blossomed. I was Letitia Hardy, Mary the Maid of the Inn. I knew that I was learning the art of being someone other than myself. In fact, being someone else was easier than being Harriet Smithson. A critic from the *Times* wrote that I have "a face and features well adapted to [my] profession; but it is not likely [I] will make a great impression on London audiences or figure among stars of the first magnitude." Their praise of my performance in the country rustic was intended to send me scurrying back to the provinces.

The French taste for curiosities was whetted by the arrival of the giraffe in May. In London we read that French streets buzzed with talk of the exotic animal, that thirty thousand people appeared from all over the country to witness the creature. Women wore their hair made tall by carefully planted sticks, à la giraffe. Men wore tall hats and neckties featuring brown and gold diamonds.

WE TRAVEL TO PARIS. I have allowed us the luxury of a cabin to mark this beginning. We are locked away from the French, who my mother says are not to be trusted. She falls asleep with an arm around my hunched sister.

In the morning I feel as though I have not slept. The sky has a smoky hue and the boards slosh with muddy water. This is not the Paris I have yearned to see. This is the first time I have been surrounded by so many foreign sounds. We queue with unshaven Frenchmen. They seem to jostle my mother deliberately, pushing her and elbowing her ribs with their thick bones. My mother grips Anne's arm a little harder; Anne winces and Mother's knuckles turn red. The men look at me. They stare at my eyes, and I look away. In their minds I know they trace my shape. They admire the paleness of my skin and the roundness of my hips; my ample figure. *I am not here to be stared at*, I want to shout. But I worry that this is not true.

Something changes the day I arrive in Paris. As soon as our carriage reaches the center of town, I know this is the city of my dreams. The magnificence of Notre Dame and the extravagance of the Opéra; the life of the Seine swelling and flowing.

Paris is a city of warmth and brilliance. There is music all around. If I could write music, I would note the cadences of the language. It is more beautiful than anything I have heard before. And yet during the night the words of Moore's Irish Melodies come to me as naturally as air. They sing me to sleep. They carry me home.

This city opens my ears. Everything happens in waves of sound. Even voices, as I walk down the street listening to their strange music, crescendo and decrescendo as evenly as they would under the hands of a conductor. I know there is only a day for me to meet this city before it must become my place of work. Paris: the center of the world. The streets are bitter with the odor of coffee and the cut grass smell of horses. The sky is ornamented with majestic statues. Above them still is an immense sky; more vast than the sky in Ireland. More vast even than London. There is room here for me to soar. It is 1827, and I am excited at the prospect of France.

Paris: December 1832

ᴍY ᴍᴏᴛʜᴇʀ ʀᴏᴜsᴇs ᴍᴇ from vivid dreams to give me bread and cheese.

"Harriet, you cannot sit around like this feeling sorry for yourself. And you cannot possibly know the nature of this situation without looking over the figures." She sets out one of my better dresses for today. It is, in fact, my evening gown of soft blue silk, and I am surprised at her choice for I have not left the house for a week. I sit at the kitchen table, and my mother unplaits my hair. She combs it gently at first. Then she takes a brush to it, and when she catches a hair or discovers a knot I grit my teeth as though this is punishment for my foolishness. I remember her words when I told her of my plans to open my own theater in Paris. "You're a woman. You have not been groomed for such things. Lord, what is to become of us?"

My mother takes such care over my appearance that it is as though she expects a visitor. It is as though she knows this is to be an important day in the story of my life. My mother has received her orders from Providence, and she has obeyed.

In stockinged feet I go to a box of papers, and my mother sighs. "Harriet, it's Sunday. Must you do that now?"

I do not answer but carry the box to the kitchen table and grab the contents as though they are autumn leaves to be scooped up in my bare hands. And I pretend not to notice my mother pulling my boots upon my feet while I order the papers. I put them in date order, oldest to newest. Then I begin calculating sums, my legs out to the side to enable my mother to pull the bootlaces tight. Somewhere behind me Anne giggles, and I am pleased to have provided a diversion for her in my reluctance to live this day.

We are taking tea after eleven when there is a knock at the door. I look at my mother who is rising expectantly.

"Monsieur Schutter," the maid says and curtsies quickly. The young man is English, and I am obliged to be polite to him because he writes for an English language newspaper in Paris. My mother has encouraged him because she likes him, she understands what he says, and she believes he has a more personal interest in me. She has already explained to me that she would prefer me to marry a man of greater wealth, though in truth she would very much like to see me married to anyone at all. For she believes a man would take care of us and relieve our troubles.

"Mrs. Smithson, Miss Smithson, and Miss Smithson." Mr. Schutter bows and smiles in that congenial manner he has.

"So kind of you to call," my mother says, and now I am quite sure she has invited him. "Please sit down. Will you have tea?"

"I thank you, yes. This needs to be a quick visit, however. I am hoping, Miss Smithson, that you will accompany me to a concert this afternoon."

"I thank you, sir. However, I have certain matters I must resolve this afternoon."

"Harriet, it is Sunday. Those matters can wait."

"You should go, Harriet." And it is my astonishment at my sister's response that convinces me.

And so it happens that I am sharing a carriage with Mr. Schutter and also with Tom Wilkins, an actor from my troupe. It is a cool winter Sunday, but the sun is shining and I own it is pleasant to watch those carefree Parisians taking turns through gardens and making sure they are seen in all the fashionable places. I smile to myself at the prevalence of black veils, the ladies with straw in their hair. This new fashion is called *coiffure à la Miss Smithson, à la folle*. I have made madness à la mode. I am not disposed to speak during the journey, and I stare silently out the window while the two men converse, slightly suspiciously it seems to me. And then I hear Tom Wilkins ask, "And what is the concert we are about to see?"

"Oh, it promises to be an important musical event. Mr. Hector Berlioz is presenting his entire symphony for the first time."

I turn to stare at them in disbelief, and Mr. Schutter thinks I have become remarkably interested in our afternoon's entertainment.

"Here is the program, Miss Smithson."

At the top of the page are the words *Grand Concert Dramatique* followed by the name of the composer. I read the words *Rêveries—Passions*. I hand the page back.

And as we near the Conservatoire I realize that we are all artists and our lives cannot help but entwine. Some force stronger than my own will is pushing me toward the man of my future, and I know not who this man will be.

The Conservatoire is a dull gray building on a narrow street. Mr. Schutter helps me down from the carriage, and I am pleased with the presence of his arm to lean on, for something strange is happening to me and I am beginning to feel quite feverish. In spite of the cold, my body is growing hot and my heart is beating fast as though I myself am about to commence a performance. We step into the Grande Salle du Conservatoire, and an usher points to the stairs that will lead to our box for the afternoon. And I wonder if I am imagining all those young men, turning to stare at me.

Although this is the largest theater in the building, it appears intimate compared with the Théâtre de l'Odéon. It is like many provincial stages I have played upon. The intricate paint and plasterwork complete the image of an elegant ballroom, and I try to study my surroundings without looking down at the spectators. For I am now sure that I am not imagining the hum of chatter and the heads turning in my direction. Mr. Schutter squirms uneasily in his seat, and Tom tries to joke. Then I look to the orchestra and I see Hector Berlioz himself, finely groomed, his mane of red hair flowing. He sits in the pit clutching two large sponge-headed drumsticks behind the kettledrum, pale and wide-eyed. He is staring at me as though he cannot believe his eyes.

My cheeks flush and I feel strangely humiliated for this is not Ophelia or Juliet but rather Harriet Smithson they are all watching and there is no opportunity for me to slip backstage. Just when I can bear it no longer, Monsieur Habeneck lifts his bow and the music begins.

Lyrical violins begin the opening melody which soothes my nerves. And though most of the spectators have turned their attention to the orchestra, I notice occasional glances in my direction as though the entire roomful of spectators longs to see my response. I fix a smile upon my face and focus on the orchestra. When the attention of most in the room is taken by the music, I chance to look around and see many faces I have only seen in the print shop windows. There is a band of long-dark-haired musicians dressed in black. I try to lose myself in the music, and even as I do so I come to understand that my presence here has been fated to occur and that it is part of the performance and that for most artists in the room this is the concert of a lifetime where art and life collide, changing one another forever.

Never before have I been so moved by music. It is ever changing; one minute quiet and soothing and the next triumphant and stirring. Sometimes I strain to hear the melody, at other times the crescendos and crashes make me jump in my seat. All the time it has an air of suspense, and a question hangs over the conclusion. For this symphony tells a story. Bit by bit I come to realize this masterpiece is the culmination of a young man's life and dreams. There is a sweetness and innocence about those sounds. The music transports me to another life.

During the interval, we remain in our box and Mr. Schutter translates for me the titles of the movements. And although I could never have articulated it, this program has already worked itself into my heart. The parody of the mass frightens me, and the "Dies Irae" brings blackness and death. I quiver at the thought that I have inspired this music, for whose death does it represent? Is it mine or his, or the death of his love? But I cannot possibly have inspired this music. For we do not know each other.

The second part, Mr. Schutter tells me, is called "The Return to Life," and I am relieved at the title. The famous actor Boccage plays the young romantic composer, and he speaks. I understand few of the words but I feel the passion in them. He shouts, he cries. Mr. Schutter is writing something awkwardly in pencil upon his program. He hands me the page.

Oh! Could I but find her—that Juliet, that Ophelia for whom my heart is calling! Could I but find the intoxication of that joy mixed with sadness that true love brings. . . .

I hear no more words or music. I sit patiently for I have all the time in the world now that I know what to do. I will go where life leads me. In my mind I begin composing a letter.

Dear Monsieur Berlioz,
Congratulations on your fine symphony . . .

Paris: December 1832

THE FIRST TIME WE MET, Hector arrived at the lodgings I shared with my mother and sister.

"You say he is a—composer?" my mother had asked for the third time that afternoon. For she sensed the importance of the occasion, and even Anne, perched on a settee in the corner from which she would have a fine view of the proceedings, was quiet. And then came a frantic thumping at the door. Some moments later he was in the room.

So like a lion he was, with his mane of red hair. As he greeted my mother, she could not prevent herself taking a step back in fright. For that pale skin had a ghostly sheen, and his eyes had a fever within them that made one wonder whether he was entirely himself.

"Bonjour, monsieur!" my sister managed. And he nodded in her direction. My mother retired discreetly to a corner of the room where she took up her sewing. The maid brought tea on a tray and placed it on the small table by the chairs in which we sat. When all was calm within the room, I dared to lift my eyes from his large hands, their fingers twisted together and trembling slightly. I looked to his eyes. He held my gaze, and without any warning tears began to flow down my cheeks.

I know not what he said. Only that suddenly he knelt at my feet, clutching my hands in his left while using his right to wipe the tears from my face with the gentlest touch I had ever known. And soon he was also sobbing, and we leaned our heads together, laughing and crying at the same time.

There were many such visits. Hector was tender and attentive. He would take my hand or kiss my cheek; I let him have no more of me for always my family lurked close by. We began to tell each other our stories. We learned to speak slowly and gently; each of us used our mother tongue mixed with words we knew from the other, and in this manner we had a certain privacy, for my mother, strain as she might, had no French at all and could not hear from the other side of the room.

"J'habitais en Irlande. Avec a priest. A father. Père." I held my hands together as though in prayer.

"Un prêtre?"

I nodded.

"Vraiment?"

At times we would pause our tales to stare at each other. He would stroke my cheek with a finger and whisper, "Ophelie, ma Juliette. Je vous aime." And these words had a solemnity and seriousness about them that stilled my body like Sunday mass.

When Hector was not with us, my mother never failed to make her disapproval known to me.

"He is young and foolish, Harriet, with not a penny to his name. You cannot make a life with this man."

"I understand, Mother," I would say, barely hearing her words, feeling his touch on me still, and seeing those eyes which held my gaze without cease.

"You must discourage him."

"Yes."

"It would be unkind to do otherwise."

"It would."

I realized my French was improving a great deal. As I went about my daily business, entire sentences in French would enter my mind where before there had been only English.

"Aujourd'hui je dois répéter," I would whisper to myself on the way to rehearsal. Each meeting we spoke more easily with fewer pauses for incomprehension. There was a lightness within me, and this new feeling was all comedy. It seemed the tragedy of my life was over.

But do not think for a moment that I was a woman free to ponder my life, my love, and my future. I knew all too well that I was not Juliet, set to make a marriage to assist her family, Desdemona, or Ophelia with a life at court. My heart pondered these questions while my mind continued to work.

After we began our more intimate friendship, there was one occasion on which he attended my performance of *Jane Shore* like a king displaying his queen to the court. He brought with him an enormous number of similarly bedraggled young men, their collars frayed, their hair uncombed, and their jackets missing buttons. Many of them brought their own friends until the whole theater was filled with artists, painters, musicians, and writers. The orchestra pit smelled like garlic sausage, and during those pitiful scenes which most pleased him he shouted "Bravo!" and clapped his hands until it was difficult for me to continue my performance.

Hector told me that our Shakespeare was a revelation. That in France, until the autumn of 1827, Shakespeare was considered barbaric. Our Shakespeare brought with it such freedom that Jeunes-France were surprised it was not banned.

I had never met a man who felt so deeply, and his response to hearing of my childhood separations was so intense that I regretted having told him.

"It was not so bad," I said, smiling, trying to halt his tears. And then I tried to tell him tales of playing in the fields around Ennis, and he smiled vaguely. It must be said that nothing ever had a greater impact on Hector than a tale with an air of tragedy.

1827

$\mathcal{M}$Y FATHER'S WATCH TELLS ME it is almost noon, and I notice daylight filtering through the streaked window of the bedchamber. This has been a strange kind of holiday filled with the heavy realization that I am putting myself through this business yet again. But this time there is a stronger anticipation. A feeling that perhaps this time it will be different.

I awake from my Shakespeare as though I have been in an enchanted sleep. This is the first day in Paris that I do not attend to my daily requirements accompanied by scripts, gesturing one hand vaguely while moving my lips to the words. It is the first time I have noticed the particular light of a French autumn.

My mother knows better than to try and accompany me on a walk so close to opening night. And while I sense she wishes to follow, she smiles and holds back, pretending she is presently occupied. I step into Rue Neuve Saint Marc wearing one of her bonnets and walk away from the center, toward the plains on the way to Montmartre. After only a few minutes my face is damp and I am slightly breathless. After some time the streets widen and give way to fields. There are no longer many people to be seen; from a distance an occasional farmer looks up from his work. When I feel sure I am alone, I furtively open the two top buttons of my gown, which swings heavily around my feet. I long to take off my boots and scamper in the grass like a child or at least to loosen my corset among the shrubs.

As I walk I sense the freedom of having my own time. My mind empties and I forget what occupied it before. I sing softly to the rhythm of my feet: "How should I your true love know. . . ." I could be Ophelia and it could be grief which seeps from me now; my father killed by my lover, orphaned and alone. "Larded with sweet flowers. . . ." And suddenly I walk around a bend in the dirt road and see a field. It is the last field before a forest, and it has been left uncultivated. Late-summer wildflowers have flourished here in burning reds, purples, and pinks. A tiny stone house is several fields away in the distance, and I see no one working the land nearby. I lift my skirts and climb over the foot-high stone wall. Clover is soft beneath my boots, and I skip through flowers. I turn and see a trail of footprints behind me. I laugh and skip some more; these are steps in my own strange dance. When I sit under an oak tree, it is as though I am on luxurious cushions. I wonder if anyone would find me if I lay here. I pick flowers outlining my shape, stripping stems of their leaves and making a bright pile in front of me. In spite of the heat, there is some moisture in the grass. I lie down to soak it in, like a cat in a patch of sunlight.

When I awake, it is to feel something poking my ribs. I open my eyes to see an elderly man staring down at me. I heave myself up, blushing, but he seems relieved that I have opened my eyes.

"Pardon . . . pardon. . . ." I do not know what to say, but he nods and grins and does not seem annoyed that I have chosen to sleep in his field.

He says something I don't understand and points at my flowers; I offer them to him, still too dazed to wonder why he would want them back. He shakes his head. Then he puts his left arm behind his back, leans forward, and begins to pluck more from the ground. Their stems are uneven lengths, and he does not remove the crushed leaves. He hands them to me with his left hand, his right palm tipped supine in a gesture of offering.

I stumble back along the dirt road, molded into my damp corset, my gown dusty at the hem. It is a Sunday dress; my mother will not be pleased. My left hand swings by my side clutching the quickly wilting flowers. After some time, I see a pond over a stone wall. I drop the flowers and bend over the water. It is icy on my fingers; I form a cup with my hands, not worrying about the drops spilling down my face and onto my dress. I lift my wet hands to my face and then my neck. I moisten my handkerchief and wrap it around the flower stems. Then I stand and stretch upward. The sun seems, finally, to be lowering in the sky. Reaching behind my head to tie my hair out of the way, I discover something rough as twine. I try to isolate the twine, but it gets caught and I wince as I pull it free. A piece of straw. I tie the straw around my hair to allow air around my neck.

On my way back to Paris I think about straw and how it is but dead grass. As a child of around eight I remember standing before a woman with long gray hair in Father Barrett's poorhouse. I am holding a small box of straw and handing her strands one by one as she plaits them into her hair. Then she moves to another woman in the room and weaves straw among her curls. They look at themselves and each other in the glass, laughing. The woman with the long hair asks me to stand with my back to her, and I feel fingers through my hair. Someone grips my arm and leads me from the room, out the front door and back to Father Barrett's house.

And so it comes about that I steal straw. Running this time, as I climb over the stone wall, for this barn is close to a house and I cannot bear the thought of being caught and having to explain such inexplicable behavior in a language I cannot speak. I only take a handful, clutching it among the flowers; I will use it sparingly. I peer out the door like some sort of fugitive and walk rather than run as my limbs are near exhaustion and I cannot help feeling speed would arouse more suspicion. Fortunately, it is Sunday afternoon and it appears the family is absent or resting. I tie the straw in a thick knot and continue my journey back to Paris.

Ophelia

I BELONG HERE AMONG the flowers. I know that I belong
here because this is the only place I can be trusted. This is the only
place I can go on my own. No one will see me here. I can remove
my shoes if I wish, or loosen my hair and roll in straw. When I am
out of sight like this, my father and my brother are prevented from
worrying about my honor and whether or not it is lost. Father told
me once long ago that a maiden requires a wedding ring as well as
a place that is warm, dark, and enclosed in which to lose her honor.
Only a heathen would succumb to temptation among flowers.

Beyond this willow tree there are crowflowers, nettles, daisies,
and long purples. The air is sweet with their scents. Follow the
brook with me a little. It is quiet here and we are free. People will
tell you stories about the straw in my hair. They will say that I
have lost my wits. But do not listen to them. You alone shall know
my real story.

I remember my mother. My father said this is impossible since
she died when I was born. He used to laugh and tell me that I was
dreaming again, then he would send me from the court out to the
woods. But I remember her very clearly. I remember our faces
smiling together in the glass in her chamber. She used to say that
this was the only way we could ever see how happy we were
together. I would tug at her curls with chubby fingers. And she
would smile, knowing I could never pull hard enough to hurt.

My mother comes to me in reflections. I see her even now,

waving to me from her chamber window while I walk in the
grounds. Sometimes I see her face in the brook, smiling and fading. At other times she stands behind me in the mirror while
Adora combs my hair.

My mother told me there was always something beyond the
frame. That was why reflections were so important, she said.
Because just sometimes, if you turned quickly enough, you would
glimpse something from the other world as it slipped beyond your
vision. And it could be captured in shiny reflective surfaces. I
should have learned to look beyond the surfaces.

Just before my mother died, she told me she would always be
close by. That I would find her in the brook, in the glass, or on the
other side of a window. Believing her was enough. Once when I
tried to explain this to my brother Laertes, he scoffed and scolded.
He told me not to make up stories. But I remember her words.

She had told me when I was very young that I was bound to
Hamlet by a promise. I no longer remember whose promise, or
when it was first made. But it was my understanding, and it was
lodged somewhere deep within my heart. Until recently I was permitted to spend time alone with Hamlet.

As children we played Peasants in the Field. Adora found us
old work clothes and made us promise to keep them secret.

"You are not to wear them in the house or to allow anyone to
see you," she had whispered. We built our home beneath an oak
tree away from the castle. Its leaves were dense enough to provide
shelter even in the rain. Hamlet tied sticks in my hair and stuffed
my apron with dry leaves. He rolled up his trouser legs.

"You must tend the garden while I kill the animals," he said.
He took a long stick and began running in a large circle around the
tree. He charged imaginary beasts. I was captivated. But already I

knew that I needed to do as I was told. On my hands and knees in the dirt I began raking the leaves with my fingers. In the moist earth I dug holes and planted acorns. Breathless and flushed, Hamlet returned to the tree. Frowning, he inspected my garden and kicked a few stray leaves.

"I am hungry," he announced.

"Sit down, husband," I told him, wondering what peasants ate. He leaned against the tree and closed his eyes. I dug frantically for acorns.

"I have cooked you a hearty meal," I said. He opened his eyes and I handed him three acorns, only slightly muddy. He popped one in his mouth and chewed for a long time. I found myself praying that they were not poisonous. I knew I could never be forgiven for killing a prince.

"A little overcooked but otherwise satisfactory," he said.

As we grew older, Hamlet's moods had the inconstancy of the wind. As I sat on his bed he would brandish his sword at an imaginary enemy. He would leap on the furniture and land with the grace of a cat. And just when I was growing weary of his game, he would turn to me with great tenderness. He would kneel at my feet and take my hand. In my sixteenth year I lay with him and he whispered sweetly while his fingers stroked my skin. His kisses were long and deep, and they carried me beyond the castle. I knew that this meant I would be his.

Hamlet was a performer. I heard stories of him playing the actor's game at university. It was said that he made a splendid villain and a handsome hero. Within him there were a thousand people; far more than I ever glimpsed. He wrote to me once that he was to play a woman and had I a dress he could borrow? I laughed when I read these words, and Adora was surprised when I asked for one of my mother's dresses to be sent to Wittenberg. He wrote back that he had made a splendid woman, that there had been much frivolity and laughter. Even the ladies had thought him convincing, he wrote. And I had wondered which ladies, for I knew there would be none at university.

For years while he was away I waited for him. I wrote letters informing him of the happenings at court. I stitched all manner of articles until every surface in my bedchamber was covered in embroidered motifs. Sometimes I did not hear from him for several months, and at these times I would seek the company of his mother, Queen Gertrude. Hamlet was busy studying at Wittenberg and would surely write when he had a moment to spare. Hamlet rarely did what was expected of him, she said. That was why they had sent him away to be educated. They hoped that by the time he returned he would have learned how he needed to behave as the future king of Denmark.

He was precocious, Queen Gertrude said, smiling. "And you are the only one who would ever bear his moods and whims, my dear Ophelia." She touched my hair. "Don't you remember the scenes he made in court?"

I remembered when he was twelve. He had often taunted me and pulled my hair. One day he had asked me to help him catch mice. I had shuddered at the very word.

"If you don't," he had threatened, "I'll tell your father that you took your clothes off and went swimming in the river!"

He had reached gently underneath his doublet.

"Touch him," he had ordered, holding a fat mouse to my nose. I had expected a foul odor, and my eyes watered.

"Go on."

I had reached out a finger and was surprised to feel that the fur was as soft as a kitten's.

We spent hours catching mice, luring them with cheese and cupping our hands around them. We dropped the animals on top of each other in a crate. Hamlet scattered crumbs in there. By the second day I could not bear to look at the mass of twitching bodies trapped in the wooden box. I would not be his accomplice, and at the hour he was to release the mice in court, I hid in a willow tree. I heard later from my father that the king had been furious at the sight of one hundred mice, a mass of fur, running in a great frenzy across the presence chamber. That several of the courtiers had stood on chairs and squealed. That the king had guessed this was the work of his young son and had beaten him. He had locked Hamlet up for a week to contemplate whether or not he was worthy of becoming king.

As Hamlet grew older, he began to spend more time alone with his father. The king had decided to teach him how to rule. It was during this time that I noticed King Hamlet's brother's attention for Queen Gertrude.

"It is as well I have my health," King Hamlet had joked, "for it will be years before Hamlet is ready to rule."

Hamlet told me he enjoyed the time with his father. Occasionally they went hunting, and Hamlet would bring his horse to a gallop until he was out of sight. Once he returned on foot with a fox on a leash trotting at his heels. Frequently they discussed literature and the art of ruling. The king would explain to Hamlet his decisions and how he had made them. He would instruct Hamlet on the correct codes of dress and behavior. And while Hamlet listened, he lived by the rules he devised himself. He once attended a spring ball dressed as a peacock; Queen Gertrude paled at the sight.

As a young woman, while I waited for him, I dreamed of our own palace and the crown that was Queen Gertrude's and would one day become mine. I imagined our own court. I had visions of the grand balls we would hold there. In my mind I saw him dancing; he performed for me alone. I heard the poetry he had written for me and the oaths from heaven that had passed through his lips. I longed for a time when I could spend all my nights in his arms.

IT WAS THE DEATH of the king that brought my Hamlet home. For days I followed him, tried to reach out to him. But on seeing me he fled. I came upon Queen Gertrude weeping once. She told me she had lost the only two men she had ever loved. Yet it was not long before she was consoled by Hamlet's uncle.

I do not remember who told me about my father. But somehow I knew he was dead. He was killed by my own lover's hand. Hamlet speared him with a sword and my father died bleeding, minutes later, staring into the face of his murderer. O cursed hour!

And there is nowhere for me to go. There is no one left for me to become. I have traveled to the end of my world. We shall cull the last of the flowers. Pansies, violets. Rosemary for remembrance of them all. Let us follow the brook some more. There, now. Can you see my mother calling? I see her in the water, reaching out her arms. Come with me now, to where my mother beckons.

Mme Harriet Berlioz

Sceaux

18 October 1844

My dear Louis,

It is quite some time since my mind has been as clear as it is today, and now I feel well enough to write to you. I want you to know how your father treated me. It will help you understand my melancholy.

Hector sent me away to the country on the pretext that it would be better for my health. I have been banished to the very place my melody was born. I wonder where is the stable where he lay among the hay, the day the symphony came. In the birdsong I imagine I hear a clarinet piping a simple pastoral tune, and I feel strangely calm. I wait for the flute's reply, yet I hear none.

I know he wants me out of the way. For some time now I have been suspecting there is another woman. I have been opening his mail and searching through the drawers of his bureau. But my only discovery so far has been his manuscript of The Death of Ophelia. *Gripping the bedposts is all I can do to stop myself tearing it to shreds. When the pain grows too great, I have been taking sips of a sweet liquid the maid found in the kitchen. Brandy:* Eau de vie. *"Water of life."*

Hector took all the bottles he could find and smashed them on the cobblestones beneath our apartment. But there are always more. I give Joséphine a coin of housekeeping money to find me another.

This liquid brought me a numbness that gave me the strength to confront your father. I knew that if I asked him enough questions, he would eventually confess. I went to him whenever I was awake and alert. And I hoped that if I caught him unawares he would admit his guilt. I went to him during the night. I wrenched him from sleep, for what could be too much punishment for a man who commits adultery?

He has sent me away, and there is still no confession.

And although I am locked away, I am strangely free here. There is no one to lament what I have become, to tell me how weak I am, how bad my behavior, how I have let myself go. I can drink as much as I like.

I am sorry to have to tell you such things. I hope you will grow into a more sensible person than either of your parents.

Your loving mother,
Harriet

1827

A SEASON OF ENGLISH THEATER in Paris. It is the first time I can allow myself to be English. The French will not hear the Irish lilt in my voice. They will not ask me to open my lips as though to swallow an egg whole. And even if they did ask, I would not understand them.

The Théâtre de l'Odéon feels vast by day. The bright light of France pours generously in through the windows, yet the building feels cold and empty. A woman sweeping the marble staircase does not look up from her feet as I enter. I hold up my skirts as I climb the stairs and pass the finely sculpted Greek women, cherubs, and angels who look as though they could speak. I wonder what they have seen and what warnings they would have for me. At the top of the stairs I pause and see my smallness reflected in the mirror. Mirrors reflect mirrors in this endless foyer. There are glints of light from all the glass and the mosaic tiles upon the floor and a faint tinkling of chandeliers. I want to garland myself in glass. I want to shine and tinkle as I walk.

The names *Racine* and *Voltaire* are etched into busts circling the foyer. There is something smug about their marble faces. My presence here seems transient: what will people say when Harriet Smithson has passed through this theater? How will people remember me? To the left of the foyer is a circular wood-paneled wall. Every now and then I see a door and realize I have climbed too high. This is where the audience will be. How will they ever find their seats when every door is the same?

Suddenly I am alone in this labyrinth, this spiraling theater. I run around and around, and it is only when I open doors and see the angle of the stage that I can sense where I am. A gentle thud to signal the shutting door. The swish of my heavy skirts and breathless panting. I feel like an insect in a glass jar. Everything is an illusion. Finally I understand the direction of the backstage area. I rush out from the stalls and find myself caught and steadied by a Frenchman. He wears a bemused expression. He says something I do not understand. By his silence I gather he was asking me a question.

"Backstage?" I ask. "I am an actress here for rehearsal." He grins.

"Downstairs," he says. "All le way. Then outside. Dere is a separate door from the side. Amongst le colemns."

"Thank you." Heat rises through me. Of course there is a backstage entrance.

Three men are setting up the orchestra pit in front of the stage, and they stare at me as I enter shakily. My new world is sweet possibility. Abbott is pacing the stage impatiently when I arrive. He is wearing a strange blue jacket, and his trousers are low on his ample waist. He says the actors were sampling the liquid taste of France until well into the night.

"We'll begin with *The Rivals*. Mrs. Malaprop and Lydia Languish. Act 4, scene 2. Lydia, reclining on the sofa, Mrs. Malaprop, standing stage right."

My mother arrived before me. She seems relieved to be thinking about her role, and I see her relax. The lines do not matter in

this strange place where emotion is everything. The absurdity of Mrs. Malaprop will be lost on the French.

"Why, though perverse one! Tell me what you can object to in him? Isn't he a handsome man?"

"More, more!" Abbott urges. "We are performing for the deaf!"

And I find myself crying and laughing with the animation of one deranged. The three bearded men are delighted as they stand only a few feet away, giggling and slapping their thighs. They do not understand a word.

By the time we have finished our scene, most of the other actors have arrived. Some are staring at me curiously.

"Everything all right, Harriet?" Bennett, one of the younger actors, asks. I nod. Abbott tells everyone to sit. I am allowed to keep my chair; my mother stands behind me. The men disturb the dust in small patches on the stage, and my mother sneezes.

Abbott paces the stage as he speaks. "What we are doing here has never succeeded before. We are presenting some very English plays to an audience which, on the whole, is not going to understand the words. We need to perform as we have never performed before. The tickets have almost sold out. We will have a large and important audience. This is a marvelous opportunity for us to show the French what English theater is."

A few hours later, the Odéon hums with noise. I cannot make out a single individual voice and wonder how I will be able to make myself heard. The lighting is dim, and backstage is a mess. There are too many of us in this small, dark place, which smells of sweat and wine.

I sit at the dresser and notice that the furniture vibrates with

sound. A chamber pot is tucked beneath a shelf. The muted music of "Vive Henri IV" pulses down through the ceiling. It is a triumphant sound, blasting trumpets and soaring strings. Then I hear applause. I grip my quivering arms to my chest. The next item is an embellished "God Save the King," and I wonder briefly which king they mean. There is wild singing outside my room.

The atmosphere on stage is different from any I have ever known before. The audience is silent, attentive. In the dim light I can make out people reading. I realize they are following the text of *The Rivals*. These people show respect, and I am grateful. I perform for them and they sob at my tears, they laugh at my joy. I am Lydia Languish, and I feel elated.

I stare out from the stage. I see muted red velvet and gold leaf. There are dimmed chandeliers. I peer blindly into the audience and see my dreams. My future takes shape before me, and I feel as though I can almost touch it. Fleetingly, I know that I will never leave.

IN SEARCH OF THE FAMILIAR, my mother and I are drawn to gardens. We walk slowly, for Anne is with us and she is unsteady on her feet. On our way to the Tuileries we pass street gardeners offering their plants for sale and shake our heads, protesting our lack of French to those who pursue us. We sit down and breathe in lilacs, we admire the perfectly carved box tree borders. From there, Paris is a fairy city sinking into a gray-blue mist. My mother tells me the gardens were planted with potatoes to feed the starving during the revolution, and I peer among flowers for those familiar great leaves and the tender flowers which would hint at the yield beneath. We Irish are not so different from the French.

And then my mother leaves me to my own musings while she takes a turn around the lake. Within seconds I am surrounded by French gentlemen as though they have been watching from a distance, stalking their pray. An elegantly dressed gentleman with a cravat and a mustache takes my hand, and I am shocked by this familiarity. I stand and try to shake my hand free while another touches my shoulder. And suddenly I am shaking and clawing at my own skin as though I have fleas. It is my mother who frightens them away. They try to take her hand, and she glares coldly back. As though stunned, they jump back and within seconds are gone.

BY THE TIME OUR MANAGER, Charles Kemble, arrives in Paris I am beginning to think I will spend the rest of my days playing pretty and frivolous maidens. That I am destined to make audiences delight at my charms and laugh at my misfortunes. That one day I will drop dead as a frivolous maiden, transforming one of these light comedies into a tragedy of the first rate.

The arrival of any Kemble is bound to bring with it a weight of seriousness. French audiences remember their admiration for Mistress Siddons, Tragedienne of the Century. They are curious to ascertain the talents of her youngest brother.

It is with great relief that I greet Kemble on the stage at rehearsal. I know that his arrival brings with it an enormous Shakespearean repertoire and that this will provide me with opportunities to savor words and passions. I will be able to immerse myself in a role once more.

In Bennett's face I read relief that we have not yet begun rehearsal, that he is not late. Then he sees Kemble and raises his eyebrows. He sits on the boards and slides over to the edge of the

stage. He dangles his legs over the edge as though he is bathing. One by one, actors arrive on the stage. By half past ten, the men are leaning against sets or sitting untidily on the boards, the women standing with arms crossed or sitting on chairs. Kemble looks to Abbott who pulls his watch from his pocket and flips it open before nodding.

"Ladies and gentlemen," Kemble declaims as though addressing a crowd. We laugh. "We are to begin a season of Shakespeare with Hamlet. I will play the man himself." He pauses. "The rest of the cast is as follows: Ghost of Hamlet—Burke; Claudius—Chippendale; Queen Gertrude—Mrs. Brindal, Polonius—Abbott; Laertes—Bennett; Horatio—Spencer; Ophelia—Miss Smithson." Mrs. Bathurst and Mrs. Gashall smile at me, and I wonder whether they are secretly rejoicing at my forthcoming downfall. They must know, all of them, that I am unable to sing.

"Others of you will be required to play members of the Danish court. Please revise this play to begin rehearsals punctually in two days' time."

Backstage is a flurry of cloaks and scripts. It seems most people are going to learn their lines at home. There is a choked feeling in my chest, and I feel as though I might cry. I cannot play Ophelia. I must not play Ophelia.

"Mrs. Bathurst." I touch her arm as she steps toward the backstage door. Light filters through cracks in the wooden ceiling. The sweet smell of fresh sawdust is in the air. "Won't you take the role of Ophelia?"

"Heavens no, Miss Smithson. My days of playing Ophelia are gone." She grins. Her eyes are sky blue and her skin is light. "Must be off," she says.

I run from one dressing room to another; all the other women

seem to have gone. How could they have left so quickly? At the end of the line I discover Mrs. Gashall in the small corner dressing room. Her eyes are bloodshot.

"Mrs. Gashall, I was wondering, would you take the role of Ophelia? I feel you would be so much better."

She sniffs. "I was not asked. It would not be right."

"But your voice is sweet, you would be far better suited to the songs." I pause. "I will pay you a week's salary."

"Miss Smithson." She clears her throat. "I do not require your unwanted roles. Thank you." She pushes past me and I am left alone in her dressing room.

In my own dressing room, confident that I am alone, I sob. It is in intimate theaters that my powers are greatest. I lack power in my vocal chords, I am not suited to vast theaters such as this one. I am lucky to make spoken words heard let alone words that are sung. What was Kemble thinking of, casting me as Ophelia? And now on top of my feelings of inadequacy I have the envy of the other actresses to bear. I cannot endure any more scathing reviews such as those I received in London. I wipe my face and blow my nose on a rag I find in a drawer. The fabric prickles my skin and allows moisture through. I have been using my black veil as a handkerchief.

For some moments I believe the tapping on my door is the sound of the boards expanding in the sunlight. Eventually I realize someone is knocking hard on my door. I sniff.

"Yes?"

"It is Charles Kemble. May I come in?"

My voice breaks as I tell him, "Yes."

"Miss Smithson," he stands awkwardly in the doorway. "I hope you do not mind me intruding. I have a daughter almost your age. You remember Fanny? Miss Smithson, may I ask, are you unhappy with the role of Ophelia?"

I watch my fingers twisting the veil. "It is just that—my voice is not strong enough to sing her songs. I fear I will not play her well."

"We have been required to make a number of amendments by the censors. The play has been shortened somewhat. To make time for the farce, you know. It ends with the words *the rest is silence*. So if you could perhaps concentrate on the mad scene. You will not be required to play many others. Make it your own, Miss Smithson. Ophelia is not an opera singer. Feel her passions." He clears his throat as though he has just revealed intimate information.

"Thank you, Mr. Kemble." I try to smile.

"Miss Smithson, please do not hesitate to seek me out if you require professional advice or additional rehearsal of that particular scene." He bows, and I thank him again as he shuts the door behind him. My knuckles ache and I look down to see my hands gripping the veil. It has left an imprint on my palms. *The rest is silence.*

1833

WITH ALL HECTOR'S REFERENCE to Desdemona, Ophelia, and Juliet, I own I wondered whether it was me he saw when he stared into my eyes. At one of my more lucid moments I asked him to cease attending my performances for I wanted him to prove it was me he loved and not the characters of my making. These doubts settled deep inside me like a cancer, occasionally reminding me of their presence with a sharp pain. I ignored them at my peril.

In the night I lay sleepless, filled with a strange excitement tinged with panic. I could not imagine a future with him or a future without him. Was I to die in this state? I prayed that this time the correct decision would become clear and I would know what to do.

I resolved to send him away. For it was true he was penniless, and he had made it clear that his family would not support our match. And fond as I was becoming of him, I could not imagine how we would live.

"It is better," I said to him, "that we end now when we have barely begun. For can you imagine the difficulties we would have . . ."

I could not finish my sentence before he sobbed like a child. He began shouting a torrent of French of which I understood not a word, and I thought I heard stifled laughter from Anne who had been apparently engrossed in her reading. I could not stop my tears.

"Hector, I am sorry. I was mistaken. Je vous aime."

He lifted his head from his hands then and stared at me, mouth agape. After some moments he pressed his salty lips on mine. I ended our kiss with my hands on his cheeks, holding his head like some fragile object.

Anne said some frightful things to Hector, and at times I was relieved his understanding of English was limited. On more than one occasion we were whispering quietly in a corner. Hector was practicing his compliments in English.

"Beautiful," he said. "Pretty eyes." And I smiled, looking down at my hands as he stroked my cheek.

"It is time you left, Hector," Anne told him. "Harriet is very busy. She has work to do."

"Quoi?"

"I said go! Leave or I'll throw you out the window!"

The suggestion would have been comical had it not been said with such violence. My mother looked up from her sewing.

"Anne, that's enough. Monsieur, I am sorry. Will you have more tea?"

While outbursts between Anne and Hector were frequent, most often he looked upon her with the pity owed to a cripple.

Anne took to mocking Hector with an acting genius I had never before seen. And though her imitations were at times clever and could make my mother laugh, I made it clear I would not tolerate such insolence from one who had ruled our lives by her very existence. Were it not for Anne and her illness, I was quite sure I would not have been forced to work from such an early age. And had she been blessed with greater health, I had sometimes imagined she would have taken to the stage with me and our work together would have been more of a happy game than a daily drudgery.

My evenings with Hector went longer and longer until finally my mother announced one evening that she needed to retire. I believe she expected Hector to leave then, but he merely stood and kissed her hand. My mother looked at me and then back at him. She nodded to us both, bade us good night, and left the room.

He kissed me hard and deep, my lips numbing as his hands pulled the pins one by one from my hair, and my locks fell to my shoulders. At first I abandoned myself to the joy of it all. My skin tingled with his touch and I could feel my very veins opening for him.

He had undone three buttons upon my gown before I realized. I stood suddenly and pushed him away. "How dare you!"

"Mais. . . ."

"No!"

He stepped toward me.

"Don't touch me! No man is to be intimate with me before marriage."

"But. . . . you are an actrice!"

"Go!" Before I knew what I was doing I was pushing him out the door. If my mother was woken by the commotion she remained in her room. And I was grateful that I did not have to explain my state of dishevelment.

I thought I had lost him then. I grieved for days. I wept in my bedchamber. My mother and even Anne became uncommonly kind to me. My mother brought me many cups of tea and assured me that I would soon meet a more suitable man.

"My dear Harriet, I am sorry you had to have this difficult experience. But now you will know the right man when you meet him."

"Monsieur wept like a girl," Anne said. "No woman could live with that."

Anne spent hours and hours sitting on my bed, keeping me company as I slept and reading to me when I was awake. I recall my mother knocking on the door a number of times. "Anne!" she would whisper. "Come, now. Let your sister sleep."

"I don't mind, Mother," I would say. "Leave her be."

"Harriet, do you think I shall marry a prince?" she said to me one day as I sat up in bed with a glass of water.

"A prince? Perhaps. Where shall we find one for you?" I asked in mock seriousness.

"In the theater. There's bound to be some princes in your theater. And when they speak to you, you can tell them you have a lovely sister waiting to meet them."

"I shall, Anne."

"Although, perhaps it would be better if I did not marry. Then we could stay together. We could see the world, Harriet. Bathe in the summertime."

"That sounds lovely." I closed my eyes.

I own it was not just the loss of Hector which upset me. I sensed that he had been my last chance of happiness. I was almost thirty-three years old, and it was growing increasingly unlikely that I would find a husband. My appearance had also altered, and I had grown more stout, similar in shape to my mother. This not only influenced my chances at marriage but also my success on the stage.

There I lay in my bedchamber, drowning in the darkest thoughts I had yet known but not the darkest thoughts I would have. I longed for the courage to gulp a poison that would bring relief. There was nothing for me to live for. Nor was there enough for me to die for. And it was nigh impossible to soften the protective shell that had taken so many years to cultivate. If this was the pain of a broken heart, I now knew I had not done Ophelia or Juliet justice. If I ever chanced to play them again, I would play them anew.

I had never before seen my mother so concerned for me, and even Anne hushed her own complaining. They sent for the English doctor, and the light from his lamp brought tears afresh from my eyes.

"I see she is weak, Mrs. Smithson," he said. "But this is no other fever than the fever of love. See she gets enough fluids and try to give her stale bread to settle her stomach."

"Will she recover?" I heard my mother ask.

"That I cannot tell you."

Jane Shore

*T*HE EMPTINESS OF MY BODY is naught compared with the emptiness of my soul. For if a woman cannot offer friendship to one who has loved her, given her all, she suffers a greater poverty than I can imagine. I cannot believe Alicia would not know me, that she would deny me in the street. What alarmed me more than her refusal to give me a little bread and water was her wild look. She pointed at me and called to a "headless trunk"; it was not me she saw when she addressed the murdered body of Lord Hastings. Even while they claw my face and spit on me, they say she loved Hastings and has been maddened by his death. They say that instead of his death she meant mine. If this be so, she shall soon have her wish.

I leave behind me a trail of blood, dripping from the soles of my feet. My hair is matted as a mane. Most of the time I can forget my aching bones as I stare upward and know heaven will soon take me. I am recognized by my burning taper. At first crowds lined the streets, as though I were royalty. My two guards were beasts with whips and sticks. They called my name so all would know me and called me many other names I have never known. And where I once stood, handing bread and blankets to the poor, now there were crowds hurling nothing but curses. I am all bone now, and I am purified by the neglect of my body. There is some peace in knowing that no man will crave me again.

I have known the death of one husband and one worthy of that name, both of whom I loved more than my own life; I will not be taken by a third. My guards have tired of watching over me; I know not where they are now. They have served their master well; the people of England no longer need to be told whom to scorn. Alas, I had hoped to save England from an evil rule. I will find a quiet doorway in which to lay my head. I hope sleep will take me with haste.

I was young when I married Shore. He took me rosy cheeked and fresh from the dances of the season. Our wedding was all wildflowers and turtledoves. He sought always to protect me; my pillows were soft down, windows were kept closed lest I be taken by a gentle breeze. Often nights I woke to candlelight, for Shore would sit by and watch me as I slept.

I planned a good many suppers and dances. We invited the very best and most important people in England. We spent few evenings in a quiet house. Always guests would arrive, whether invited or no, and we would sit around the fireplace reading and conversing. I was at my most animated on these occasions; words and laughter slipped from my person with the slightest provocation. It is true I spoke my mind more than most other ladies. Men would start in delighted surprise at my quick wit. They warmed to me, begged to be allowed to escort me to dinner. It is surely my tongue that has cost me my life.

It was my mother who first married well. As I grew, she conveyed to me the sense of my fortune, that I never knew hunger or cold. While I was still a child, she whispered to me tales in quiet lamplight, of babies taken in the night by the bitter ice, of my own grandmother starving to death to feed her nine children. My fortune was a burden I must always carry with me. I asked my husband to allow me to work for the poor. Whenever he returned from his own duties, he never failed to ask after my own work, writing petitions and collecting funds. I had a hospital built; people soon knew of it, and it became easier to raise funds for a second. I began planning a charity school. Shore encouraged me to ask our guests to give what they could spare. And our friends gave generously.

A good number of my husband's friends were noble by birth, and thus I was not surprised to find myself at gatherings with the king.

"Mistress Shore," King Edward said to me one evening. "I hear you are keeping our poor from the streets."

"We are helping them with firewood and food in the wintertime, Your Highness."

"They have been far less trouble to me this year. Pray, tell me of your work?" And so while I had spared His Majesty my petitions, I began to tell him of the army of ladies; some writing, others providing food and firewood from their own kitchens and estates. When I had finished, he said to me, "What sum would prevent any English child from starving this winter?"

"One moment, Your Highness."

As I stood, all eyes were upon me. I left the room for my bureau where I sat calculating sums. My hand shook as I gripped my pen. That winter the king provided more than twice our previous sum.

His Majesty asked to see me after this meeting. And then again. Each time, I took my sums and my letters, ready to show him should he ask. He poured over my papers and admired my longhand. I can love any man who is kind to me. That is both my greatest strength and weakness. Men ask much of those who love them.

Edward said I must give myself to him or my husband's life is forfeit. I dared not hesitate. I was allowed one final audience with my husband. Shore kissed the tears from my brow and swore I did not need forgiveness. He prayed the king would keep me safe and said his own love for me would remain unchanged.

The king came for me in his own chariot like a peasant with his master's horse. I was handed up to him, and I blushed like a bride. He saw me hesitate, and he sought to calm me before the journey.

"You do your country a great service, madam," he said, taking my hand. I stared down at my gown as he spoke, my spine rigid. Then I chanced to look up at some movement from the horse before me, and I saw my husband standing but a short distance away. I grew cold and then I burned, as though encased in ice. I was not myself when I screamed, wringing my hand like a widow, tears pouring from some secret place within. And I imagine Edward looked annoyed, grasped me possessively to him, and whipped the horse into motion, beginning the journey away from all I had known and loved.

And though I sensed some courtiers were in jest when they now referred to me as "Mistress" Shore, my life with King Edward was largely a happy one. I had moments of deep melancholy when I recalled my husband who had allowed me so much freedom. On the night I was told of my husband's murder, I locked my room to Edward. I could not bear the thought that one man who had possessed me had caused the death of the other. There was talk of political secrets, Shore could no longer be trusted. The king whispered through the keyhole late at night. I had no reason to doubt the truth of his claims.

I never forgot my previous life with Shore, nor did I cease to mourn my dead husband. I sought solace in my quick wit, my new life, and the king's warm hand sensing the quickening in my belly.

When we were together, I tried not to think of Queen Elizabeth. There had been occasions when I had seen her glare across at me from the other side of a room. Always I smiled back. I had no reason for bitterness. In truth I pitied her.

I had tasted almost every royal privilege. Every night of the week a different feast was planned with minstrels and masquerades. I had gowns and masks to the dozen, each of my own choosing. The king lavished jewels and furnishings upon me. After the birth of my son, estates were put in my name. I still remember Edward's rarely serious face, some days after my confinement, telling me where the papers were kept.

"The land is yours, my Jane," he said. "Let no one take it from you." Little did I know how easily the casual jottings of a scribe could pass these deeds to another.

On occasion, the king's brother Richard was present at the palace during supper. He was a surly, serious man. He walked aided by a stick and rarely smiled. He never spoke directly to me, but I could not help noticing the anxious way he glared at me, then at the king and back again. It would take all my concentration to keep my eyes upon my soup, and I would retire as soon as it seemed polite to do so.

When my Edward grew ill, we all suspected fever. Richard was one of a small group who visited every day to discover the king's state of health. When I saw Edward, shrunken by fever, sobbing like a child while sweat poured from his face, calling my name, I could do nothing but run to him. For a time his illness was not identified. When the doctor called it a *fever*, some kept away. But not Richard, nor I. I can only guess what passed between the two men when they were alone. Whenever I chanced to pass

Richard about the palace, he stared through me as though I were not there. It was not long before the doctor became aware that no one else had caught the king's fever. And then I heard whispers of poison. Richard was assembling his allies, and the queen was assembling her own. I was left alone nursing my suspicions.

There was no place for me in the battle for England. Now I realize that had I valued my life, I should have fled when I saw that Edward would not recover. England was to be ruled by a madman who had cut off all the men I loved, who ripped the crown from dear Edward's skull while he still breathed. Soon followed my lands. I was taken into protection by Lord Hastings, that loyal friend of Edward's, who appeared to lose the quickness of his step during those weeks when he had to tell me of my lover's wilting and dying. And while he protected me, I knew he spent a good deal of time with Elizabeth who had been queen, consoling her in her grief.

Hastings worked tirelessly for England. I could see the glow from his candle until late into the night; he left the house in the early mornings before I arose. For my part, I spent my days at softly weeping, refusing to leave my chamber, failing to take anything other than a little bread and water. I sensed fortune leaving me and knew I had had my share. I waited for something to happen, yet I dreaded that it would.

Did I ask for beauty that kings would love me? In trying to do right I have done much wrong. Fool was I to trust all men and what they asked of me. Hastings was my fortune turned from good to bad. I had felt safe within his refuge, but then he asked my body in payment for his protection. What sin, what abomination, what pollution have I known. Ever since the death of the only one who was good, my Shore, I have been a vessel for all that was bad in man. Even kings can spew forth wickedness, I learned. Hastings was sent to teach me. It was under his protection that all became clear. My life without love was worthless, there was nothing to fear in chastening my body. Without my desire to live, Hastings had no power over me. I sought only to make my peace with God before my life was taken from me.

Gradually, I learned a great darkness came over the palace when my Edward died. There were disappearances and whisperings. Hastings did not tell me he was afraid, but I sensed it the night he tried to draw me to him, and I turned away. His palms were cold with sweat and his face the paleness of wax, maddened by fear.

His voice softened, his words melted, there was a frenzied look about him that I had never before observed. I begged him gently at first, for this was a man who had offered genuine friendship, one of the few to remain loyal to Edward after his death. I did not think to doubt his honor. I looked away and begged him not to speak to me thus. His words sharpened, his voice grew in anger, and I stepped away from him.

"How canst thou give this motion to my heart," he shouted, fist clenched, sweating, shivering, "and bid my tongue be still?"

I breathed deeply, calming myself, wondering if he would strike me down and force himself upon me. I begged him look upon the highborn beauties of the court, for he was worthy of them, could take any he chose. I was lowborn and soiled, he a gentleman of the court.

I would know no other man. I fell to my knees, begging God to see what was in my soul, begging to be taken from this life immediately, to be prevented from knowing Hastings. Had I a sword I would have used it upon him. And then those words that haunt me still: "Ungrateful woman! Is it thus you pay my services?"

At this moment, God intervened in the shape of Dumont, who saved me from Hastings's advances.

That lowborn Dumont blithely pinned down my noble attacker with his sword. I knew some moment's peace then. For as Hastings was sent from his own abode, Dumont told me of a kind of paradise that could be mine. There was a cottage near the woods, he said, with flowering garden, simple neighbors, and an old priest. He promised to convey me there with haste. Alas, the haste was not great enough. I could only quiver and hide when Hastings returned with his men to take Dumont away.

The evil of that man Richard was confirmed when he took me to his court in pretense of politeness. He said Hastings would support those royal children who should be kings. And I was surprised for we had never spoken of the matter. But at this moment I forgave Hastings all. For even in spite of what he had done to me, he had remained loyal to my Edward. And so I told Richard that Hastings was right and he grew angry until the words spat from his lips like molten lead. "Harlot," he called me, and words far worse, as he bade me have my way with Hastings to sway his loyalty toward Richard. For Richard wanted all the court to endorse his yearning for power. To be king was more important than to live. And then I spoke those words which sealed my fate:

> Let me be branded for the publick scorn, turn'd forth, and driven to wander like a vagabond, be friendless and forsaken, seek my bread upon the barren, wild, and desolate

waste, feed on my sighs, and drink my falling tears, e'er I consent to teach my lips injustice, or wrong the orphan who has none to save him.

The man who would be king and the heavens listened.

Methinks I see my husband, Shore. I believe not. I have not eaten these three days, and the visions are before me. He is there, in the crowd, strange. He is there. There, the face that has known my dawn. He is there, running to me, reaching his arms out to catch me as I fall.

1833

*T*HAT NIGHT HE CAME. My mother was like an overexcited girl as she called me to dress myself. "He is come!" she said. And I saw that she hoped this would bring a recovery.

She lifted my arms one by one into my gown, and I felt that she had not tightened my undergarments. "You must have plenty of room to breathe, Harriet. The doctor said so."

My mother led me out from my sickroom, and he ran to me in alarm when he saw my frailty.

"Malade? Oh, ma pauvre. . . ."

My mother sat, not so far away this time.

I sat in my armchair for some time, exhausted, just watching him. I could no longer remember whether I felt anger or remorse. I no longer knew what I wanted from him. Hector did not seem to realize that he had been the cause of my distress, and the reason for his absence soon became apparent. He had been thinking and writing.

Once he had completed his greeting, touched my hands and kissed my brow, he pulled some papers from his pocket. Gradually I realized that he had written a letter to his parents. The letter was forceful and gave scant information about me. He did not expect them to give it, but he demanded their consent to our marriage. I smiled weakly and gave him my hand in a symbolic gesture I did not intend as such. For Hector had not yet proposed, and I saw no reason to make a decision. But I was pleased his intentions were honorable, and after he was gone I would tell my mother. For she could not have instructed me better on the way to woo a man.

1827

I COLLECT GRIEF LIKE A SPONGE soaking up bitter juices. It is there in the faces of the defiant poor walking the streets, collecting scraps of coal for their fires. I drink it like poison in my thick early morning tea, my mother watching as though waiting to see if I drop from its force. I absorb it from Anne's angry words and my mother's complaints. We are left man-less in a forbidding city.

And then I lift the blanket of calm to search within myself. I hear echoes of a lonely child with a still unknown future. Led always for the convenience of others. Surrounded by a strange family of stagefolk with inconsistent loyalties. Dragging the ill and elderly behind her from country to province. Confused about what it means to love.

At rehearsals I am quiet, conserving my energy. I deliver my lines accurately, but I do not hint at what I feel. I use only slight gestures. During a break Kemble tells me I must not be afraid of exaggeration. "Remember that many audience members will not understand the words, Miss Smithson."

Alone in my dressing room I sing Ophelia's songs.

How should I your true love know
From another one?

The dirge-like minor key is enough to start the tears, before I have even begun work on the gestures. I know my voice is soft and not the voice of a singer. It is the voice of Ophelia.

The king and queen are to my right, the dead king and Polonius to my left. In front of me at an angle is Hamlet, and behind him the audience. This will allow me to have greatest power because I will seem to be addressing the audience. Slight gestures for the songs; my quiet voice in the minor key will create most of the effect. I will lay my black tear-stained veil on King Hamlet's grave. It is the sweet flowers that I must work on. As though in a trance, I stand. I half speak, half sing the words:

Larded with sweet flowers;
Which bewept to the grave did go
With true-love showers.

I whisper the words and begin to walk around in a small circle, staring down, imagining the purple flowers. And suddenly my life has followed a different path. I have remained in the Ennis countryside where I have found and lost love. Grass smells sweet, and the sun warms my hair.

In years to come my mother will remember coming to find me that night, making her way through Paris in the darkness past suppertime. She will remember wondering whom she could alert as to her daughter's disappearance and how she could find the lodgings of Charles Kemble without knowing his address. She will remember her despair at what would become of her and Anne, of who would support them in their grief. She will recall arriving at the Odéon on a night of no *représentation*, breathless and tearful, and then apprehensive that the stage door moved with her weight. She will relive that journey through the dark bowels of the theater, arms tight around her chest to protect herself should she need it. She will forget that she did not knock, that she was so sure something was wrong, all she could do was force the key in the lock.

My mother told me afterward that a chill went through her when she first saw me prepare for *l'apparition* of Ophelia. I was transformed, she said, the grief of a long lifetime heavy in my bones. My face glistened with tears as though someone had died. My mother said it was as though I had received new knowledge that evening.

1833

*H*ECTOR COURTED ME with songs and flowers. And when I promised him my strength and my energy for his fight, it was as though it was all a play. For I wished his parents' approval and their consent because I felt it my right. But I had not yet decided that Hector should be my husband.

I had known Hector but two months when our courtship turned from a thing private between us to a crude public battle. The battle so consumed him that we ceased progress in our knowledge of each other.

Hector had always sought his father's approval, but his music, his very lifeblood, was a decision taken against his father's wishes for which he would never be forgiven. And so he became accustomed to such continuous battles. Every day he would come to me more and more exhausted, thick lines under his eyes but a greater fury within him. He would bring the latest communications from his father, or a copy of the letter he himself had written. And so it became like a war, and I was always told who had charged and who retreated; whose weapons were newer and in better repair. Hector now spoke of nothing else but our terrible situation, of how much we were to be pitied. He wanted nothing more than to marry me, and yet this was the one thing denied him by his family. In his darkest moments, he spoke of taking his own life.

And so my mother was spared voicing her own disapproval

and could appear all goodness and kindness when she offered Hector tea and told him that he really must obey his parents' wishes but that he would surely find a nice girl to marry, one carefully selected by his family. She cared not that she slandered me and my profession with such words, but only that she was keeping me to herself and saving me for a wealthier man at the same time.

My role was changed from storyteller to comforter, from lover to mother before we were wed.

Hector's father tried to talk Hector out of our union in his letters. I still do not believe it was necessary for me to hear every detail. For Monsieur Berlioz was critical of his son, and from his words it was apparent that he did not know or understand me at all. I once suggested we visit his family, and Hector paled at the thought. Such a long journey only to be greeted with rudeness? It was out of the question. But Hector had fought his parents before and had, in a sense, won. And so he resorted to his friend Rocher, who worked as a lawyer. Rocher told him he could take legal action against his father to prevent being disinherited. This was what Hector resolved to do. I told him I had had enough.

"What passes between you and your family is your own concern," I said. "From now on, I do not wish to know of it."

We spoke of returning to England; I wondered if I would finally find my fortune there and hoped, meanwhile, to secure some well-known actors for the following season. Hector stared solemnly as I told him of these plans.

"I shall come with you," he said.

"Not if we are unmarried," I told him.

"Then I shall blow my brains out."

"Don't be ridiculous."

Mme Harriet Berlioz
Rue Blanche, 43
Montmartre, 25 May 1849

My dear Louis,

Last night I dreamed your father was at my graveside and a gravedigger had come to move my bones. The coffin came apart in the man's hands and he was left holding my skull like Hamlet and poor Yorick.

I have been very ill, and I fear my time is near. Today my mind is clear and it is like a miracle sent from God to enable me to write this. I have had a number of fits. Hector says I writhed like someone ridding herself of demons. The gurgle in my throat was like a death rattle, and my face turned black. And after each attack a little more of me was gone. It is a long time since I have felt this tenderness toward your father. For he has been by my side a good deal; he makes the journey from Paris on foot, and I see him rubbing his heels when he thinks I am sleeping. He is always by me during treatment, especially when I am bled. He brings newspapers and flowers and occasionally something sweet to eat. When I am awake he reads to me.

I have trouble remembering any words of French at all. My left side is paralyzed, and my words are halting and awkward as though I am trying to speak with someone else's jaw. But I shall not complain anymore, Louis, because today I am able to think and to clutch at my pen and write. For this I am grateful.

Your loving mother,
Harriet

1833

I WAS DISAPPOINTED to realize that I was performing on the evening of Anne's birthday.

"We will celebrate together next week," I promised her. "Just us. You will have a wonderful evening with Mother. And I'll see you when you get home."

My mother said to me, "I know not what to do for your sister on her birthday. Or where to go."

"You could take her to a concert. I have heard the young virtuoso Franz Liszt is performing on the pianoforte. You know how Anne loves music. And she has so few opportunities to hear it."

And so although I did not manage to hear Liszt play, I saw his performance every evening for a week. I would have given a month's wages for the joy and spirit with which this concert imbued my sister for the next few months. The night of the concert, I crept in as quietly as I could manage, only to find her sitting by a single lamp sewing, a pot of tea waiting for me on the table beside her. It was a great effort for Anne to manage such objects as kettles of boiling water and tea leaves, so I knew she had spent much time preparing for my arrival.

"How was your evening?" I asked, kissing her.

"Oh, Harriet, it was marvellous. That Liszt is princely. So noble and tall, with long dark hair and sharp features. I'll show you how he was."

I sat down on one of the armchairs, untying my boots and rub-

bling my feet as I watched her. It was only then that I noticed my
sister was wearing an old jacket of my father's over her gown. She
pulled the ribbon from her hair and let it tangle around her face.
She had a collection of bootlaces on the kitchen table, and she held
our her hands, asking me to tie one to each finger. Then her performance began.

She stood slowly and stretched herself as straight as she could
manage. She took great steps as she walked from the armchair to
a small side table nearby. Her earnest expression made me laugh,
but she remained serious as she turned her head to me and then
back to her table. She began shuffling the table and stool until she
was finally satisfied with their positioning. Then she bowed to me
and I applauded. Once seated, I saw that Anne had ensured I could
see her in profile. She made no sound, but how she swayed as her
fingers flew up and down! And the string was a truly ingenious
effect, almost convincing me that it was fingers a foot long, flying
up and down independently on a wooden side table that did indeed
resemble a pianoforte. I began to giggle, and after some moments
Anne also lost her composure. She swayed so hard that she lost her
balance and tumbled to the floor, the bootlaces tangling around
her. I ran to her quickly, kneeling beside her, fearing she had
injured herself. But she was laughing as hard as I had ever seen. I
pulled her up into a sitting position, and we spent the rest of the
evening disentangling her bootlaces.

We began to look forward to these evenings. I would collect
and embellish characters for my sister to perform. Anne took to
waiting up for me to return from the theater in the evenings.

"How was it, Harriet?" And her eyes would bore into mine,
longing for stories and characters. And so I began to tell her of the

artists of Paris. Anne absorbed my stories as though she were reading novels. And bit by bit she began constructing characters from my descriptions, devising costumes from my mother's rag basket. It was not long before she performed my stories back to me in the evenings before the dying fire: my own private theater.

"Who are you this evening, Miss Smithson?" I would smile as I walked in the door and kissed her. Once she even mimicked Joseph; no one was safe from her mockery.

Another evening it was a version of Mademoiselle Mars, the older French tragedienne, I discovered in our drawing room when I returned home. Anne had stuffed rags under her clothing and particularly over her chest which made her body look strangely out of proportion. From this solid trunk emerged spindly limbs. She had used some of my skin paints to draw lines upon her face, which from a distance made her look aged and close up gave her the appearance of the kind of performer usually allotted the second greenroom. And in this bizarre outfit, she fussed over me with a heavy French accent.

"Mademoiselle, this Ophélie is parfaite. Such madness I have never before seen!"

Anne's enduring favorite character was Hector Berlioz. Again she donned the old clothes of my father's that my mother had kept. And somewhere she had found a tangled blond curly wig. Sometimes she would merely wave one of my mother's wooden spoons frenetically in front of her, conducting an imaginary orchestra. Other times she was more cruel. She began to involve me in her dramas.

"Mademoiselle," she would grab my hand and try to kiss it, clutching at my skin until she scratched and I pulled away. She would mock his tears and his explosions of rage. Always her Berlioz was alarmingly thin with the air of an elderly woman. One night I told her to stop.

"It's cruel Anne. We shouldn't laugh at him."

"Why not? We laugh at everyone else."

"He is sensitive."

"Nonsense."

"It's true. He's very kind hearted. You wouldn't understand."

"*I* wouldn't understand? Choose *him* if you prefer!" She shuffled as quickly as she could to her room and slammed the door behind her.

The following evening, she tried Berlioz again. I had had a particularly difficult evening, performing in both dramas, and I longed for sleep. My sister was standing by the window in her blond wig when I walked in the door. I pretended not to notice as I kissed her cheek. "I'm going to bed, Mouse," I said.

"Going to bed? I've been waiting for you."

"I'm very tired. I'm sorry."

"Let me play for you."

"Anne, show me in the morning."

"I've been preparing all afternoon. Why do you spend so much time with him and not me?"

1833

I COMMENCED PLANS for my benefit concert, which we all hoped would relieve some financial pressure. Meanwhile Hector tussled with his family and we continued to meet, though slightly less often. In my situation, it fell upon my shoulders to undertake most matters of business, and thus it happened that I attended an appointment with the Ministry of Commerce in which I sought the permissions required for my concert. Such men were not accustomed to working with women and were a little shocked upon my arrival. But after their initial surprise they spoke to me tolerably well, and my aims were achieved.

As I returned home, my mind was more filled with work than it had been for some time. I compiled lists of actors and musicians I could call upon to perform for my benefit concert. I tried to imagine a program that was diverse yet unified. In my mind I planned the afternoon. I needed to look through my own roles to choose which one I wanted for myself. I was impatient to work and did not wait until the carriage had stopped before standing. I did not see the hem of my gown catch in the wheel.

I heard the bones snap as I landed on my left ankle. Pain shot through my foot and up through my body. I was light-headed and screamed in pain as though I could force it away. The carriage was gone. I clutched my swelling ankle, which now felt as though it would burst. It was as though I had taken too much drink. Suddenly all was black.

I do not remember the young men who carried me upstairs, though I imagine they struggled for I was no longer thin or slim-waisted. However, I do recall the doctor tugging at my boot as I screamed. And then my mother handing him her best kitchen knife, tears rolling down my cheeks as I felt the pinching and watched him saw through that soft, expensive leather.

This accident was almost the end of me. I could not leave my bed for almost four months, though occasionally Hector would carry me to the sofa to relieve the monotony. I wept at the thought of how burdensome I had become. The English doctor visited often, and we could barely pay his fees. My mother told me I would soon work again, though I heard the doctor say otherwise when he thought I was sleeping. Then she said to me that she imagined it would not be long before Monsieur found a more able-bodied girl and that I was not to distress myself over him. I watched him keenly, for I had little else to do. And I saw that for some days he wavered. But then he brought a box of names and addresses. He began to organize my benefit concert for later that year.

We knew some peace during that time. Whenever I cried over my predicament, Hector would console me with stories of how successful my concert would be, of how well I would be received, of how the money earned would pay off my creditors with some to spare. Not a day went by when he did not tell me of George Sand or Liszt or Chopin asking after my health and praying for my quick recovery. He brought Franz Liszt to see me without any warning one afternoon. My mother and sister stood dumbfounded in the doorway. The man was tall with a prominent forehead and a serene face. Although my mother had helped me dress, I was wearing one of my older gowns and my hair hung loose about my crepit state

.lthough he
grew more

sommations

ctor, I need

a, you need
l waved his
e left, slam-

future with
mily of our
ny hand, he

ctor helped
we returned
on the floor

st can't bear
ng. He knelt
he same rev-

nce she had
"

o have to greet him in my

one of his enormous hands
admired your Juliet, Miss
. Mind Hector looks after

finding her voice.

venom I had never before

old me one day.
level. And though the very
something I could ask him
or. But then she told me he
l and committing unspeak-

ursting into tears.
e insisted he was, I should
He himself could fly into a
. And if he did not under-
im.
le wooden crutches. In the
from one room to the next
but it was a delight to move
I did learn to move more
could lead me slowly, walk-
din des Tuileries where we
shoulder. Prostrate months
nother did not feel it neces-

sary to accompany us; Hector's gentleness and my
presented no threat whatsoever.

In this way I became accustomed to his presence.
would not have been my mother's choice for me, sh
accepting of our courtship.

One day in the apartment he told me that th
against his father were over. We were free to marry.

I stared at my hands when he said this to me. "F
more time."

"More time? After everything I have done for y
more time?" He began to shout in angry French a
hands about, knocking some scripts off a table. Then
ming the door behind him.

That night I did not sleep. Still I could not see th
him or without him. I knew better than to tell my
changed situation. The next day he returned. Taking
looked me in the eye. "I have the papers," he said.

"Which papers?"

"The forms we need to sign before we marry."

"Put them down a minute. Let's read a little." F
me to the small bookcase in my bedchamber. When
to the sitting room, I noticed the form in torn piece
while my sister sat nearby attending to her sewing.

"Oh, dear God, Anne, what have you done?"

She began to cry. "I'm sorry," she whispered. "I
it." She left the room, and Hector, for once, said noth
and silently retrieved the patches of parchment with
erence as he showed for his music scores.

"Why do we have to marry now?" I asked him,
left. "Why can't things stay as they are a little longe

"We are not united completely," he said. "I cannot support this waiting. If you will not marry me, you will never see me again."

I felt the tears sting my eyes.

"Why do you hesitate?" he shouted. "One more day! I give you one more day. Tomorrow I must have an answer." With this he suddenly threw the shreds in the air, turned, and left, parchment raining down on his head.

That night I decided. I would be free of him. Now that my leg was better, I could travel to London and if not perform then at least employ some actors for the next season. My travels would distract me and perhaps introduce me to a more suitable man. It was just a matter of telling him.

When he arrived, he was paler than usual and there was a wild look about him. We said nothing for some moments as I tried to find the words I needed. He reached into his pocket and pulled out a large vial. I looked around the room, wondering what to say. He tipped his head back and swallowed. A groan escaped him.

"What was that?"

"Quoi?"

"That liquid? What did you take?"

He took my hand. It was as slippery as wet soap.

"It was opium."

"But Hector, so much? It will kill you!"

"Will you marry me?"

The commotion brought my mother running, and she watched the proceedings unfold like some bizarre type of pantomime. *A young musician of morbid sensibility and fiery imagination poisons himself with opium in a fit of amorous despair.*

"If not I shall die here."

"I. . . . Oh, God! Hector, of course, I love you."

"There . . . in my bag . . . the remedy."

My leg ached as I dragged myself to his bag. It contained a few coins and a crumpled page of manuscript. There was a large hand-kerchief. Down at the bottom was another vial. I could not make out the words.

He had crawled to me, and now he snatched the vial from my hand like someone possessed. He sucked the liquid from the glass and licked the rim for good measure. Then he collapsed, groaning on the floor. My mother brought him a pillow, and the maid brought a chamberpot.

"What's wrong with him?" Anne asked. I slapped her and she howled.

For three days I did not know whether he would live or die.

1827

*D*URING THE LAST FEW DAYS before *Hamlet*, Paris is airless and it holds heat like an oven. There is nowhere to escape. On my way to rehearsal I see sleepless ladies fanning themselves in early morning patches of green or shade. I am too tired to lie tossing beneath my sheets and instead fall into dangerous, still, and heavy sleep from which it is almost impossible to wake. I relish the late evening when the sun is briefly hidden.

The Théâter de l'Odéon, due to its size, heats up rather more slowly than other buildings. But each day, more and more actresses appear with fans they have bought in the streets, garish and fashionable. I have nothing but my script with which to fan myself, and it is not done to appear with a script three days before opening night.

After rehearsal one afternoon my mother gives me a gift. She is rosy cheeked with droplets of moisture on her forehead. She has sacrificed some clothing and locked herself in our airless apartment to construct a fan for me. It is white with a pattern of pale blue flowers.

At the final rehearsal Charles Kemble twitches like a child bitten by flees. "I am still not satisfied with the stage directions!" he says. "Miss Smithson, would you kindly improve your posture."

I open my eyes. I have been furnished with a sofa for the viewing of the play within *Hamlet* and, fanning myself, had begun to doze. I sit up straight. For a moment all eyes are upon me, shadows beneath them.

"I have it!" Kemble lifts his index finger as though he has solved a puzzle. We all watch as he lies down at my feet, his right shoulder against my knees.

"Miss Smithson, may I borrow your fan?" He takes it with his left hand and begins to fan behind him, in my direction, while watching the miniature stage.

"The beginning of act 3, scene 2, please."

On opening night my mother will be delighted to see how her fan has become the center of the scene, how Kemble fans both me and himself, how he walks the stage with it, brandishing it like a sword. She will be proud when someone explains to her that Monsieur Dumas, the playwright, has renamed this scene "La scène de l'éventail." "What a gentleman that Mr. Kemble is," she will sigh.

IT IS A WONDER anyone can summon the energy to leave their homes on Tuesday the 11th of September. I travel by coach to hasten the journey, but still the driver cannot deliver me to the backstage door on account of a jam of carriages blocking the road for several streets. I pay him and walk the final two blocks in the heat, carrying a white muslin dress, my scalp dripping and heart fluttering as I realize it is none other than my own theater troupe that has stopped traffic in the middle of Paris.

I have arrived in good time, but already there is a crowd of people all along the Place de l'Odéon jostling each other in the heat. Some of them are extremely well dressed and looking slightly put out that they, too, should have to wait their turn. I hear hurried and animated French and the occasional smattering of the king's English. I stumble my way among them to the backstage door.

Backstage, Mrs. Vaughan is peering through the sets into the auditorium.

"Look at them all squashed together in the pit," she says. "Bless them." And sure enough, quite a number of ragged young men in tailored suits have already claimed the few inches that will be theirs for the night.

"A very important audience this evening," Kemble says later in the greenroom. "Almost all the English in Paris as well as many young French artists, I've been told. They've come to learn about Shakespeare."

I make my way to my dressing room, realizing with relish that it is one of the cooler parts of the building on account of its lacking windows. There must be some advantage to having to prepare in near darkness. I light the candles and fill a bowl with water from the jug. I push a chair against the door and begin peeling back my clothes. It is slow work dressing myself, but I forbade my mother to accompany me. Being alone enables me to imagine myself to be Ophelia. When I stand in my underclothes, I sponge myself down and dab lavender water behind my ears. I pull on the light muslin dress and line up my properties on the table: my wildflowers in water, the straw, the fan, and my long black veil, stretched and ironed with dried wildflowers fastened to it.

In the greenroom, everyone is rigid with anticipation. The benches are empty, and we all stand as close to the door as we can manage. Every now and then we hear roaring from the audience, and we know not what to make of it.

I first enter the stage as Ophelia with Laertes in scene 2. As Ophelia I listen to his advice to be wary of Hamlet and to remain guarded in my behavior. Although I cannot see many members of the audience and I daren't be distracted by them, I am aware of their silence and attention. It is true, what they say about how other countries provide spectators yet it is only the French who will provide an audience. And although I fear they barely hear let alone understand my words, there is a silence within the hall, as though one thousand people hold their breath.

Later that evening, in my dressing room, I take much time to prepare for my third entrance. I let my hair fall loosely and untidily down my back. Slowly I weave strands of straw among my hair so that I rustle when I shake my head. I pin the veil and stand to let it fall over my shoulders. I sit quietly until I am called to the greenroom. Some of the other actors snigger when they see me with dark veil, straw, and wildflowers. It is as though I have entered a different world.

I walk slowly onto the stage, turning my head to look all around. I am clothed in black; the veil flows behind me.

"Where is the beauteous majesty of Denmark?" I ask Queen Gertrude breathlessly. And she turns to me in concern.

"How now, Ophelia!"

I fall to my knees thinking of Hamlet and then my dead father and then Hamlet again. I sing slowly and softly. I have no voice, it doesn't matter. My right hand lifts ever so slowly.

How should I your true love know
From another one?

And I am looking to the dead on my left, and Hamlet in front of me. And then suddenly I am unpinning the veil, laying it gently over my father's body. I am shuddering and sighing, sobbing for my father. I am drawing circles among flowers with my feet, looking down in grief.

Back in the wings I hear roaring, and I fear I cannot face the audience's disapproval. "My God, what are they saying? Do they like it or hate it?" I ask.

"It is a marvelous success," someone shouts over the audience's roaring, and pushes me back on stage.

The basket over my arm swings as I return to the stage.

"I hope all will be well," I say sadly. And with my right hand on my heart and my left hand moving up to join it as though in prayer, I say, "But I cannot choose but weep, to think they would lay him in the cold ground. My brother shall know of it."

Then I see I am surrounded by ladies and gentleman, still and watchful. A wave of sobbing washes toward me and I look up, puzzled. I smile and spread my hands, the basket knocking against my left hip.

"I thank you for your good council." I turn to my basket and lift flowers one by one. There is lavender, rosemary, and sky blue forget-me-nots. I lift a sprig of lavender between two fingers and hand it to Queen Gertrude who forces her lips into a smile. A daisy for the king. "There's a daisy: I would give you some violets, but they withered all when my father died. . . ."

I swing and turn to my ladies in waiting. "Good night, ladies; good night." One by one I hand them forget-me-nots. Then there is a wave of sobbing again. Then it is gone as I speak, "Sweet ladies; good night, good night."

I notice that there are still flowers in my basket. I scoop up the petals like seed and fling them into the darkness, over the edge,

and I fancy there are people there; women weeping into handkerchiefs and men sobbing as they stumble out a door, petals falling
like rain. Someone takes my arm and leads me away.

HAD CHARLES KEMBLE not gripped my arm during the curtain
call, I am sure I would have collapsed in the heat, the stench of
perspiration fanned by plaudits, the air heated by shouting and
tears. As I stared into the vast hollow of the Odéon, I fancied I saw
the stone walls trembling.

Backstage everyone possessed a new energy in spite of the
temperature. Other actors tried to drag me straight to the greenroom, but I shook my head.

"In a minute. I must change first." Once in my changing room
I locked the door and unpinned the veil from my head. The tops
of my arms were streaked in a rash which I hoped would soon
clear. I struggled from my gown and began sponging myself, trying to return sensation to my limbs for the small room was airless
as a closed oven. Wearing only my underclothes, I fell into the
chair and lay my head on the table.

A steady firm knocking woke me from dozing, and I grabbed
for something to cover myself.

"Just a minute!" I called, expecting a voice to indicate whose
presence it was. The person did not speak, but I sensed there was
someone there waiting; occasionally I heard heavy breathing as I
pulled my day dress over my sticky skin. I did not have time to fix
my hair and must have looked a sight standing there, bulging in all
the wrong places for I had not had time to adjust my clothing. My
hair was partially caught under the dress, the rest of it flowing

untidily around my face with wildflowers and straw caught in it. I unlocked the door and a stately older woman examined me.

"Mademoiselle!" she took my hands in hers and kissed both my cheeks.

"Merveilleuse!" she looked me in the eye, and I feared I would not understand her.

"Madmoiselle Mars," she said, holding her right hand to her heart.

"Oh," I said. "Miss Smithson. Harriet Smithson."

She smiled. "Very good, Miss Smithson. Zis Ophélie she is merveilleuse! You play vell. I shall come tomorrow."

I nodded. "Thank you. Yes, please come again."

After she had gone I dabbed rose water behind my ears, caught my hair in a bun, and adjusted some wildflowers for ornamentation. I wondered who had let that woman come backstage.

MRS. BRINDAL TAKES MY ARM in the greenroom, as though she is still Queen Gertrude and I am Ophelia and she is worried about my health.

"A drink, Harriet?" she asks, pouring me something deep red. I resist the urge to drink quickly, each sweet sip adding to my haziness. "That was lovely," she says. "Original and quite beautiful. The audience loved you."

"I really think you should learn to sing Ophelia's songs, Miss Smithson," Mrs. Gashall says. "But apart from that I gather it was a reasonable—"

"Ah, Miss Smithson, Miss Smithson." Charles Kemble is striding toward me, around the food table which I have just spotted and walking quickly as though he has been seeking me for hours. "Excellent performance!" He takes my hand. "The French seem to love our Shakespeare—I was thinking about *Romeo and Juliet* for Saturday night. How would you feel about the role of Juliet?"

"Well, I—all right."

"They are very taken with you, Miss Smithson." He winks. "On my way backstage I could still hear them calling for La Belle Irlandaise!"

"Mr. Kemble, a woman came to speak to me in my dressing room. I had never seen her before. She said her name was . . . Mademoiselle Mars."

At the mention of her name, it is as though all conversations in the room cease.

"Mademoiselle Mars?" Kemble asks.

"Ahh—yes."

"Well. The great French tragedienne. She is known for her portrayal of madness. She was paying you a great compliment, my dear."

Charles Kemble escorts me to my carriage around the back of the theater, urging me to walk quickly with my head down.

"They will not harm you, but it is best to avoid any unpleasantness," he says, and I realize that there is a gathering of young men lurking around the backstage door hoping to catch another glimpse of me, this time out of costume. There is a slight breeze now, and the sky has the evening lightness of summer. There is a hint of celebration in the air. Here in Paris, members of society walk in certain streets in the evenings, and they nod to me as I pass. I see coffeehouses, and there is an occasional waft of garlic and cream, bursts of laughter from open doors, excited chatter. On this night I feel that I am the subject of every conversation. I stretch my legs under my gown and slouch back in my seat. Charles Kemble has advised me I am not required at rehearsal tomorrow. Act 5 is to be altered slightly to make Hamlet more acceptable as a hero. Ophelia touched them to the very core. I will be able to rest.

I climb the steps to our lodgings, and my mother is already standing in the doorway, beaming. Anne stands behind her in her nightgown. I hand my mother the pastries Mrs. Brindal packed for me when I left. I feel as though I have not eaten for a day.

"Harriet, you were marvelous! What generous people these French are. And what a magical city! Oh, you will have great success here. And we will never have to worry again! Come, sit down. Tell me of your evening."

For three nights I sleep fitfully, my waking thoughts blurring into dreams. For the first time I allow myself to believe everything in my life has led me to this moment.

MY FAMILY HAS MOVED into more comfortable lodgings at Rue Neuve Saint Marc; there are three bedrooms, a withdrawing room, and a parlor. Monsieur Tartes is a very helpful doorman, and we also have a maid and cook. Although I have ensured my mother is freed from almost all domestic duties, I still find she enjoys sewing in the evenings, though it cannot be good for her eyes.

Anne collects newspapers and journals looking for my name. Soon there is a whole box of clippings describing me as pure and beautiful. The French write "Miss Smithson nous a montré une véritable folle!" and "À la fin de la pièce, Miss Smithson meurt de douleur. . . ." They like me best when I am mad or dying.

I would have expected my mother to delight in our newfound fortune, but she has found other anxieties with which to occupy her mind. I am not to receive guests in my dressing room, she says. I must always travel by carriage. And it seems that my inaccessibility drives the Parisians to fury. Almost every day there are callers at the front door leaving cards and letters. Monsieur Tartes collects them patiently, assuring visitors he will pass them on, and sends the callers away.

Madmoiselle Mars calls each week to help me with my mail. At first I wondered why she would give of her time so generously for such a tedious occupation, but now I have seen how her eyes light up as she reads those sweet young words of love; sometimes I have to call her name three times to remind her to translate the words. I gather it is some years since Mademoiselle Mars received such letters. Even after she has translated the meanings for me I am usually left wanting, for I cannot believe all the letters are nearly identical.

"Love," she says, nodding. She instructs me to write *Merci* and sign my name. She spells their names to me in halting English mixed with French.

"Who is this Monsieur Berlioz?" I ask her one day when she has spelled his name for the third time. "Why does he write me so often? What does he say?"

"Fou," she says. At first I think she curses. Then she says it again. "Musicien et fou. Mad. You must be careful." I shiver as though I have heard a prophecy. I put his letters in a drawer together with my unsent responses and wait for Mr. Turner who meets with me weekly to discuss my business affairs.

After we have finished discussing financial matters, while he sips his tea, I say, "Mr. Turner, I have received three letters from a Frenchman and I wonder whether you could help me decipher them?"

"Certainly, Miss Smithson." He beams, and my mother blushes as though he has whispered something indiscreet in her ear. "I would be delighted."

He sits back in his chair, leaning his chin upon his right palm while holding the letter in his left hand. And when he finishes I expect him to turn to me. Instead, he begins the second letter and then the third. He stares at his teacup as though deciding what to say.

"This young man takes liberties in what he says to you."

"What does he say?"

Mr. Turner clears his throat. "He claims to be in love with you, Miss Smithson."

"All the young men are in love with her!" my mother states proudly. "She has had some fine proposals!"

"Hush, Mother."

"He seems rather—Miss Smithson, I must tell you I have heard of this Berlioz. He is a student of composition at the Conservatoire. He approaches all work and life with great determination and passion. A very talented young man but a most unstable character. I advise you to avoid him. I believe he may suffer from epilepsy."

"Is he a danger to her, then?" my mother asks.

"I believe he can be dissuaded from his affections if Miss Smithson is careful not to respond to his advances. Tell the servants you wish to receive no further correspondence from him." Mr. Turner looks from me to my mother and back again. "I think we are best rid of these," he says, dropping the letters one by one into the fire. Each letter flares briefly, as though it has been dipped in lamp oil, before collapsing into ash.

And suddenly I realize that this Monsieur Berlioz is the red-headed young man who watches my performances with such anguish, the same man I have seen among the columns of the Odéon as I arrive for rehearsal.

1827

$\mathcal{N}$ow that i have become someone who is noticed in public, I can no longer bear to wear those worn and scrubbed dresses and the whalebone corset made for narrower hips, which I inherited from Eliza O'Neill so many years ago. I am vague about my salary when my mother asks; I have given her enough to put some away. I take almost all I have left, with promises of much more, to a small boutique near the Opéra. My mother thinks I am attending rehearsal.

I enter beneath the sign *Modiste et Corsetière*. Two extremely well dressed women are standing behind a table speaking. The shorter woman raises an eyebrow at me, as though she believes I belong in the *épicerie* down the road, but the other one bustles over and begins chattering in quick French I do not understand.

They take me into a small room where they undress me in a business-like manner and stand me on a pedestal. The thin woman does not flinch as she pulls her tape measure around my hips and waist, then measures the distance from my hips to bust. And when she has finished I gather she is having corsets made for me; she asks me to write my address, and I know she will have them delivered.

And although the corset I am wearing is obviously inadequate, bent out of shape and slightly gray, the shorter, wider woman takes great delight in sweeping gown after gown off the rack. One by one she holds them against my body, squints, nods, and beckons me to floor level so she can slip the shiny fabrics over my arms and fasten them at the back. I begin with one gown for each day of the week, silks and satins in pale blues and pinks, a deeper navy and bottle green, a light mauve, a white, and a cream. Many reveal my neck and arms; they have capped sleeves and can be fitted with short jackets during the day in summer or cloaks in winter. Without saying a word, simply nodding and smiling, I purchase the gowns, wordlessly communicating my approval. Finally, the short woman sits me before a mirror and begins emptying the jewelry cabinet. I laugh and shake my head, and eventually she remembers a word of English. "Try," she says. "You try." There are heavy diamond earrings, perfect pearls, gold bracelets that sparkle like chandeliers. All these riches a woman of my station must not purchase for herself. Particularly a woman who two weeks earlier could barely afford to feed her family. But I admire the glittering against my skin and stare deep into sapphires which match perfectly with the navy gown. And I dare to hope that one day I will love a man who buys me such jewels. When I have pushed every trinket to one side, the woman places a small wooden box before me. I am tiring of her game, but I open the box so as not to offend her. Inside is a gold bracelet ornamented by a gold shamrock. Clutching the small wooden box, I wave to the two women as I leave.

EACH NIGHT AFTER OPHELIA, it is as though the grief and madness have sucked the very life from my bones. It takes longer and longer to return to my own world. Most evenings I return home and my mother grips my arm to ask what has happened. Wearily I tell her it is just Ophelia. Only sleep wipes the melancholy from my brow, and in the mornings I lie awake and grin to myself, remembering the carriage at my permanent disposal and how the young men from the Latin Quarter run after it shouting "I love you!" They have taught themselves those three words of English.

One morning I ask Pierre to deposit me and my mother in one of the cobbled streets leading like points of a star to the Odéon at their center. I am going to attend rehearsal, but punctuality is no longer of the essence and I wish to examine the lithographs of my performances in the windows of the tiny bookshops that Mrs. Vaughan told me about. Although the weather is cooling now, and brown leaves are beginning to scatter over the streets, I carry my parasol elegantly over my left arm. My mother clutches my right arm and walks beside me as a man would, shielding me from the road in case the carriages should splash mud in our direction. In the first bookshop there is a large print on an easel. It shows act 3, scene 2, in which all members of the court are present to watch the performance by the traveling players. It is a poor likeness of me, sitting forward in my seat, my arms bent awkwardly. And there is something comical about Charles Kemble, who has been depicted as youthful and quite handsome as he lies fanning at my feet.

Suddenly the bookseller is before me, all in brown with an animated face speaking in rapid French as though he wants to get every word in. Then he pauses. I smile, and then my mother looks alarmed as the man takes my left hand and kisses it. My hand is moist and he will not stop; I tug at my hand, but he will not let go. Suddenly in place of the man I see dogs from childhood, and I try to withdraw my hand with a feeling of distaste. And then suddenly there are more men like him, surrounding us, and I can no longer see the theater, my destination. The men are staring, mouths agape, some trying to separate my arm from my mother's. One is kneeling at my feet, another is trying to kiss my boots.

"Excuse me," I say firmly. "We must go." And they stare with furrowed brows. I push forward, and they do not move. I begin to feel trapped, fastened tightly into my new corset and gown, surrounded by these tall men who will not allow me to leave. It becomes difficult to breathe, and now my mother is shouting. Eventually our arms are separated, and I raise my parasol high in the air. I have only to poke one man in the ribs to cause them to begin to disperse. I grab my mother by the hand and walk her quickly toward the theater. Suddenly I notice Pierre and the horses trotting next to us, his brow furrowed.

"Allez, allez!" he shouts at the men on the street, cracking his whip.

It is this incident which teaches me that my days of anonymity are gone, and I begin to look back nostalgically to the days where my presence on stage was barely noticed and I could walk where I chose.

I HAVE BEEN IN PARIS some weeks when I feel settled enough to find a church. When I think of Father Barrett and all that he taught me, I feel a deep shame that I have been such an irregular attender of church these past years. But I have always believed that it is familiarity that makes church such a comfort, and when one spends so much time traveling from one town to another, working all the while, both familiarity and time can be difficult to come by.

And though I do not remember saying the words, I have a feeling that somehow I did promise Father Barrett that I would never neglect my duties by God. I must say that I rarely forget my evening prayers, and at times it is Father Barrett's voice I hear in my mind when I remember the words. I pray that God will care for me and make decisions clear in my mind and cure my sister and look after my brother. But prayers do not seem enough, so some weeks after my arrival in Paris I ask my mother to wake me on Sunday morning in time to attend mass. And although my mother is not familiar with mass, she agrees to attend with me.

By the time we arrive at Église Saint-Roch, there is a crowd of people on the stone steps making their way inside. Some small boys are running around the statues inside the iron gates, and two women stand nearby, deep in conversation, occasionally looking toward the children and shouting, "Robert! Jacques!" As we near the entrance, I fancy the crowd of people has fallen silent to stare at us. Some girls have reached the front of the line. They turn behind them, look at me with large brown eyes, turn back, and slip through the doorway. An elderly woman with a stick pauses and hisses, "Actrice!" Then she shakes her head, mutters under her breath, and disappears through the doorway. A slightly thinner man, who might be her husband, stops on the step and begins addressing me in rapid, angry French. He points at me and then toward the doorway. It is not that I am unaccustomed to being stared at. It is just that I am usually watched in the process of being someone else. And I feel strangely vulnerable on a Sunday morning, washed and neatly dressed, standing as myself outside the church. My body stiffens and heats. The man turns, and I am briefly relieved that he is going to enter the building. But suddenly he turns back and a lump of spit flies through the air and lands on my cheek.

I have barely registered the offense when my mother has wiped the filth from my skin with the lace handkerchief I planned to use as Desdemona. And while I am wondering whether to stay or go, she grabs my arm and drags me through the heavy doors. The church is all arches, domes, and columns. But the smell of sweat and the noise remind me of the pit after half-price entry. I begin to realize it is not by accident that people on the ends of rows stick boots in front of me. They are standing all around us, pointing and shouting. On the column to my right is a carved wooden Jesus on the cross. I see his ribs struggling to rise and fall, his rounded muscles, his knees bent weakly trying to support his weight. More men are spitting, and a rotten tomato splatters my mother's arm. A priest stands at the altar; he does not speak, and his inaction passes like judgment. Above me are whitewashed walls, sunlight tinted the colors of stained glass, and a mosaic of Jesus in Heaven. As I lift my arms to shield my face, I see the priest out of the corner of my eye, watching the congregation hit, spit, and throw, and my mother, head down, pulling me after her out the door.

Later, my mother pours tea and we sit somberly at the kitchen table. "You know, Harriet, Talma had to renounce the theater before he was allowed to marry in the church. Remember that it was people and not God who prevented you attending mass today."

DURING THE DRESS REHEARSAL Charles Kemble wears black face paint, but even so he is more a Roman than a Moor. It is as well the stage lighting is so poor or the audience would see the patches of black on my face like mud after his embraces. In general the casting is somewhat comical, and I wonder whether people find me as miscast in the role of Desdemona as Kemble is as Othello.

I am not at all sure about Desdemona. It is one thing to be mad or passionate on stage, another thing altogether to be smothered.

However, it is easy to see that no other of the actors is suited to the part. I have requested the removal of the "Willow Song" for I can only manage a song if sung in madness or jest; the soft earnestness of my voice travels only to the curtains and back again without reaching the crowd.

There is much interest in this latest Shakespearean play, and this time I make sure I arrive well in advance so as not to get caught up in the crowd. They know the story from Rossini's *Otello*, and there are raucous renderings of choruses from the pit. I fancy the red-headed man with the mad eyes is there, and sometimes he stands and waves his arms about as though conducting the others. I see this through cracks in the curtains and in my imagination. For I am loath to go near the audience before a performance.

And so I sit through several scenes in the greenroom. This more than the others is a play of men. Of male friendship, war, and rivalry. Desdemona does not appear until it is time to defend her husband against her father.

Next time I am on stage it is the heart of the drama. Desdemona has been speaking to Cassio, for she enjoys the company of men. And then I am offstage while schemes are plotted and men cease to be what they seem.

It is difficult to lie serenely on my stage bed when I know that any minute Kemble will come at me with a pillow. It is a strange thing to lie there in a nightgown, my hair aflow before an audience. Kemble embraces me, and I smell his sweat. Then he is like a man possessed, with blazing eyes and all that face paint, and I scream and scream, holding out my hands. I tell him to stop and remind myself that I must weaken, I must allow this to happen, for it is in me to fight. And then the pillow is gently over my face and I feign weakness, falling limp into the bed. Enraged, Kemble mimes striking me twice with his dagger. I am lying still for some seconds before I hear pandemonium. There is sobbing, cries of "Non! Non! Affreux!" and furious chatter. I hear boots on boards and someone backstage whispers, "They are leaving! The audience is walking out! They are covering their eyes!" And I wonder if this has been an immense success or a failure.

THERE IS A LETTER awaiting me in my dressing room one morning, and Mr. Turner informs me that Achille Deveria wishes to meet me and to paint my portrait. I have only met Monsieur Deveria in passing before, but I know he is responsible for the scenes from Shakespearean plays in the windows of the Parisian print shops. He has sketched me lightly as Ophelia, Juliet, and Desdemona, but he has not yet attempted to create a likeness.

My mother insists I must be extremely elegant for my portrait; she spends hours the previous evening putting my hair in rags, creating fine ringlets. In the morning I wake with a headache, and she dresses me in a gown crawling with heavy woolen lace and hemmed with frills. Deveria completes the appearance of a peacock with an enormous feathered hat. My mother sits in a corner of the studio and is soon asleep. I sit slightly forward on my chair, my right hand dangling finely over the armrest. Monsieur turns his head first one way, then the other. He is close to my age and has a slightly ragged appearance, a slight beard as is the fashion, and a dark filth that could be paint underneath his fingernails. He instructs me to pinch some dress fabric between the thumb and forefinger of my left hand and asks me to point my left foot out from underneath the gown. A heavy sleepiness comes over me as I wonder how long I shall have to sit like this. He has seated me before the mantel, and I ask him to allow the logs to burn low. I notice he has a line of moisture across the top of his lip.

Achille speaks more English than most, and I learn from him that he has already painted many important Parisian figures. "I should like to perfect your features, Miss Smithson. Boulanger and I are thinking to compile a book of lithographs on the English theater."

"You are very kind."

"Do you like Paris?"

"Very much."

"This Shakespeare! He is—beautiful. You are very liked here, Miss Smithson."

"Thank you."

"Especially Hector Berlioz, you know."

"Berlioz?"

"Yes. He speaks of you often."

"What does he say?"

"You inspire him. Miss Smithson, Hector Berlioz is a genius."

HECTOR BERLIOZ BEGINS to haunt me both awake and in my dreams. I am strangely drawn to him though paralyzed in fear of what he would do to me given half a chance. Whenever I take my carriage through the streets, I seem to see his face in a crowd. He is there in the pit staring at me in anguish when I perform. Once I even see him staring up at my window from the street. I fancy I hear him humming, and this tune calls me to him in my dreams. I drag the curtain across the window, exposed as though inadequately clad. What a strange thing it is that public figures are so easy to find in this city. I do not know what to do, for the man has not defied the law and I have trouble distinguishing Berlioz in flesh from Berlioz in my imagination.

I agree to perform in a benefit concert for the poor. I am grateful that the Salle Favart is within walking distance for it means I do not have to wake early and it seems I am always tired. We are to perform the final act of *Romeo and Juliet*, and when I first see the program I notice that an overture by Hector Berlioz is to open the evening. After my soliloquy I spend a good deal of time dying and being dead. At rehearsal, Kemble is holding me limp in his arms when I hear a door close. Then suddenly there is a great scream and I open my eyes to see that man Berlioz, shrieking and running from the theater. I struggle, and Kemble helps me to stand. I point at Berlioz. "Beware that gentleman." The words spill from my lips before I realize what I am saying. "Beware that gentleman with the eyes that bode no good!"

Kemble laughs. "Come, come Miss Smithson. That is the composer of our overture. He is merely one of your admirers, that is all."

1833

*I*N ALL MY CHILDHOOD DAYS it never crossed my mind that I would marry anywhere other than a church. I had watched Father Barrett prepare so many young couples for marriage. Occasionally I had attended ceremonies. I had simply thought that a wedding, like mass or a christening, was a happy ritual that must be witnessed by God. Hector had been raised Catholic, and though it was not important to him, it was very important to his family. And though in my soul I was more Catholic than he, no Catholic church would have admitted us. He made all the arrangements with the British Embassy, and I wore my best silk gown. I could not afford the extravagance of a new one when I still owed so much money in unpaid bills. Silently my mother helped wash and style my hair.

There were only five guests at the ceremony: Hector's friends Liszt, Hiller, Heine, and Gounet, and my mother. Anne refused to attend. The Reverend Luscombe spoke English and kept a stern countenance.

HECTOR GRIPPED MY ARM firmly and half lifted me into the carriage. Ever since my accident I had been wary of carriages. I blamed them for my limp, the affliction which made my movements jerky and took away the gracefulness of a young woman.

He sat there with me as we began the few hours' journey to Vincennes for our wedding tour.

During the course of the journey, Hector began to teach me his Symphonie Fantastique.

"Sing with me, my sweet Ophelia," he said.

"No, no. Hector, I have no voice."

"Sing with your heart." He said. He started again, and when I thought he was not looking, I opened my lips and sang as quietly as I could, still staring out the window. I did not wish to meet his eye, but when I eventually turned to him, he beamed.

When our carriage deposited us at the front gate, it was difficult to see the cottage for all the shrubs and flowers. I wondered if he had delivered us to some sort of paradise, and suddenly I did not mind if there were no cottage and no roof. All my life until that day had been concerned with finding a roof. And now, finally, I was free. Parts of my skin that had never seen sunlight would go ripe and soft in the warmth. We would be like Adam and Eve there in our nakedness in the sunshine. Finally alone. We would wear the sweetness of rose and jasmine. We would adorn ourselves in lilacs and magnolias. *Sweets for the sweet.*

He led me through the smell of sweet tea and cinnamon. There was blue, yellow, white, and pink. With each step I saw a new tangled corner. The warmth of the sun on my eyelids made me squint at the creeping, towering, carpeting green.

Hector pushed open the wooden door which had been left unlocked for us. The kitchen was cool and shadowed by the foliage masking the windows. It was a simple cottage with a rough wooden table in the center of the room. I was grateful for the dimness. It would give my mind and my eyes some due rest.

He led me gently, as though I were a small child. He took the hat and case from my hands and laid them on the bed. Then he drew me into his arms. He trembled, and I felt his warmth and his moisture. There was little pleasure in those new, wet sensations. But he made me feel tall and graceful and more womanly than I had ever felt before.

I remember very little of our first private meal together. We ate at an inn not far from the cottage, but I could not tell you which one or what we ate. There must have been other people at the inn, yet I recall only that we were there together.

Afterward, Hector tried to carry me home. I must have had too much wine with my meal to have allowed this, for it nearly caused him permanent injury. However, he insisted, and I must have been flattered by his attention. Every few feet he stopped again and set me down, and we both giggled so hard we could barely stand. In the end he carried me like a child, my legs wrapped around his slender hips to keep from falling and my heavy skirts drooping beneath. He led me around the back of the cottage where we found an orchard. I formed a basket with my skirt, and Hector filled it with apples, pears, and figs. Next to the cottage was a grapevine. Hector fed me fat grapes peeled with his teeth, juice dripping down our chins. And his sweetness mixed with the sweetness of the fruit.

We felt our way back to the bedroom in the darkness. A single candle created a dim glow on a desk near the window which was open, filling the air with the scents of flowers. Crickets hummed loudly, and occasionally a moth flapped in through the window. The open curtains billowed slightly in the wind, and between the branches of a tree I could see glittering stars.

In the morning I was surprised to hear one of his melodies singing somewhere inside me.

MY MOTHER PREPARED our lodgings for us while we were away. On our return she embraced Hector; however, I could not help but notice the suspicious way they eyed each other. Mealtimes were a strain, for Hector and I could sit silently staring into each other's eyes between mouthfuls, words of English and French shooting between us like sparks from a fire. Since our marriage, my sister no longer looked me in the eye or spoke with me; my mother soon took to staring at her plate until the maid removed it, and then retiring immediately to her bedchamber.

One morning my mother came to me in the drawing room. "Harriet, there is nothing for us in Paris," she said.

I could think of no reply.

"I am thinking to take Anne back to Ireland."

"To Ennis?"

"Perhaps Dublin. I will find somewhere we can live."

"I see. Mother, I shall speak to Hector. If you choose to go, I will ask him to send an allowance after you. You must do what you think best." She walked slowly over to my chair and took my hand. She leaned over and kissed my forehead, her lips resting upon my skin.

Hector accompanied us to the poste restante from where my mother and sister would begin their journey. They had but one case; we would send a trunk after them once they sent an address. The journey would take several days, and I wondered if any of us would make it again. I embraced them both, and each time it was difficult to let go. I clung to them as though to my life. "Mother, thank you for all you have done," I whispered to her.

In the end Hector had to peel my arms away for the driver

was impatiently cracking his whip. Hector lifted Anne to her seat and gave an arm to my mother. He kissed each of them quickly on the cheek.

"Look after my girl!" I thought I heard my mother's voice break as the carriage drew away.

"Remember to write, Anne!" I called, my voice breaking.

Hector held me firmly. He kissed the tears from my cheeks. He led me home.

1828

THERE IS A LULL in the season, and I have hours of time to myself. The sweetness of such days! The season is turning slowly from winter to spring, and it is nearing my twenty-eighth birthday. My mother allows me to open our house some evenings to guests, and I become a hostess for the first time. Charles Kemble, Mademoiselle Mars, Mr. Turner, all these people take tea with us and bring friends, and our lodgings take on the air of a fashionable salon.

In the daytime I read every Shakespearean play I can find and imagine roles for myself in all of them. I am less familiar with the comedies, and I wonder what it would be like to play a fairy or a princess or a duke's daughter who finds herself happily married at the end. I attend public balls, a new gown and often a new trinket to wear to each. I meet elegant gentlemen who kiss my hand in the European fashion and lead me on their arms as though they would protect me from the world.

But even as my days have such lightness, a disquiet lurks beneath the surface. For I know not what the future holds. I wait for some sign, some offer or invitation to guide me. But nothing comes. I see an end to this season in Paris, and I do not know where to go next. I cannot bear the thought of returning to that unwelcome city of London. My mother urges me to find a husband. She says I may not know such success anywhere ever again and that I must make good use of it. "Befriend a gentleman of means," she says. "And you shall never have to work again." I imagine such a life of ease and contentment. I know I could be a good wife to a man of society. But Shakespeare has taught me to follow my heart without fearing the consequences. With every touch of my fingers and kiss of my hand I wait for a fluttering in my chest that will give me an answer. But none comes.

At one of my evening gatherings, Mademoiselle Mars takes me aside and says it is time I had a benefit concert. When he hears, Kemble claps his hands together. And so I begin composing a letter to the minister, requesting permission. It is my custom to write such letters in English for I would require a good deal of assistance to write so in French and most government officials are proficient in English. My colleagues begin petitioning for the evening's entertainment and I decide we will perform the third act of *Romeo and Juliet*.

Mademoiselle Mars sits with me a whole morning during which we compile an extremely ambitious guest list. She writes every member of royalty she can think of, and at the end we have the names of the Duchesse de Berry, the Duc and Duchesse d'Or-léans, the Duc de Chartres, the Prince de Saxe-Cobourg, and the king. I blush and shake my head, but Mademoiselle is insistent and soon we have a pile of invitations signed by us both, ready to be posted by Monsieur Tartes.

Tickets are to be sold directly by the theater, and I am pleased to be divested of such a tedious responsibility. When I arrive for rehearsal I am told they are selling extremely well and that my concert is expected to be sold out by the end of February, a week before it is to take place. It is only when entertainment has been confirmed that I am informed Mademoiselle Mars has requested the Théâtre-Français perform the comedy *Le Manteau* and the

Théâtre-Italien a part of *Il Barbiere di Siviglia*. I feel that I am feted by all the arts of Europe.

I am almost sleepless, but excitement pulses through my veins. My mother predicts great things for us: travel without work to make us weary, a house in the country full of servants, friends of rank in every corner of the earth. And when I tire of her chatter, it is my sister she tells, muttering to her even as she helps her dress, for Anne will not allow the maid to touch her.

Something has come over my sister. She questions my every move as though there is important business being kept from her. She wants to know exactly with whom I have spoken at every ball. She begs the details of my performances and what I observed of audience response. Anne has her own bedchamber now, and I lend her copies of my plays and books. It is only at intimate family gatherings that Anne is allowed to be present, and for this I am sorry. My mother is sure to lock her away in her bedchamber in the evenings whenever we have company. She fears Anne's weakness will dampen our prospects. At such times I can almost weep for Father Barrett and the kindness he showed to all unfortunates.

And so it happens at one of our suppers, we are all sitting in the parlor. At Mademoiselle Mars's instigation, Madame Pasta has done us the honor of attending and she is midway through an unaccompanied aria when all is silenced by a piercing scream. My mother freezes and turns pale. I run to Anne's bedchamber. My sister is lying twisted and sobbing on the floor. There is a wound on her head, and a small statue given to her years ago by my brother is lying on the bed. Even as I try to lift her, I wonder whether she has done this to herself. Mr. Kemble and Mr. Turner have followed, the other guests are murmuring quietly in the parlor. If the men are surprised at the existence of my sister, they do not indicate so, and together they lift the girl gently back to her bed. I remove the statue and watch my mother thank them as she touches my sister's stockinged legs looking for injuries.

"Harriet, a compress for your sister," she says as Anne weeps softly and my mother wipes the blood from her brow with a lace handkerchief.

"Shall I call for the doctor, Mrs. Smithson?" Mr. Kemble asks.

"That will not be necessary. Thank you, Mr. Kemble."

For some moments he remains in the doorway, and I brush past him to see the maid looking helplessly between the guests, my mother, and Charles Kemble.

MY MOTHER GIVES ME a string of pearls, and I do not dare ask where she found the money to pay for them. She kisses my cheek and says Father would have been proud. And I have a tear for him and also for Father Barrett that they could not live to see me like this, at my most beautiful, the beloved of all Paris. I travel in a coach alone while my mother finishes preparing herself and Anne.

My family has a box for the evening of my benefit concert, and I am able to join them from time to time, though I take care to arrive in the darkness of a scene for fear my presence will draw eyes away from the stage. I cannot concentrate on the drama or the performances for I am buoyed by the crowd and amazed at all the royalty within that theater. I remember my father's fears of his theater burning down, and I wonder at all the disruption to the running of France if this theater were to burn at this moment.

I have purchased a new gown for the evening. It is a cream silk, and I wear it even as I am Juliet dying in the arms of Romeo. And as I lie there I start suddenly at the memory of an agonized cry.

And I find myself as Juliet, in a lull between life and death, opening and shutting my eyes, weeping to the sighs of the spectators.
Kemble does not protest at my inspiration. Romeo touches my
face and weeps. The moment is perfection.

At the end of *Le Manteau*, Abbott speaks to the crowd in a
French slow and ponderous; in it I can hear the roundness of English, yet the crowd roars. He speaks my name a number of times,
and afterward Mr. Kemble tells me Abbott praised my talent exceedingly. There is warmth and merriment in the air and the roar of the
crowd. I stand shaking with emotion in the wings; the audience
calls my name and I am drawn to them. Mademoiselle Mars has her
arm around my shoulders and will not let me move. It is good she
does so, for at that moment I do not care that it is against the law for
an actor to make a reappearance. Eventually the crowd quietens, and
I know from the breeze touching my skin that the doors have been
opened. There are many people coming in, I am told. They are the
crowds who missed out on tickets and who hope for a glimpse within.

Mademoiselle Mars leads me quickly to my dressing room
where she straightens my hair and reapplies my scent. And then I
am in the greenroom, all garlanded in the most brilliant of early
spring flowers. There are daffodils, tulips, and the flowers of
daphne, and the air is as sweet as cake. Within seconds there is a
line of royalty all awaiting my attention. They greet me like a
friend. The Duchesse de Berry kisses my cheek with such innocence it is difficult to believe the scandals that will soon befall her.
And then a young man standing beside her hands me an enormous
porcelain vase, white and blue with dramatic curves. My mother
is there to take it from me and place it in a corner where it is soon
filled with flowers. And throughout all the other conversations of
that evening I cannot resist turning back to look at the vase, three

feet high, the most beautiful object I have ever received. I imagine it traveling with me wherever I go, and I wonder what words and music it will hear during the passing of years.

I recognize some journalists from the *Courrier Français* examining the vase. I am handed discreet envelopes and small boxes of trinkets and jewelry. Mr. Turner takes me aside and whispers that the young man Hector Berlioz is at the backstage door wishing to offer his congratulations. I shake my head and he nods, leaving to convey the message. Many people bring flowers, and my mother begins removing them from the crammed greenroom, piling bouquets on top of each other in my dressing room until there is nowhere to step and it looks like a flower shop. And when the crowd is beginning to lessen, I become aware of my aching cheek muscles and that my knees wish very much to sit down. I look around me for a chair, and then suddenly an extremely well dressed gentleman bows before me and says he comes from the king. And I wonder whether I am part of a fairytale when he hands me a purse of gold.

It is early morning when my mother, Anne, and I return to our lodgings. None of us wishes to sleep, and we sit in the drawing room discussing the evening until late. Anne cannot help but mimic the French in gushing tones.

"Incroyable! Sublime! Elle est pure et jeune! Si belle!"

I smile.

We count the gold coins over and over again, and I am impatient for my other gifts to arrive by coach.

It is light when I make my way to my bedchamber and begin to undress. I open the curtains a crack and stare down to the street. My carriage is there, and I imagine that Pierre is here delivering my gifts. And then suddenly I see the carriage move off down the street. On the side are painted the words *My kingdom for a horse.*

1827

HERE IS A BUZZ in the air that first night I am Ophelia, a palpable electricity that makes my arms tingle if I move them too quickly. And it is as though the angel of destiny is there, hovering over the stage where the curtains should be. She wishes to reward me for making the less than obvious decisions. For being an Irish girl playing an English girl playing a Danish girl in the city of Paris. And so she will now lead me, freeing me from the concerns of this wandering life.

And while my heart and mind are absorbed in the madness of Ophelia, there is a part of me standing still and silent, staring out into the crowd and hungry for what she can absorb from there. First she stares out into the boxes; there are tailored gentlemen and ladies with fans. She notices the red and blue of the British flag, and then she realizes this is bigger than theater. This is politics, the stuff of revolutions. This night could change British and French relations forever. She is momentarily puzzled and wonders if she will have to choose a side. She chooses harmony and wonders if this night will change the world.

Then she lowers her eyes to the pit, and there she sees count-less young men. These are the artists, she has been told. And these people have all bought the English-French text of *Hamlet* from the stand that was being set up earlier in the day. They are flipping backward and forward, mouths open, their eyes wide. The action of looking constantly between the stage and their books makes their heads nod, giving them a slightly comical appearance, like strange waterbirds. But she has never seen anyone as serious as those men, quivering with emotion, overwhelmed by Shakespeare.

She notices that many of the young men are staring right at her, and she shivers, simultaneously thrilled and exposed, as though their eyes are fingers. There is one man who does not look at his text at all. The booklet is untidily crushed into his pocket, allowing him to clutch at his seat with white knuckles. His mouth is agape, and he does not try to conceal his feelings. A line of ginger whiskers crosses his cheek, and a mane of red hair tumbles around his ears and neck. Fiery strands wave almost vertically from his head, and it is as though he is possessed by the electricity in the air. He is like a madman, unkempt with fire in his eyes. Every now and then he lets out a great sob, and it is as though he has foreseen his own death.

HER WORDS CREST and break on the heads of the gaping onlookers, dissolving, dispensing their magic, like the golden dust of fairies' wings, until—

The rest is silence.

And she sees a world of sighs climb to the rafters.

And there in the cascades of applause that wash through the darkest corners, she tastes the sunshine and the earth and the clover, and she hears—"Good night. Good night."

And now she sees the sweet prince.

And as she curtsies, she feels the flights of angels singing.

Acknowledgements

HARRIET SMITHSON lived from 1800 to 1854. Her significant influence over French Romanticism has largely been overlooked; she is known today mainly for her role as muse to Hector
Berlioz. This novel attempts to recreate her life and work in its
own right. While I have tried to remain true to documentary
sources, this remains a work of fiction.

This project would not have been possible without the support
and assistance of several individuals and organizations.

Research in England, Ireland, and France was undertaken with
financial assistance from the Foundation for Young Australians
(formerly the Queen's Trust for Young Australians). I made particular use of the British Library; British Library Newspapers at
Colindale; Birmingham Library; Drury Lane Archive at the
Theatre Museum, London; National Library of Ireland; Clare
Local Studies Centre, Ennis; archives at the Bishop's Palace,
Ennis; Freemason's records, Dublin; La Bibliothèque Nationale
de France; and La Bibliothèque de l'Arsenal. I am indebted to the
thorough research and generosity of Peter Raby and David
Cairns, biographers of Harriet Smithson and Hector Berlioz,
respectively. Without their work I would not have known where
to begin. In particular, I thank David Cairns for his detailed proof-
reading of this manuscript. Any remaining errors are, of course,
my own.

County Clare local writer and historian Seán Spellissy gave his time generously and provided crucial background on the town and people of Ennis. Anne Hignett provided friendship and the space that made it possible for me to spend as much time in London as I needed.

I am grateful to staff and students at the School of Creative Arts, The University of Melbourne, for their interest and support of this work, which formed the basis of a Ph.D in creative writing. In particular, I thank Dr. Kevin Brophy, who cast a gentle eye over early drafts.

Crucial polishing and structuring work was undertaken during a three-week fellowship at Varuna, the Writers' House. I thank Peter Bishop, executive director of Varuna, for giving so generously of his time and helping the novel take form.

I am grateful to Helga Hill for her patience in teaching me the basic principles of historic gesture. Thank you to Anne Radvansky, who put a lot of time and thought into reading drafts and giving detailed feedback.

I thank my Australian agent, Fran Bryson, for her continuing hard work, enthusiasm, and encouragement; and Maria Massie of Witherspoon Associates, my New York agent, who has worked tirelessly to bring this novel to publication. I also thank Amy Cherry, my editor at W. W. Norton, for her patience and understanding, and for believing in this project from its early stages.

I thank my parents as well as the Smith and Talbot clans for their interest and encouragement of my work, and for living with Harriet and Berlioz over the last five years. Finally, thank you to Rupert for his unfailing support and assistance.

Court Journal. "Covent Garden." 16 May 1829, p. 43.

Dramatic Magazine. 11 May 1829.

Examiner. 7 October 1821.

Fyvie, John. "Eliza O'Neill (Lady Becher) 1791–1872." In *Tragedy Queens of the Georgian Era.* London: Methuen, 1908.

Garrick, David. *Romeo and Juliet: A Tragedy.* Oxberry's edition with prefatory remarks, as performed at the Theatres Royal, London. Covent Garden: Simpkin and Marshall, 1819.

Hazlitt, William. *Liber Amoris: or, The New Pygmalion.* London: Woodstock Books, 1992. Originally published 1823 by C. H. Reynall, London.

Jackson, Russell, ed. *Victorian Theater: The Theater in Its Time.* New York: New Amsterdam Books, 1989.

Lamb, Charles and Mary. *Tales from Shakespeare.* London: Bancroft Books, 1967 (reprint).

Maassakker, Jean-Pierre. *Berlioz à Paris.* Paris: Edition Aug. Zurfluh, S.A., and Association Nationale Hector Berlioz, 1992.

Marshall, Dorothy. *Fanny Kemble.* London: Weidenfeld and Nicolson, 1977.

Moore, Thomas. *Moore's Irish Melodies.* London: Longman, Green, Longman, Roberts, & Green.

Murray, Christopher. *Robert William Elliston, Manager.* London: Society for Theatre Research, 1975.

Oxberry, William. "Memoir of Miss H. C. Smithson of the Theatre-Royal, Drury Lane." In *Oxberry's Dramatic Biography and Historical Anecdotes.* London: Simpkin & Marshall & Chapple, 1825.

Raby, Peter. *Fair Ophelia: Harriet Smithson Berlioz.* Cambridge: Cambridge University Press, 1982.

Select Bibliography

Berlioz, Hector. *Symphonie Fantastique*. Compact disk and program notes. Sony SM3K 64 103.

Berlioz, Hector. *Correspondance Générale*. Vols. 1–8. Ed. Pierre Citron. Paris: Flammarion, 1972–1975.

Cairns, David, ed. *The Memoirs of Hector Berlioz*. London: Victor Gollancz Ltd., 1969.

Cairns, David. *Berlioz: Volume 1: The Making of an Artist: 1803–1832*. London: Allen Lane, Penguin Press, 1999.

Cairns, David. *Berlioz: Volume 2: Servitude and Greatness: 1832–1869*. London: Allen Lane, Penguin Press, 1999.

Clare Journal and Ennis Advertiser. Numerous issues, 1800–1808.

Clark, William Smith. *The Irish Stage in the Country Towns, 1720–1800*. Oxford: Oxford University Press, 1965.

Clark, William Smith. "The Limerick Stage 1736–1800." *Old Limerick Journal*, no. 9 (1981) and no. 11 (1982).

Cone, Edward T., ed. *Berlioz: Fantastic Symphony. An Authoritative Score Historical Background, Analysis, Views and Comments*. New York: W. W. Norton & Co. 1971.

Corish, Patrick J. *Irish Catholic Experience: A Historical Survey*. Dublin: Gill & Macmillan, 1985.

Le Corsaire. "Théâtre Anglais. Hamlet." 12 September 1827, p. 2.

Le Corsaire. "Butin." 11 October 1827, p. 4.

Le Corsaire. "Théâtre Anglais. Venus Preserved—Blue Devils." 7 November 1827, p. 2.

Rowe, Nicholas. *Jane Shore: A Tragedy*. Oxberry's edition with prefatory remarks, as performed at the Theatres Royal, London. Covent Garden: Simpkin and Marshall, 1819.

Shakespeare, William. *Hamlet: A Tragedy*. Ed. William Oxberry. Covent Garden: Simpkin and Marshall, 1818.

Spellissy, Seán. *The Ennis Compendium: From Royal Dún to Information Age Town*. Ennis, Ireland: The Book Gallery, 1998.

Stockwell, La Tourette. *Dublin Theaters and Theater Customs, 1637–1820*. Kingsport, Tenn.: Kingsport Press, 1938.

The *Times*. "Miss Smithson." 11 October 1828.

Tomalin, Claire. *Mrs Jordan's Profession: The Story of a Great Actress and a Future King*. London: Penguin, 1995.

White, Patrick. *History of Clare and the Dalcassian Clans of Tipperary, Limerick and Galway*. Dublin: M. H. Hill & Son, 1893.

Wright, William Aldis, ed. *The Complete Works of William Shakespeare*. Garden City, N.Y.: Garden City Books, 1936.